BOOK ONE OF THE ⦶IGIL SAGA

VIGIL

EVERYONE HAS AN AGENDA

P.B. OBENG

ASCENDANCE PUBLISHING

Published by

ASCENDANCE PUBLISHING

ISBN: 978-0-9998186-3-3

Cover design & interior formatting: Mark Thomas / Coverness.com

I would like to dedicate this novel to my wife and family who have been especially pivotal in making this novel a reality.

*"The love of liberty is the love of others;
the love of power is the love of ourselves."*

-William Hazlitt

(1778-1830)

PART ONE

UNKNOWN ORIGIN

PROLOGUE ONE

June 1st
Delohar, Lemalia

Three bullets. With only three bullets a world leader's life is snuffed out. Just three bullets are all it takes to throw a nation into chaos and set the world on fire.

Mohann Aldessa was the newly elected president of the small eastern Mediterranean nation of Lemalia. As a nation it is as much a melting pot as the United States, with ethnic origins in Europe, North and East Africa, and Southeast Asia. Today was inauguration day for the country's first democratically elected president in over fifty years. Sadly, what was meant to be a joyous occasion devolves into chaos.

As onlookers react in horror and disbelief, Aldessa's security detail immediately converges on his body, instinctively brandishing their automatic weapons as they look to return fire. The police make a failed attempt to maintain calm. Hysteria overtakes the crowd and a major stampede ensues, with dozens trampled in the tumult.

Amidst the confusion, a sniper on the rooftop of the adjacent parliament building meticulously field-strips his weapon, a Remington 7.62 mm M4OA1 sniping rifle. The man, dressed in cargo pants, a black t-shirt and a well-worn M65 field jacket, carefully places the disassembled rifle into a rectangular weapons case. He pulls a small silver-colored cell phone from his inner coat pocket and presses #7 on the touch screen. As he lifts the phone to his ear, his coat sleeve slides back, revealing a distinctive tattoo of a bald eagle clutching lightning in one claw and arrows in the other.

The call is answered. "It's done," the sniper says in a sterile tone.

He nods in acknowledgement of the orders given by the other conversant. "I understand." The sniper ends the call, grabs his belongings, and quickly retreats from the rooftop. As he leaves, the man fails to notice the security camera perched on the satellite tower above him.

PROLOGUE TWO

June 3rd
CNN Headquarters
Atlanta, Georgia

"How are things on the ground in Lemalia, Giles?" Wolf Blitzer, anchor of *The Situation Room*, asks foreign correspondent Giles Woodbridge.

Reporting from Delohar via satellite, Woodbridge responds in his unapologetically thick British accent.

"There's been rampant unrest since the assassination of the newly elected president, Mohann Aldessa of the moderate People's National Democratic Party. His opponent, Emerante Legaud, seized power shortly after the assassination."

"As I understand it, Legaud is a well-known hard-liner from the New Revolutionary Party."

"That's right, Wolf. He has called for the nationwide expulsion of all foreigners as well as the immediate nationalization of all foreign and domestic business interests."

"That's a pretty bold step, considering that he wasn't the one elected to office," Blitzer retorts. "What's been the UN's response?"

"The Security Council ratified a resolution condemning the assassination," Woodbridge replies. "The secretary general issued a statement saying that the UN will not formally recognize Legaud's presidency."

"So what's their next move?"

"It's believed that economic sanctions will be levied against Lemalia."

"Is that wise, considering the fact that Lemalia provides the bulk of Duritium to the global market?"

"It seems the Security Council has decided to take a harder line since Legaud's rise to power," Woodbridge answers.

"From what we've gathered so far stateside," Blitzer adds, "the White House has not released a statement concerning the recent turn of events in Lemalia."

CHAPTER ONE

WHERE ALL MY TROUBLES BEGAN

July 3rd
Office of the Secretary of Defense
The Pentagon
Arlington, Virginia

Secretary Charles Hanahan is a middle-aged man with a shaved bald head and mid-sized frame. Even though he's gained a little weight over the years, he's still quite fit for his sixty-three years. With the demands of his role as defense secretary, he has to be. He pulls a stack of manila folders from the file cabinet behind his well-worn leather chair and plops them onto his already cluttered desk.

"Well, Captain, here's your team."

Even sitting across the table from him, Captain Alicia Conrad cuts an imposing figure. With a five-foot, nine-inch frame and athletic build, she's a formidable sight. Although possessing the defined physique of a soldier, Conrad is still able to maintain an hourglass figure.

She has been an army officer for over ten years and comes from an esteemed military pedigree. Even with the expectation of constant readiness that military service fosters, Conrad still does not appreciate short notices. When she received a phone call the previous day from the Secretary's office, all that she was told was, "You have a meeting with SecDef at 0800 tomorrow at the

Pentagon." No further elaboration, no courtesy, just an abrupt "click." Given all this, it is no surprise that she responds as she does.

"Come again, Mr. Secretary?"

"You've been selected to lead a group of superhuman operatives under the jurisdiction of the United States government," Hanahan responds.

"Selected by...?" The ergonomic chair creaks ever so slightly as she leans forward to hear Hanahan's response.

"The whole NSC[1]: DNI[2] Norton, Joint Chiefs Hoppert, Secretary Nichols, both POTUS[3] and the VP, and of course yours truly."

Conrad smiles. "A unanimous decision, huh?"

"Yup."

"I'm curious, who else was on the NSC's short list?"

"A few senior-level Marines, a guy from the NSA, and a couple of others who aren't worth mentioning," he says flatly.

"And Blankenchip? I know he's been dying to get his own special ops team for the longest time."

"Are you serious?" Hanahan responds incredulously. His tone is somewhat expected given that he and Lieutenant Aaron Blankenchip are not exactly on the best of terms. "We need someone who can manage a mix of egos and personalities—not a hard case like Blankenchip. Don't worry though; he's also on the team."

"I see," Conrad responds.

"Why are you so worried about that anyway? What matters is that we picked you."

"I understand, and I'm thankful for the opportunity, sir."

Sensing the hesitance in her voice, Hanahan probes further. "But?"

"I just don't want it to seem like you picked me because of my dad."

"Please, it's not like nepotism wasn't alive and well in this town long before

---

1 National Security Council

2 Director of National Intelligence

3 President of the United States

your family showed up," Hanahan responds. "Look, it has nothing to do with that; we picked you because you have what we need."

"That's reassuring, sir," she says, her voice lightening up a bit.

"Besides, I couldn't have you languishing behind a recruiter's desk. That was just temporary until you got yourself together."

Conrad nods in acknowledgement.

Hanahan continues, "You were always meant for greater things, Alicia."

"Thanks."

"What did your dad used to say when you were a kid?"

She glances down and quietly responds, "Be better than yourself."

"Exactly. Your dad, God rest his soul, knew how great you could become." He reaches over to grab a framed picture of him and John Conrad and their 82nd Airborne Division unit. He gazes upon it. "He trusted me to watch over you and the twins. There is no way I'm going to allow your potential to go to waste."

Conrad could see the conversation going to an uncomfortable place so she quickly shifts back to topic.

"So, why this? Why now?"

Hanahan pauses briefly before speaking. "The Minneapolis event."

Three years prior an al-Qaeda operative named Mahmoud El-Hayek leveled the Mall of America single-handedly. This was accomplished not with a bomb but with his superhuman ability to generate localized nuclear fission reactions. He single-handedly unleashed the equivalent of a megaton yield nuclear bomb. The death toll exceeded 50,000 and left the rest of Minnesota a virtual wasteland due to the residual radiation.

"We live in a post-human era now, Alicia," Hanahan continues. "Since the beginning of the space race, people with unbelievable abilities have popped up all over the world. Some are harmless, others pose a threat."

"Like me?" she jokingly responds.

Hanahan smiles. "No. You are our best asset in dealing with this emerging threat."

"You're being too generous, sir."

"It's true. You're the best investment ever made in military research."

"I see."

"Any threat to our security must be dealt with swiftly and lethally," he says, his tone becoming noticeably grimmer. "I figure when you're in a fight with a pit bull you get your bigger, meaner pit bull to deal with him."

"So... I'm America's attack bitch now?" she says sarcastically.

"No. It's just an analogy, Alicia."

Taking the opportunity to display her vocabulary acumen she counters, "It's actually a metaphor, sir."

"Same difference," he snaps back.

She smiles. "OK, so what have we got?"

"First things first. The name of the team is Vigil."

"Vigil?"

"Yeah, it's the only thing we could agree on at the NSC meeting."

She raises her eyebrows. "OK."

"It's essentially a task force created for the sole purpose of protecting US interests and allies."

"So, it's like a super-powered CCI squad?"

The Crisis Conflict Intervention unit—or CCI for short—was a sub-division of the Army Special Forces. Several top Green Berets couldn't even meet the strenuous requirements for membership. Their original intent was to perform, for lack of a better term, politically gray missions. For all intents and purposes, CCI is essentially a black-ops division of the Special Forces. Both Conrad and Blankenchip are former members.

"Not quite," Hanahan responds. "CCI was strictly covert ops; this'll have more of a public face. And we're pulling in civilian agencies as well."

"I see."

"It's one of the most ambitious interagency initiatives like it since the creation of the Department of Homeland Security."

He notices that Conrad's attention is drawn to one of the files. "Still with me?"

She looks up. "Yes, go on please."

"These people aren't ordinary—much like you."

"So I'm a weirdo. Thanks, sir, didn't know you cared."

"You know what I mean."

She flips through the pages in one of the folders. "OK, Cynthia Fighting Bull, formerly Cynthia Sorrell... Codename Pseudo." She pauses to make an editorial comment. "We're using codenames?"

"For now." Hanahan replies.

"The NSC was really into the whole superhero motif hungh?"

He responds peevishly. "Maybe a bit."

"Maybe a bit *too* much." Conrad continues reading. "She's a CIA agent in the Directorate of Operations' Spyscape division. Age twenty six, genetic endowment: metamorphosis. Genetic endowment? We have genetic mutants on this team?"

"I believe the politically correct term is 'Variants'," Hanahan admonishes.

"Whatever."

"There are two, as a matter of fact."

"Who's the other?"

"FBI agent by the name of John Arrowhawk."

"The one who cracked the Kerrington case?"

"Yup—one of the youngest ASACs[4] to crack a case of that magnitude."

"Isn't his brother some kind of eco-terrorist or something?"

"Or something."

"I see. So, what's his power?"

"He's essentially a human power cell. He can absorb, convert, and manipulate all energy forms. You name it: nuclear, electrical, kinetic, whatever. He's your heaviest hitter in terms of raw power."

"Hmm, and this one?" She picks up a 4x4 inch photo of a large-framed man.

Hanahan takes the photo from her hand and draws it closer for a better look. "He's a Secret Service agent by the name of Terrell Morrison."

4 Assistant Special Agent in Charge

"I've never heard of him. What's his story?"

"He was caught in the Houghton Biomedical Research Lab accident and was exposed to a synthetic Duritium-based reagent. As a result, he can take on the physical properties of any substance he comes into contact with."

Conrad points to the final photo. "And the last one's good ol' Blankenchip. Is he the only complete normal on this team?"

"He's not so normal, with that Battle C.A.T.[5] suit he designed."

"Tell me about it. How much did it cost to design and manufacture that thing?"

"About fifty million."

"And they say we have a national debt of over 30 trillion."

"Hey, it's one of the perks of being in the service for as long as he's been."

"When I get twenty years of service can *I* get my own high-tech body armor?"

"Why? It's not like you need it."

With a smile that could melt the fiercest of hearts, Conrad replies, "That's why you picked me for the job, right?"

"That, and you have one of the best military minds I've ever seen since your father," Hanahan adds.

"You really know how to flatter a girl, sir."

"I try. There's a press conference at the Pentagon at 1400. I'll see you then."

Taking this as her cue, Conrad salutes the secretary, gathers her beret and briefcase, and promptly leaves his office.

As he clears off his desk, he glances at the ominous headline on the front page of the *Washington Post* that reads, "Turmoil in Lemalia continues to send world stock markets into tailspin." Hanahan folds the paper in half and throws it into his desk drawer.

---

5 Cybernetic Armor Technology

CHAPTER TWO

BUREAUCRATS

Interstate 495
The Washington Beltway

Conrad navigates the perpetually congested Washington Beltway in her late-model Ford SUV, with the intent of getting to her Silver Spring home before lunchtime. Although her eyes are fixed on the road, her mind drifts back to the meeting with Hanahan. The thought of being active again is both appealing and honestly quite frightening—*How would she transition back to active duty? What would she do to keep them all on the same page?* These thoughts run through her mind just before the ringtone of James Brown's "The Big Payback" from her cell breaks through her fugue. She looks at the caller ID and sees that it's Maurice Hodges, case officer with the Montgomery County Department of Child Welfare Services. Hodges has been a constant thorn in her side since the beginning of her custody case with the county. Her disposition immediately changes as she lifts the phone to her ear.

In a flat voice she answers, "Conrad."

Maurice Hodges's voice is the perfect amalgam of the character Steve Urkel from the 1990s television show *Family Matters* and comic actor and economist Ben Stein.

"Yes, Ms. Conrad, this is Maurice Hodges from the Department of Child Welfare Services."

She can't help but grit her teeth every time he opens his mouth.

"Yeah, I know who you are. What exactly is it that you want?"

"Just calling to remind you of your pending court date."

"Yes, I do remember, Mr. Hodges. Is there anything else you would like to waste my daytime minutes on?"

Hodges is put off by the curt response and pauses a moment to gather himself before responding.

"No, nothing else, but considering that you're one of our decorated servicewomen I have to say, your tone and manner are quite rude—"

She interrupts him mid-sentence. "Look, I'd love to listen to your diatribe on proper phone etiquette, but unlike some people—such as yourself—I use the air I breathe to do work that actually matters. So if you'll excuse me…"

She presses the "End" button on her phone and flings it into the lap of the passenger seat. *The absolute nerve of him… he seriously needs to invest in getting a life. I promised mom that I'd keep us together. There is no way they're taking Camille and Cameron away from me.*

Conrad turns on her multimedia player. Her SUV is suddenly immersed in the sounds of James Taylor's "Fire and Rain". Little does she know how prescient that song title is.

CHAPTER THREE

SUPER SLEUTH

SVR[6] Headquarters
Yasenevo 11 Kolpachny
Moscow, Russia

The Cold War has been over for decades, but the CIA still has a penchant for keeping tabs on its Russian sister agency. This provides covert operations officers like Agent Cynthia Fighting Bull a world of job security. Her current assignment—retrieving files on former Soviet nuclear scientists from the SVR archives—is going smoothly so far. Her ability to shape-shift no doubt helps this along. She operates under the guise of SVR Security Chief, General Anatoly Andropov.

Her operations officer, Dalton Clemens, talks to her over the radio earpiece, addressing her by her call-sign.

"Chameleon, your exit window closes in thirty seconds. Have you secured the package?"

"That's affirmative; I'm almost done," Fighting Bull responds.

After downloading the file, she pulls the jump drive out of the computer's USB port and tucks it into her coat pocket. Clemens comes back in her ear.

"Chameleon, infrared is picking up movement in your direction."

She taps her earpiece before responding. "I'm leaving now."

---

6 Sluzhba Vneshney Razvedki—-Russian Foreign Intelligence Service

As she proceeds to the exit, much to her surprise (and chagrin), she bumps into the genuine General Andropov.

"What the hell?!" Andropov blurts out in his native Russian.

Fighting Bull hesitates briefly as Andropov reaches for the H&K P-10 pistol in his left shoulder holster. Regaining her mental bearings, she kicks the pistol out of his right hand and follows through with a forceful roundhouse to the chest. The impact knocks the wind out of Andropov. He loses his balance and tumbles to the ground. She sprints out of the room just as the back of his head hits the floor.

A trio of security guards walks by to find one Andropov sprinting out of the archive room while another is sprawled on the floor. The guards are understandably confused by what they see. The real Andropov, struggling for air, orders the guards, "G-get him."

The men pull out their Kalashnikov rifles and begin firing on Fighting Bull, as they chase after her. She deftly navigates a myriad of corridors and stairwells. Shattered pieces of plaster splatter across her face as bullets pierce the walls, just narrowly missing her.

She reaches the roof, where her extraction team hovers above in an MH-60 Enhanced Black Hawk helicopter. Clemens motions for her to jump in. Just as she leaps for the helicopter, a bullet grazes the side of her right leg. Fighting Bull stumbles and barely grabs hold of one of the landing skids with her left hand as the helicopter begins its ascent. As she dangles from the skid she draws a black Sig Sauer P-225 from her shoulder holster and returns fire. The bullet pierces the chest of one of the guards, and his body crumples to the ground.

Fighting Bull loses her grip, but before she can fall, Clemens snatches her left wrist and pulls her into the cabin. Their gunner returns fire with two mounted 7.62mm miniguns. The pilot releases burst flares from the M-130 flare dispenser, disorienting their attackers and covering their escape.

Fighting Bull hands the jump drive to her operations officer.

"That was too close, Cynthia," Clemens comments.

"I know," Fighting Bull counters. "It won't happen again."

"You said that in Sarajevo, and in Kandahar before that."

Fighting Bull nods contritely. Deep down though, she wasn't truly penitent. The fact is that she thrives on episodes like this. To her, the rush of being on the precipice of death is like being high on cocaine. One could rightly assert that Cynthia Fighting Bull is an adrenaline junkie with no intention of ever going into rehab. Competent as she is at her job, her love of excessive risk-taking is her one major flaw as an agent.

Clemens inserts the jump drive into his laptop's USB port and begins transferring the encrypted files to Langley's server. The on-board medic bandages Fighting Bull's leg wound. Thankfully for her, there is just superficial damage with minimal blood loss.

With the release of superhuman growth hormone from her anterior pituitary gland, she transforms from the Andropov identity back into her original slim five-foot, five-inch frame. Her protean ability is both amazing and unsettling to witness, best described as wax melting, with Andropov's visage liquefying away to reveal Fighting Bull's true face. Clemens looks up from his laptop to catch this process.

"No matter how many times you do that it still gives me the creeps," he comments.

Fighting Bull smiles and ties her long, light brown hair into a pony tail as she takes a cabin seat. She grabs the duffle bag with her change of clothes from the side of her chair and places it in her lap. An unfortunate downside to her ability—she can't transform her clothes whenever she shape-shifts. Thus, constantly requiring a change of clothes to fit her original body frame.

"It's what helps me do my job, sir."

"Yeah, but you were this close to not making it out, Cynthia," Clemens says.

"We secured the package and made it back in one piece. I'd call that a success, boss," the pilot says. "Cynthia, you want to grab something to drink before we head home? You know, to celebrate."

"You know she doesn't drink, Barton," Clemens says. "Just worry about getting us home."

Fighting Bull nods at Clemens then looks down at her phone. She notices the time and sees that she is almost late in giving her video debrief to her handler. She touches the overhead flat-screen monitor above her. Agent Tony Dickson appears onscreen.

"How was it?"

She responds with a smirk. "Smooth as a baby's bottom. They didn't have the slightest clue that I was even there."

"Yeah right, and there's a bridge in New York that I'd like to sell you. I saw your little fiasco from the SATVID.[7] Next time, leave when Clemens tells you to!" Dickson chides.

"Now where would the fun be in that?"

"It's all fun and games until I'm reading your eulogy."

"I understand. I won't make that mistake again, sir. So when's my next assignment?"

"You won't have one. You have a press conference to go to, remember?"

"Uh, no. When did this come about?"

"Didn't you get the memo about being sanctioned into that new special task force?" Dickson retorts matter-of-factly.

"No, sir."

"You sure?"

"Positive."

Back at Langley, Dickson clicks the *Microsoft Outlook* icon on his computer screen and retrieves the errant email. He pauses as he reads.

"On second thought, scratch that. There's no way you could've gotten that memo because I'm staring at the copy I was supposed to email you. Sorry, I must've forgotten to send it. My bad."

"'My bad?' Sir, isn't it *you* who always reminds me that *this* CIA stands for the Central Intelligence Agency, not the Center for the Inept and Amnesic?"

---

7 SATellite VIDeo

CHAPTER FOUR

FEDS

Shadyside Café
Venice Beach, California

Agent John Arrowhawk grows impatient by the minute. He sits alone at a wire-framed table covered by an umbrella shade waiting for arms dealer, Derrick "D-Tech" Sylvester. *What kind of stupid nickname is D-Tech, anyway?* Arrowhawk wonders as he checks his watch. The arms dealer is more than thirty minutes late, and Arrowhawk fears that the deal may have already fallen through before it's begun.

Sylvester supplies weapons to many within Southern California's criminal underworld. Posing as a rising cocaine trafficker in the L.A. underworld, Arrowhawk has arranged a buy with Sylvester. He's been working on this meeting for weeks, with hopes of not only apprehending Sylvester, but also obtaining his client list. Arrowhawk taps his earpiece.

"He's got cold feet, the deal's off—"

His field leader interrupts. "Don't get your paranoid thong in a bunch, we got him on surveil, he's heading right for you."

At that moment, a thin man with a close-cropped hair, and dressed in an Armani suit, arrives at Arrowhawk's table. His appearance comes off more like a *GQ* cover model than an arms dealer. He pulls up a chair across from Arrowhawk.

"You got the money?" he asks calmly.

"No money till I see the merchandise," Arrowhawk answers.

Sylvester nods and the two get up from their outdoor table and head inside the café. They walk past numerous café patrons and into a side room just across from the kitchen. In the room is an oval wooden table with three chairs.

Sylvester places a two large metallic suitcases side by side on the table. He releases the latches on the sides and the suitcase lid springs open. Within the foam-lined cases lies an assortment of weaponry, including two Glock-36s, one Walther 9mm submachine gun, and an Uzi.

"This is just a sample," Sylvester says. "I'll take you to the rest once I see the cash."

Arrowhawk looks at the weapons and then at Sylvester. "Thanks, but that's all I needed to see." He presses a button on his wristwatch.

The door is kicked open, and suddenly, Sylvester is accosted by a slew of café patrons. Unknown to Sylvester, most of the café patrons were in fact undercover agents. He slips his right arm free to grab the Glock from one of the suitcases. Sylvester trains his weapon on Arrowhawk. Before Sylvester can squeeze the trigger, Arrowhawk swiftly grabs the second suitcase and uses it to bat the weapon out of his hand. Sylvester is then slammed face-first into the ground with his arms pulled behind his back.

"You set me up!" a bewildered Sylvester blurts out.

"Way to state the obvious, Tech," Arrowhawk replies.

"I'll get you! You ain't seen the last of me!"

"'You ain't seen the last of me'," Arrowhawk mocks. "Do you know how utterly unoriginal that sounds? You sound like a perp from a bad cop drama."

"Go to hell!"

"Let's be honest, you're just mad 'cause you got caught."

He slaps Sylvester on the back of the head as he's lifted off the ground by one of the agents.

"You gotta be slick, my man."

Arrowhawk motions to the agent. "Get him out of here. I want him in interrogation within the next half hour. Also, make sure we get a team to the industrial park to recover the rest of his caché."

"Right away sir," the agent says. "But, I'm just curious, why didn't you just zap him when he pulled the gun on you?"

"Because it would've been too dangerous. I can't risk one of our guys getting hurt." As he turns to walk away, one of his colleagues pulls him aside.

"Samuels is on the line for you, John."

He takes the cell phone. "Arrowhawk."

L.A. office Special Agent in Charge Kevin Samuels comes on the line. Arrowhawk worked briefly under Samuels as his ASAC, but stepped down shortly after the Kerrington affair. The two still maintain a fun yet professional relationship.

"How did it go?"

Arrowhawk responds in his own slightly satirical way.

"As well as it could have. Some of these arms dealers aren't that bright. They wouldn't recognize a sting operation if it ran up and bit them in the crotch."

"You know, I really could've done without that mental image, John."

"Sorry."

"Anyway, make sure you write up your field report before your hot-shot press conference."

"The Vigil thing?"

"Yeah."

"What time was it again?"

"Do I look like your secretary?"

"No, sir, but you are one of the most informed and astute people I know," Arrowhawk responds.

"Enough with the brown-nosing. It's at two o'clock, east coast time."

CHAPTER FIVE

MISTER PRESIDENT

Oval Office
The White House
1600 Pennsylvania Avenue

T he White House is intended to be one of the most secure buildings on the planet. Common sense says it would have to be, considering that it houses the most powerful person in the Free World. Yet, two would-be infiltrators from the militia group, the National Freedom Alliance, have managed to infiltrate the Oval Office. The men, one of them armed with an H&K P-10 pistol and the other with a Mac 10 submachine gun, train their weapons on the back of the president's chair. They think they have the president right where they want him.

The pistol-toting infiltrator speaks up. "All right, Mr. President, you're gonna listen to our demands or we're blowin' this building sky high."

No response comes from the man in the chair. The two men look at each other in exasperation, agitated by the president's seeming disregard for the threat they pose. The second man reaches over to turn his chair around.

"Hey, listen to the man when he's talkin' to…you…" The militia man's voice shrinks to that of a preadolescent boy as he discovers that the person sitting in the president's chair is actually Secret Service agent Terrell Morrison. The men stare at him dumbfounded. Morrison responds to their obvious shock with some levity.

"What? You were expecting someone a little lighter and thinner?"

They quickly compose themselves and fire their weapons. Before the first bullet can pierce his body, Morrison converts his six-foot, eight-frame from flesh into solid steel.

The bullets tear through his clothes but ricochet off his steel skin. Without hesitation he quickly grabs the submachine gun from the man closest to him, and flips it around to the butt end. He delivers a devastating blow to the infiltrator's left temple. The impact knocks the man unconscious. The second man, being the wiser, makes a beeline out of the room, but not before letting off a few rounds as he retreats. When he reaches the exit, to his mortification, he's greeted by three Secret Service agents. The agents waste no time tackling him to the ground and clasping handcuffs around his wrists.

Morrison converts his body back to its natural state; gleaming steel skin recedes to reveal warm flesh and blood. He frantically pats down his suit.

"What's wrong?" his colleague Jeff Garner asks.

Morrison reaches into his right breast pocket and pulls out a gold wedding band with the engraving: "T&D."

"There it is," Morrison says with a smile.

He kisses the ring and puts it back on. Then he looks at the remains of his suit and laments. "I paid over two grand for this thing. What a waste."

"Next time, you might want to leave the Dolce and Gabbana at home," Garner comments.

Feigning shock at his friend's lack of designer-brand savvy, Morrison says, "It's actually Kenneth Cole."

"Sorry," Garner replies with eyebrows raised, as if to say, "Excuse me."

Morrison smiles and quickly changes the subject. "Did you guys get all the audio on that?"

"Yes, we did. Those idiots won't see the light of day for a long time."

"What about the planted explosives?"

"We retrieved and deactivated all of them."

"Good. Tell Stiles he can bring the president back in from the safe room now."

"Copy that." Garner taps his earpiece lightly. "All clear, let the eagle out of the nest." He shifts his attention back to Morrison.

"So, are you ready for your big press conference today?"

Morrison lets the corners of his mouth betray a warm smile. "Yeah, but not until after I get a bite to eat. I'm starving like you wouldn't believe!"

CHAPTER SIX

ACID DREAMS

Eight Years Ago
Jakarta, Indonesia

*U*nder the cover of a moonlit night, an MH-60 Apache helicopter descends silently onto the rooftop of a skyscraper in downtown Jakarta. Four CCI operatives descend from the helicopter. As soon as the last person is clear, the helicopter ascends once more and disappears into the night. The top level of the building is the headquarters of former high-level Jordanian intelligence operative Omar Al-Khatib. He previously served as a Defense Intelligence Agency liaison until going rogue a few months earlier. Al-Khatib was in possession of the highly sensitive Missile Defense Protocol (MDP) discs. The discs outline the entire US missile defense infrastructure, including launch codes, missile silo sites, and mobile units. This information would be invaluable to a number of American enemies abroad. Al-Khatib's apparent duplicity has severely strained relations between Jordanian and US military intelligence. And both the Americans and the Jordanians wanted him back, badly.

This CCI unit was specifically tasked by the DIA to retrieve Al-Khatib by any means at their disposal. Their strike team is small but lethal; consisting of Conrad, Blankenchip, and team leader Major Paul James, with support officer David Breslin. Breslin breaks away from the trio to the main building's main circuit breaker to override the failsafe mechanism. The other three deactivate the roof's cameras and motion sensors before quickly moving in to observe Al-Khatib's office through the skylight.

Major James turns to Blankenchip. "Do we have visual confirmation of the package?"

"Affirmative," Blankenchip replies as he peers through his night-vision-enhanced binoculars. "I spot four bogies—three security guards and Al-Khatib."

"Good." Major James turns to Conrad. "Do you have the flash-bang grenades?" She nods.

"All right, the package is isolated." He radios Breslin. "Lights out on my count." "Copy that, Major."

The three of them strap on their AN/PVS-5 night-vision goggles in preparation. James begins the countdown.

"We go in on three. One... two... THREE!"

Breslin cuts power to Al-Khatib's office and the once brightly lit space is suddenly immersed in darkness. The trio bursts through the skylight with shards of glass dispersing through the air like stardust. Conrad reaches inside her tactical webbing to pull out three flash-bang grenades. She hurls them into the midst of the security guards, disorienting them. One of the guards draws his Uzi and shoots wildly through the smoke. Bullets ricochet off the walls and floor, with one of them barely missing Blankenchip's head. He fires back with his Beretta M92F pistol, wounding the guard in his shoulder. Conrad dispatches the second guard by plunging her Night Force knife into his midsection before he can let off a shot. The guard collapses to the floor without an utterance. James shoots Al-Khatib's last guard in the right flank and leg. After the chaos settles, he turns his pistol-mounted flashlight on Al-Khatib, who takes refuge behind an overturned desk chair.

"Put your hands up!" James orders.

Al-Khatib staggers to his feet as he gathers himself. Aside from some coughing from the smoke, he seems otherwise unfazed by the intrusion.

"So, this is the famed CCI squad? Hanahan and Davis must be getting lax in their recruitment standards," Al-Khatib says with contempt.

Not at all pleased with his glib tone, Blankenchip gets right to the point. "Cut the crap, where are the MDP discs?"

"Now why would I want to give you that information? They have to be worth at least a billion dollars on the black market."

"Look, we can do this the hard way or the easy way. The choice is yours," James says.

"Way I see it," Blankenchip chimes in, "he doesn't have a choice."

"I believe you're right," Al-Khatib replies, seemingly at ease with his fate.

He turns to the computer console on his bullet-ridden desk and types in his security password. Thankfully, the computer was still operational. The disc tray under the console opens and a rotating array of discs slides out. Al-Khatib removes the tray's contents and walks toward them.

"Here are your discs."

James grabs the discs from him and hands them to Conrad, keeping his eyes and weapon steady on Al-Khatib. "I want authenticity verification."

Conrad inserts the discs into her mini-laptop. Within seconds the analysis program reads the discs to confirm that they are the originals.

"They're legit. All the protocols and countermeasures are present and intact," she replies.

"Any copies made?" James inquires.

"I checked the duplication history and it's clean. No extra copies were made."

"Good." Major James turns to Al-Khatib. "Now, Mr. Al-Khatib, I think it would be wise of you to come with us without a struggle."

Al-Khatib complies with the order. Major James pats him down for any weapons before turning him around. James pins Al-Khatib's chest to the wall, and places handcuffs on him.

Conrad radios Breslin. "We've obtained the package. We're heading up."

"Copy that," Breslin replies. "I'll rendezvous at the extraction point."

The quartet leaves by way of the stairwell; Conrad and Blankenchip lead the way, closely trailed by Al-Khatib and James, who are roughly fifteen feet behind them. The Apache helicopter is in clear view as they reach the rooftop. Just moments before entering the helicopter, Al-Khatib turns to look at James.

"You honestly thought that I would go this easily?"

Al-Khatib taps on one of the cuff links on his shirt, detonating the micro-explosives within the lining of it.

The explosion's force hurls Conrad and Blankenchip into the side of the helicopter. Their ears ring so loud they can't even hear each other. Blankenchip struggles to get to his feet as Conrad tries to make out any body through the thick smoke from the explosion. Her goggles were more of a hindrance than a help. She rips them off to get a better view and turns to see James lying lifeless on the ground just a few feet from her, his body burned to a nearly unrecognizable degree. She rushes to his side and starts to perform vigorous chest compressions, trying to bring him back. Ultimately, her effort proves fruitless.

Breslin yells at Blankenchip to get on the helicopter. He nods and runs to gather Conrad.

"We gotta go!" Blankenchip says as he pulls her away from James's body.

"But we can't just leave him!"

"He's dead, Alicia," Blankenchip says coldly. "PJ knew the risks when he signed up. Now let's get the hell outta here!"

Blankenchip forcefully yanks her away from James's body. As he does so, James's dog tag is ripped from his neck as Conrad clutches onto it.

* * *

Conrad Residence
Silver Spring, Maryland

"Get up, Alicia," are the words Conrad hears as she's woken from her dream by her younger brother Cameron.

"What happened?" Conrad mutters as she shakes off the effects of sleep.

"You were screaming."

"I was?" She's still slightly disorientated.

"You were having a nightmare, Alicia." Cameron's concern for his sister is evident in his voice.

Even though he's seventeen years younger than his sister, he takes it upon himself to assume the dual roles of watchful brother and man of the house. It's an unnecessary burden, but nonetheless he's chosen to accept it.

"I guess I was," Conrad says, now settling down from being jolted out of her dream state.

He glances at the digital clock on her bedstand.

"It's 12:45. Didn't you say you had a meeting at two?"

"Yeah, but what are you doing home so early? I thought you had AAU practice?"

Playing competitive basketball has been in the Conrads' blood for years. Their father, John Conrad, was an All-American during his high school years. Conrad herself was also an All-American at Springbrook High School, so it's only natural that Cameron would follow suit. He's been playing on the AAU team since he started middle school. He's pretty good too, averaging sixteen points, ten rebounds, and five assists per game. Just like his big sister was, he was highly sought after by dozens of Division I colleges.

"We ended an hour early," Cameron answers. "I called and left a message on your phone for a ride."

Conrad picks up her cell phone from the bed stand and looks at the screen to see that she indeed missed Cameron's call. She puts her head in her hand.

"I'm sorry, Cam. I was at a meeting this morning, and I crashed as soon as I got home."

Cameron has sadly grown accustomed to being let down by his older sister. It always seems that affairs of work always take precedence over family for his sister. At least, that's what it felt like to him.

"I figured as much."

The young man exits the room, leaving Conrad alone.

CHAPTER SEVEN

SMALL TALK

Underground Parking Garage
Sublevel One
The Pentagon

The drive back to the Pentagon is not as bad as the morning commute. Noticeably absent is the high traffic volume of rush hour, which gives Conrad plenty of time to arrive in the sublevel parking lot. After providing the guard with her credentials, she parks her SUV between a midsized sedan and a red Hummer. She heads toward the elevator. Thankfully, it doesn't take long for the elevator to arrive after Conrad presses the up button. It stops on the next floor. The doors open to Cynthia Fighting Bull waiting just outside.

Dressed in a suit jacket and long trouser ensemble, Fighting Bull looks a tad more polished than the file photo Conrad had previously seen.

"Hello, Captain," Fighting Bull says.

"Hi," Conrad replies, reacting slowly to the greeting. "Agent Fighting Bull, right?"

"You don't have to be so formal. Just call me Cynthia."

"OK, just call me… Captain."

At first, the young CIA agent looks at Conrad as if she has lost her mind. Then, a smile creeps up the corners of Conrad's lips. Finally coming to the realization that Conrad is attempting to be humorous, Fighting Bull starts to smile. They stare at each other with comical looks on their faces before chuckling.

"Just kidding," Conrad finally relents. "Call me Alicia."

"So, when did you hear about all of this?"

"This morning, as a matter of fact."

"Yep, that's our government for you, always the model of timeliness. I found out about it on the way back from an assignment."

"So, how long have you been in the CIA?" Conrad asks.

"This is my fourth year. You saw my file, right?"

"Yeah, but I'm just trying to make small talk."

"An annoying yet necessary nuance of social interaction," Fighting Bull comments.

Conrad is thrown by her statement. "What's that?"

"Small talk; it's one of those things we just feel compelled to engage in once we meet new people," she answers. "It's our way of making an awkward situation less awkward."

Conrad looks at Fighting Bull quizzically. "Psych major in college, right?"

"Actually it was one of my minors," she answers. "So, Captain, how does it feel to become the most powerful black woman in America since Condoleezza Rice?"

"Or Oprah Winfrey?" Conrad says without missing a beat.

Fighting Bull laughs. "Including her."

Conrad pauses for a moment to ponder Fighting Bull's comment. Growing up, she never truly viewed the world through the lens of race. Her father was biracial and her mother was Ghanaian, but it wasn't something that she dwelled on. She knows who she is ethnically, but hasn't allowed that fact to dictate her life. "You know what, though, I never really thought of it that way."

The elevator finally arrives on the lobby level where the remaining members wait. The two women introduce themselves to the rest of the group.

Conrad walks over to greet Morrison. "Agent Morrison, nice to meet you."

He grasps her hand. "The pleasure is all mine, Captain."

She turns to her old colleague, Blankenchip. They acknowledge each other in a way that only old army buddies can.

"Glad to see you haven't hit the retirement home yet, Aaron."

"I can still run circles around your considerable ass, you stupid broad," Blankenchip utters. "Nice hair, by the way. You sure that's AR-670 approved?" referring to Conrad's dreadlocks which she had recently begun growing. He gladly points out that her hairstyle is not Army regulation approved.

"It is now," Conrad snaps back.

Meanwhile, the two youngest members of the team get acquainted.

"Cynthia Fighting Bull," she says as she stretches out her right hand to greet Arrowhawk.

Arrowhawk takes her hand. "John."

"Good to meet you."

"The pleasure's all mine. Believe me."

"I know," she replies assuredly.

Fighting Bull's confident response is a surprise to Arrowhawk. Normally, his charm elicits a giggle and a blush from the opposite sex. Fighting Bull's cocksure attitude is new territory for him.

Within a few moments, Hanahan arrives with a tall, thin, blond-haired man with gray streaks on his temples.

"Good afternoon, everyone. I believe you all know me. To my right here is Chandler Ramsey; he's the NSA's Director of Operational Planning and Programming. He'll also be serving as your operations officer."

Conrad interjects, "But I thought we'd be reporting directly to you."

"Being the Secretary of Defense is tough enough; I can't take on the extra duty of serving as your operations officer. Don't worry, I hand-picked him for the job myself."

"I see," Conrad replies in a tone that belies her lack of enthusiasm for Hanahan's choice.

Ramsey finally speaks up. "I have to say that it's a tremendous honor to be involved with such an accomplished and talented group. I look forward to working with you all."

CHAPTER EIGHT

MEET THE PRESS

Pentagon Press Room

The pressroom is packed to the brim with reporters, bloggers, and correspondents. Those who arrived just minutes late were relegated to standing in the back. News outlets from every medium are eager to get the chance to see the debut of America's new superhuman defense initiative.

Pentagon Press Secretary Dana Person walks into the room, followed closely by Hanahan, Ramsey, and the rest of the team. A crescendo of camera flashes erupts as they take the stage. Those reporters fortunate enough to have seats available to them sit down as Person takes to the podium.

"Welcome, ladies and gentleman. We appreciate you all coming out to this press conference." Person shifts her tone of voice. "As we all know we live in dangerous times, and they're made even more perilous with the emergence of unlawful superhumans. Our founding fathers could never have foreseen these imminent threats to our national security. Consequently, we have created our own superhuman defense deterrent: Vigil. At this moment, I'd like to introduce Secretary Hanahan to discuss the initiative."

Person retreats from the podium as Hanahan steps forward with a pat to Person's shoulder. A few camera bulbs flash as he pulls out note cards from the inner pocket of his sport coat. He puts on his bifocal glasses and adjusts the microphone to his height before speaking.

"Thanks. As Dana just said, we live in perilous times. Humans are no longer human, they're superhuman. And terrorism is no longer terrorism, it's super-terrorism."

Hanahan clears his throat. "In the face of these impending threats, we have taken the preemptive step of forming our own superhuman defense initiative. Individuals from the military and several federal agencies have been recruited to create the core of the team."

Hanahan points to each Vigil team member individually and names them. They nod or raise their hands in acknowledgement when their names are called. Mild applause accompanies each individual's introduction.

Hanahan continues, "I would like to praise the interagency cooperation that's gone into forming this team. Who'd ever think that government could actually get things done for once?"

His comment elicits a few chuckles from the audience.

"All right, enough of my bad jokes. I'm free to answer questions."

ABC news correspondent Brian Dawson raises his hand.

"Yes, Brian."

"Mr. Secretary, we're in a financial slowdown right now. At this moment the country is running a thirty-trillion-dollar deficit. Where are you getting the funds to pay for all this, and is it even necessary?"

"We're being funded through a separate revenue stream." Hanahan turns to Ramsey for confirmation of what he's said. Ramsey nods in agreement.

"As for necessity, it's very necessary. We can't have what occurred in Minneapolis to ever happen again."

"With all due respect sir," Dawson responds, "that was an isolated event. The superhuman community, by some census figures, is about 3 percent of the total US population and about 1 percent globally. Are they a credible enough threat to warrant such a vast initiative?"

"One percent of over 7 billion is still a lot of people, Brian. Look, what happened in Minneapolis was the superhuman equivalent of 9-11. It's my duty, and this Department's duty to defend this nation against any present and potential threats. That includes superhuman threats, and we have recruited the personnel who can do the job."

Hanahan again looks sternly into the crowd. "Next question," he says, as if daring any of them to challenge him again.

After an awkward pause that almost seems like an eternity, Luke Matthews from CBS raises his hand. Hanahan points to him.

"Mr. Secretary, aren't you afraid of escalation?" he inquires. "With the deployment of our own superhuman initiative, what's to keep China, North Korea, or Russia from responding in kind?"

"That's just speculation, Luke," Hanahan says dismissively.

"It happened with the development of the nuclear weapon. Initially only two nations had it, and now it's mushroomed to several dozen. Mr. Secretary, is America willing to start a superhuman arms race?"

"Look, you're simply being an alarmist. We don't have silos full of superhumans waiting to be deployed. Other nations are free to do as they please, but our policy is one of preemption rather than reaction. Vigil will be a deterrent to any outside superhuman threat to this country. Period. Next question?"

In the farthest reaches of the press room, Mavis Nixon of NPR speaks up.

"What about the UN and NATO? As a member of both organizations, would the US be obligated to use Vigil in support of them?"

"Mavis, Vigil will gladly assist any US allies on request, but make no mistake, Vigil was and is intended for the protection of Americans."

Nixon quickly responds with a follow-up question. "So we can take it that the administration is adopting a renewed policy of unilateralism? Similar to what we saw during the first decade of the twenty-first century?"

"I am not the official spokesperson for the White House, so I can't comment on that. Anyway, I think the question and answer session is over. At this point, I'd like to ask Captain Alicia Conrad to step up to the podium to say a few words."

Just as she prepares to take the podium, Chandler Ramsey's cell phone vibrates. He pulls it from his breast pocket and quickly glances on the screen. He presses the ignore icon and puts it back into his breast pocket. Conrad notices this just before Hanahan motions for her to step up to the microphone to speak.

She walks up to the podium and opens up the pad folio tucked under her left arm.

"Good afternoon, ladies and gentlemen. As we all know, we live in very dangerous and uncertain times. After the terrorist events of September 11, 2001, we learned that we are all too vulnerable to forces seeking to end our way of life. Now we live in a new era, a superhuman era. And with this come new dangers. The Minneapolis event was evidence of this. America now more than ever needs people equipped to confront these new dangers. I am proud to say that we are those people. We hope that America can sleep a little easier knowing that someone is watching over her. Thank you."

As she steps away from the podium, Matthews blurts out a question. "How does it feel to be continuing the family tradition?"

She turns to look at him. "Excuse me?"

"Your father was one of the most decorated military servicemen of the modern era. It must be satisfying to be continuing his legacy."

"I appreciate that, but I'd rather not talk about it right now."

Tom Edwards from the Washington Times then shouts, "Captain, would you like to comment on the custody case with your siblings?"

Conrad's blood begins to boil. Of all the things that could have been asked in this setting, this is the one question she's feared the most. She's aware that an expression of anger is clearly taking shape on her face. Before she can respond though, Hanahan blocks her with his left arm. Noticing that things are going sour fast, Dana Person swiftly steps up to the microphone to try to salvage the situation.

"I think that'll be all the questions for today. Thank you."

As the room empties, the rest of the team is somewhat perplexed by what just transpired. Then they are promptly ushered along to sublevel two to begin their orientation.

CHAPTER NINE

CORPORATE AMERICA

Vigil Headquarters
Sublevel Two
The Pentagon

The elevator carrying the contingent of the newly formed team and their handlers, Ramsey and his personal aid, Lauren Price, arrives at the second sublevel. The ride down is notably quiet after the closing moments of the press conference. As the doors of the elevator open, Ramsey begins the orientation.

"As America's foremost national security force, you will have the full resources of the US government at your disposal."

"I have a question for you, Mr. Ramsey," Fighting Bull says.

"Shoot."

"I'm just curious, how are we being funded? There's no provision in the defense budget for this initiative, and we're not covered under the president's discretionary fund."

Ramsey pauses to clear his throat before answering. "Actually, the Vigil project is being funded through a joint corporate/government agreement. We have a few friends on Wall Street who wanted to see this project come together, so they lent their financial support. It's their way of carrying out their patriotic duty."

She nods. "Interesting."

Ramsey continues, "Let's head over to the main operations room."

As they walk, Price, intrigued by Conrad's hair, reaches from behind to touch it. "Wow, Captain your hair is—"

Conrad swiftly grabs Price's hand before it can make contact with her mane. "Do *not* touch."

Price pulls her hand back apologetically.

They arrive at a large circular door underneath a sprawling archway. The entrance requires a security card and biometric retinal scan for entry. Ramsey provides the appropriate credentials, and the large doors slide open, revealing an elaborate array of high-tech equipment. He looks in Price's direction. "Lauren, if you'd please."

The attractive brunette begins speaking. "As Mr. Ramsey mentioned earlier, this is the main operations room, or 'war room,' as some of you army brass like to call it." She turns to look at Blankenchip and Conrad as she says this. "This room is equipped with some of the most sophisticated technology of this century. From here you can access real-time video feeds from around the world through your specially designated satellite system."

"Our own sat system?" Arrowhawk says in amazement. "That's dope."

"It's true," Ramsey responds. "Lauren, go ahead."

"Not only do you get real-time video feeds around the clock, but intelligence reports will be streamed here directly from all divisions of our military and intelligence agencies through an interdepartmental interface."

Conrad asks a question on a topic that up until this point no one has brought up. "What about support staff?"

"You have approximately six direct support staff members and over a hundred ancillary staff. We're still in the process of hiring a pilot."

The need for a pilot is minimal at best. Their ship, the Avian, is equipped with an artificial intelligence auto-pilot feature. Also, with the exceptions of Morrison and Arrowhawk, everyone else on the team has extensive flight training.

"When can we meet them?" Conrad asks.

"We're on our way to do that now."

"After you meet your support staff, your orientation will be over," Ramsey tells them. "I suggest that you all get a good night's rest because you have a big day ahead of you tomorrow."

"For that National Mall thing tomorrow?" Morrison asks.

"It's not just a thing, Agent Morrison. You're going to be feted by over half of DC tomorrow."

Ramsey and Price lead the team to a large rotunda within sublevel two. Banks of computers, flat-screen monitors, and holographic projectors line the walls. Dozens of technicians mill around filing reports, conducting threat assessments, and working on intelligence analysis. In the middle of this controlled chaos stand six people. Ramsey introduces them.

"Captain, you asked earlier about support staff? Well, it's my pleasure to introduce you to Nick Weiss, Andrea Drake, Alysande Mendoza, Erick Anderson, Winston Jordan and last but not least, Daniel Portis."

Each of the introduced individuals wave as his or her name is called, then they formally greet each of the Vigil team members.

"Nick and Andrea will serve as your tech division chiefs," says Price. "They've worked for some of the top software and hardware companies in the world. Nick was a senior software writer, at both Microsoft and Google, and Andrea was a head engineer at Raytheon for the past fifteen years."

Price turns toward Mendoza and Donaldson.

"Alysande and Erick will head up the Public Relations and Diplomatic divisions respectively."

Arrowhawk makes one of his trademark comments: "Spin doctors."

"'Spin doctors' is a term for amateurs, Agent Arrowhawk. We're professionals," Mendoza protests.

"Sorry," Arrowhawk says, smiling. Mendoza reciprocates with an equally warm smile.

"Anyway," Price interjects, aiming to steer the discussion back to the orientation, "Winston and Dan head up the Weapons and Equipment division.

They'll be in charge of everything from outfitting your aircraft with the latest weaponry to designing your uniforms."

Winston Jordan jumps in. "Funny you should mention uniforms. We were just finishing preliminary testing on them."

"Can we take a peek?" Ramsey asks

"Sure," Jordan answers giddily.

The contingent moves from the inner rotunda through a doorway with metallic sliding doors. They enter a small darkened room with a large plate glass viewing window. Behind the window are the team's uniforms displayed on plastic mannequins on a rotating platform.

"We were tasked with designing uniforms that are functional, yet complement each individual," Jordan says. "We looked to the sports apparel market for inspiration."

Fighting Bull comments, "They look like the Dri-Fit or Under-Armour stuff the pro-athletes wear."

"The material's similar in fact," Jordan tells her. "We made your uniforms out of a microweave blend of biosteel, Duritium, and high performance nylon."

"Biosteel?" Blankenchip says. "Isn't that the stuff that's supposed to replace Kevlar?"

"Yes," Jordan answers. "It's derived from a recombinant form of spider silk protein synthesized in the milk of transgenic goats."

"Seriously? Body armor from goat's milk?" Arrowhawk comments.

Jordan chuckles. "Yeah I know it sounds weird, but biosteel is twenty times as strong as conventional steel and has the flexibility of elastic."

"Can it stop a bullet?" Morrison asks.

"From point blank range," Daniel Portis, who has until now been silent, interjects. "In fact, it can withstand fire, knife attacks, and to a small degree, directed energy weapons."

"In addition to its protective features, each uniform is outfitted with a microclimate conditioner," Jordan continues, "to keep you comfortable in all types of environments."

"How does that work exactly?" Fighting Bull asks.

"Through the electro-textiles woven into each uniform. We integrated micronized computer chips into the fabric. It's also through this mechanism that we're able to monitor your vitals while you're in the field."

Portis adds, "And that's also how the BiSC feature of your uniforms works."

"BiSC?" Conrad asks.

"Bio Synchronous Complement feature. To put it simply, it allows your uniforms to work with your powers. For example, whenever Agent Fighting Bull performs a shape change, she'll be able to transform her clothing as well—"

"As opposed to constantly carrying around a change of clothes as she's had to do in the past," Jordan blurts out, finishing Portis's sentence.

"Finally," Fighting Bull sighs to herself.

"And whenever agent Morrison alters his density, his uniform will change with him," Portis adds.

"Very nice," Morrison remarks approvingly.

Jordan turns to Arrowhawk with the look of a happy fan boy. "And your uniform, Agent Arrowhawk, your uniform is designed to withstand energy emissions in excess of a million joules. That way you don't have to worry about your uniform melting on you when you let loose with your powers."

"Thanks," Arrowhawk answers. "But I don't think I'll be letting loose anytime soon."

Ramsey looks at his watch. "Thank you, gentlemen. I think that should wrap up the orientation. See you all tomorrow."

CHAPTER TEN

THE SET-UP

July 4th
WJLA TV Studios
Washington, DC

"In world news, there was another car-bomb explosion outside the Presidential Palace in the Lemalian capital of Delohar," news anchor Donna Michaels says. "This marks the third major car-bomb explosion on the island nation in as many weeks."

Her co-anchor, David Kellen, continues. "The civil instability in Lemalia reflects the economic instability occurring in the global marketplace. To talk more about this is our economics expert, Sendhil Srivathsan. Sendhil?"

"Well, Dave, today the New York Stock Exchange dropped by 100 points and there was a steep decline in the Nikkei average. The sharp market losses were largely attributed to the Legaud administration's business nationalization plan."

"How have business interests within Lemalia been affected by this?" Kellen inquires.

"Many of them have seen considerable losses in their bottom line due to this initiative. As the major natural source of Duritium worldwide, multiple business sectors have taken a tremendous financial hit."

"What makes Duritium so special?"

"It's believed that Duritium ore is non-terrestrial."

"You mean from outer space," Kellen says.

"Exactly. It's similar to the meteoric iron that's naturally found in our environment. Scientists think that its non-terrestrial nature is what gives it the ability to be used in multiple ways from medicines to machines," Srivathsan says. "And Lemalia is where the bulk of this Duritium ore is found."

"They export, what… about 70 percent of the world's Duritium?"

"Exactly, and that's why it's such a big hit to not only durable goods, but also to the tech and automobile sectors." Srivathsan answers.

"Thanks, Sendhil," Kellen says.

Michaels transitions smoothly to the next topic. "In other news, today marks the debut of Vigil, the country's first superhuman task force. We go live now to the National Mall, where Rick Stevens is reporting."

* * *

The National Mall
Washington, DC

The Mall green is congested with admirers, on-lookers, parade participants, and emergency personnel. Stretching from the Capitol Building all the way to the Washington Monument, the Mall crowd rivals that of the forty-fourth president's inauguration.

As he gets the cue from his producer, Rick Stevens begins speaking. "Thanks, Donna. As you can see, thousands of people have come out to celebrate the debut of Vigil. Many of DC's finest and brightest are here to celebrate the event." The camera pans the crowd and then zooms in to focus on Vigil onstage.

The team sits on the stage with various dignitaries just in front of the Lincoln Memorial. The emcee begins giving the introductions while the team members talk amongst themselves. Morrison, who is seated to Conrad's left, asks her, "How are you feeling?"

"A little bit overwhelmed," she replies. "I'm not used to being in crowds this big."

"It took me some time to get used to the crowds after I started working on presidential detail. Saying a small prayer usually calms me down."

"I'm not really a praying person."

"Now's not a bad time to start."

Conrad pauses at this comment. "Funny, I never pegged you as a religious guy."

"Well, I am a Christian, but I wouldn't call myself religious," Morrison tells her. "To me, it's about my personal relationship with Jesus Christ. I just try to live my life according to His will."

"Oh, I see." She says, not quite sure how else to respond.

Just to Morrison's left sits the rest of the team. Arrowhawk is seated between Fighting Bull and Blankenchip and he leans in and to make an unsolicited remark.

"So, Cynthia, what does a guy have to do to peel you out of that skin-tight uniform?"

Unamused, she fires back. "They'd have to come up with a better line than the one you just spat! A criminology degree from UCLA, six years in the FBI, and you *still* can't come up with a halfway decent pick-up line? Pathetic."

Leaning in on the conversation Blankenchip says, "Ooooh, Pocahontas got you gooood, kid."

They both look in Blankenchip's direction.

"Kid?" Arrowhawk exclaims.

"Pocahontas?!" Fighting Bull chimes in.

The mayor steps to the podium to deliver his address. As he pulls out his note cards, the sounds of plane engines fill the sky. He looks up to see five Predator drones swoop in low from the eastern sky and descend upon the Mall.

The afternoon sun gleams off of the drones as they fire ten Hellfire II missiles into the crowd gathered around the Reflecting Pool. The missiles find their targets. Dozens are injured or killed from the explosives' impact.

One of the drones breaks formation and trains its machine guns on the occupants on stage. The mayor flinches as the flurry of bullets erupt from the machine gun's barrel toward him. He cowers down expecting to be hit. After a moment he realizes that he's unharmed and he looks to see a sold-state force field absorbing the bullets. The mayor then looks behind him to see Arrowhawk with energized hands raised, straining to keep the field up.

Reflexively, the officials on the stage then look to Conrad for direction. Without any vacillation, she takes control.

"Arrowhawk, expand your defensive force field over the crowd. Morrison and Fighting Bull, assist in the civilian evacuation. Aaron, you're with me. We're taking out those drones."

The Predator drones double back. One of them breaks formation and flies straight toward the Lincoln Monument. As the drone prepares to fire, Conrad aims her assault rifle and fires three shots straight at its left wing. It breaks apart, with its remains careening toward the team. Arrowhawk instinctively lifts his left hand and instantly raises an energy force field that deflects it.

The remaining drones fire five more missiles into the throng of people gathered at the section of the Mall between Jefferson and Madison Drives. Conrad hears the bystanders' screams as they are wounded by the shrapnel from the concussive force of the missile blasts. She taps the keys of the remote control panel embedded in her left glove, which activates their ship, the Avian.

Just a few yards from their location, the Avian hums to life, its engines roar as it flies in above the podium. Three rappelling rope lines descend from its hull to the team standing below. Fighting Bull, Morrison, and Arrowhawk secure themselves to the lines using the attached harnesses. The Avian utilizes a rappelling system that's a variation on the surface-to-air recovery system used by the CIA and Special Forces in the late twentieth century. It facilitated the rapid extraction of operatives in tight spots. And in this case, it comes in handy for situations such as the one the team is encountering. With the exception of Blankenchip and Conrad, the team members are flown to their assigned crisis points. The dignitaries on stage are immediately evacuated from the stage as the team goes into action.

Arrowhawk detaches his harness and takes a post atop a high-mounted scaffold overlooking the Reflecting Pool. The structure was originally intended to mount large speakers, but serves as a good vantage point from which to see the crowd below. A surge of bioelectric energy crackles through his hands and out of his fingertips, creating a tight network of interweaving energy beams that surround the entire expanse of the Mall greens and forms an almost impenetrable shield around the civilians down below. He grimaces and stumbles momentarily under the strain of performing such a feat.

Arrowhawk has never pushed his powers this far before—an energy blast here or a small force field there are about as far as he's gone with his powers. And although he knows the necessity of it, there's a small part of him that resents Conrad for asking so much of him.

Oblivious to Arrowhawk's plight, Fighting Bull helps clear civilians from small pocket fires that have started as a result of the previous explosions. During the chaos, an elderly couple tries to escape the flames, but is quickly overtaken by them. Seeing this, Fighting Bull grabs one of the blankets out of the back of a nearby ambulance and quickly smothers the flames engulfing the couple. With the exception of some superficial burns, the couple is unharmed and grateful for her assistance.

Just a few feet away from her, Morrison helps injured civilians fleeing the aftermath of the explosions. He lifts an overturned tour bus off the ground and uprights it. As the bus is placed back on its wheels, a small boy falls out of one of the bus's side windows and into the middle of a fleeing crowd. Just before the inattentive crowd tramples him, Fighting Bull grabs him up and places him on the top of one of the nearby police cruisers.

While the trio is taking care of civilians, Conrad and Blankenchip focus on the cause of the attack. Taking cover behind an overturned news van in front of the Lincoln Memorial, Conrad aims her Colt Commando assault rifle at the tail wing of the drone heading towards her. With the buttstock of the rifle pressed firmly against the inside of her shoulder, she fires multiple rounds at the drone. The bullets tear through its right wing and hull, setting the plane ablaze. A burning mass of debris tumbles to the ground in the path of a crowd of bystanders by the Reflecting Pool. Thankfully, most of it is deflected by Arrowhawk's protective force field.

Conrad gets up from her crouched position to see a red beam trained on the center of her chest.

"Oh sh—!" Before she can complete the expletive, the second drone fires a laser-guided GBU-12 Paveway II missile. She darts for cover behind the Korean War Veterans Memorial just as the missile is launched. She turns her head to see it land barely thirty feet away from her, and the ensuing blast hurls her through the concrete statues of the Memorial. She lands awkwardly on the left side of her neck and hears an audible snap. With her ears ringing and her shoulder stinging, Conrad pulls herself up off the ground. She flexes her neck from side to side and another audible snap is heard. She picks up her rifle. As the drone closes in on her, she points her weapon in the drone's direction and lets off a salvo of bullets. With near flawless aim she hits the drone's right wing and engine, causing it to spiral to the ground in a flaming heap.

On the opposite end of the Lincoln Memorial, Blankenchip uses his helmet's built-in targeting computer to home in on the last two drones. His armor is a unique exoskeleton composed of nanofibers derived from Duritium. It also has a full complement of offensive weaponry and an onboard computer that relays real-time field data to his helmet's heads-up display. It was intended to be the next generation of the US military's Future Force Warrior combat armor. The integrated laser-guided sights on his weapon mark out his targets. He fires incendiary rounds at the drones from his modified M16/M203 assault rifle. The first one is hit in its rear tail and sputters off course and into the force field. Blankenchip's second incendiary round hits the last drone squarely in its nosecone, causing it to explode on impact.

As the turmoil begins to subside, Arrowhawk is hit from behind with a focused sound wave blast from an antipersonnel acoustic rifle. The blast knocks him off the scaffolding. The drop is a good fifteen feet. He descends to the ground below, violently flailing his arms as he falls. Seeing this, Morrison makes a run for him. As Morrison leaps to grab Arrowhawk, he transforms his density in mid-air into solid gold—a wise decision considering that just a few feet below lies twisted metal and concrete debris. The pair land with a crash, but with little else in the way of bodily harm. The man wielding the acoustic rifle aims his weapon down on the two men. Before he pulls the trigger, Arrowhawk shoots a thin plasma beam at him that knocks him unconscious.

"Thanks for the save, Terrell. Can I call you Terrell?"

"Don't mention it, and yes, you can," Morrison replies, transforming his molecular density back to its normal state.

Gunfire erupts from the tops of the buildings on the east end of the National Mall. Gunmen brandishing semi-automatic guns indiscriminately fire into the crowd below. Conrad hears the gunfire over her earpiece and immediately sends for the Avian. Rappelling lines descend upon her and Blankenchip, and the Avian flies them over to the site of action. As they fly in she notices that the gunmen are stationed at posts on the roofs of the Museum of Natural History, the Gallery of Art, and the Smithsonian. She radios the rest of the team.

"Arrowhawk and Fighting Bull, take care of the hostiles on our north flank. Morrison and Blankenchip, cover the east flank. I'll use the Avian to take care of our south flank."

Immediately, Fighting Bull grabs Arrowhawk's arm.

"What are you doing?" he protests.

"Shut up. I'm trying something." As she touches him, Arrowhawk receives a mild static shock.

"Ow! That hurt."

"Oh, man up, John!" Fighting Bull retorts.

She immediately morphs, her face melting away as Arrowhawk's replaces it. With the transformation, she also adopts his ability. Wasting no time, she emits an electrical burst from her hands that is so powerful it jolts her back about ten feet. One of the gunmen takes advantage of this and fires his H&K rifle at her as she tumbles backward. But before the bullet can reach its target, a solid energy force field—courtesy of the real Arrowhawk—deflects it. He looks in her direction.

"Not easy, is it?" he says snidely.

Fighting Bull ignores the comment and emits a broadband electrical burst from her hands. The directed blast electrocutes the four gunmen on the roof of the Museum of Natural History.

Morrison grabs a damaged projector monitor and lobs it at two of the snipers atop the Gallery of Art building. The projectile hits both men in their midsections, knocking them unconscious. Four more gunmen continue shooting at him, but the bullets deflect off of his molecularly-altered metallic body.

Blankenchip returns fire on these men with Special Purpose Low Lethality Anti-Terrorist (SPLLAT) shells. The shells incapacitate the gunmen, clipping them in their legs and arms. A stray gunman, located behind damaged scaffolding, continues firing on the two men. Morrison looks at Blankenchip and gives him a smile. Blankenchip nods his head in acknowledgement.

"Allow me," Morrison says. He peels off the front left tire of a damaged police cruiser and flings it at the sniper. The tire slams into the sniper's forehead the force of the impact nearly takes his head off but he still lives.

The last gunmen fire on Conrad from atop the stage scaffolding just in front of the Smithsonian's facade. She takes cover behind some debris and remotely activates the Avian's weapons system. The aircraft hovers in behind the gunmen. As they turn to fire their weapons on it, the Avian fires multiple beanbag rounds on the two gunmen, knocking them off their perches. Both fall into the rubble below. Another pair of gunmen takes cover behind the Smithsonian's front pillars as they continue firing on Conrad, their bullets whizzing just past her head. The snipers move in. As they inch within twenty feet of her, she suddenly emerges from behind her cover and unleashes a salvo of bullets on her attackers. The bullets hit their targets. One of the men is hit in his left shoulder and thigh, the other in his right hand. The second one still manages to reach for the tactical knife in his thigh pocket. He lunges at her with the weapon. She swivels around, dodging the strike, and connects with a karate chop to the back of her attacker's neck. She finishes him off with a knee to the abdomen and a right uppercut.

Conrad radios the rest of her team to check on their status.

"Sit rep."

Blankenchip answers first. "East flank is secure."

Arrowhawk replies next. "All's clear on the north flank, Cap."

"Good work, everyone," Conrad replies.

She pauses briefly to catch her breath. Behind police barricades, a large crowd of evacuees on the sidelines applauds them. The team takes it all in, now realizing that this is the just the beginning of their time in the limelight.

CHAPTER ELEVEN

LIFE IN MARVELOUS TIMES

July 5th
WJLA TV Studios
Washington, DC

"We are just getting new information regarding the attack on the National Mall," Anchor David Kellen says.

"That's right, Dave," Co-Anchor Donna Michaels says, "There are reports from the FBI that the attacks were orchestrated by members of the militia, the National Freedom Alliance. The FBI states that the Predator drones were commandeered from a Ground Control Site in Colorado Springs. It's believed that these drones were obtained on the black market."

"Also it's believed that some of the gunmen involved were disgruntled former Special Forces operatives who aligned themselves with the Alliance's agenda," Kellen says.

"The FAA and the FBI have launched a coordinated investigation looking into how Predator Drones could be deployed on US soil without the knowledge of multiple military and security agencies. We'll keep you informed on the latest updates into the investigation," Michaels concludes.

* * *

Santa Monica Place
3rd Street Promenade
Santa Monica, California

Alysande Mendoza sits on an uncomfortable plastic bench just outside the fitting room as Arrowhawk takes his time shopping for a new pair of jeans. Mendoza shifts her body to keep her butt from going numb while Arrowhawk makes up his mind between a lightly faded pair of boot-cut jeans or a dark blue pair of carpenter pants. He walks out of the fitting room.

"What do you think?"

"Honestly, John, I don't care," Mendoza replies. "This is what, the fourth pair of jeans you've tried on? Seriously, you're worse than a girl. We've got places to be."

"Oh come on, Aly, work with me here. You of all people know that when you're in the public eye you have to look fly." Arrowhawk pauses. "And yes, I did intend for that last part to rhyme."

"'Fly?' What are you, from 1975 or something?" Mendoza grudgingly snickers at his intentionally corny joke.

"Look, just hurry it up, OK."

"Funny, if I recall correctly you were saying quite the opposite last night," Arrowhawk counters with a roguish smile.

Trying to keep from blushing, Mendoza attempts to alter the topic. "Like I said, we've got appointments to keep." She pulls out her touch-screen Blackberry and begins rattling off the day's agenda. "I've got you booked for an autograph signing at the Staples Center at 2, and an interview with Vanity Fair at 4:30. And it's already 1:30!"

Without even turning away from the full-length mirror in front of him, Arrowhawk says, "What's up with all these engagements anyway? I thought we were supposed to be civil servants, not commercial heroes."

"Well, it's what the public demands and it's what we'll give them."

As Arrowhawk continues admiring the way his backside looks in the jeans, a trio of twenty-something women by the Misses section stare at him from afar. He is totally oblivious to the giggling and whispering going on just a few feet away from him, although Mendoza's keen ears pick up the chatter. She turns to look at these young women standing by the mannequins adorned with the fall season line. One of them, a five-foot-five brunette, walks towards Arrowhawk. All the while, Mendoza's eyes are trained on her like a watchful mother eagle.

"Excuse me, are you Agent Arrowhawk from Vigil?" the young woman asks, a bit of hesitation in her voice.

He turns. "Please, call me that only when I'm on the job… or when I'm handcuffing you. Otherwise, you can call me John."

It takes just a second before she begins screaming at the top of her lungs like a crazed fan. Her friends now run up to Arrowhawk as well.

"Oh my God, you are him," a second woman in the group exclaims. "You were awesome during the DC attack!"

Arrowhawk nods in acknowledgement, trying to come off as aloof, but he's surprised and appreciative of the compliment. He thinks, *If she saw the part where I got blasted off my behind, she wouldn't think I was so awesome.*

A third woman in the group, an attractive well-endowed redhead, presses up against Arrowhawk and pulls a Sharpie pen from her purse. "Can I have your autograph?"

He takes the pen. "Sure, where do you want me to sign?"

Without any hesitation (or even modicum of modesty) the woman unbuttons the top three buttons of her tight-fitting blouse, exposing her cleavage to just above the bra line. She points to a spot in the upper inner quadrant of her left breast and smiles provocatively. "Right here."

Arrowhawk smiles and obliges. He makes certain to take his time as he completes the arduous task of signing his name on her silicone-enhanced flesh. Mendoza is in no way amused. She gets up from her seat.

"That's all, girls. Agent Arrowhawk has a long day ahead of him," she says, literally dragging him away from the trio of adoring women.

"Sir, you haven't paid for those jeans yet!" a store associate blurts out.

"Bill it to my office," Mendoza says, handing her card over to the associate.

"Jealous?" Arrowhawk asks, as he's forcefully extracted from store.

Mendoza turns to look at the women still gazing and waving at him. "Of those skanks? Hardly."

* * *

Buffalo Jump Auditorium
Blackfeet Council of Business Leaders' annual ceremony
Great Falls, Montana

The Young Leaders of Tomorrow ceremony is an annual event intended to recognize outstanding achievement within the Blackfeet nation. The banquet hall is packed with community leaders and well-wishers. This ceremony is particularly special because of the chosen award winner.

Council president Jim Bradford opens the ceremony.

"Ladies and gentlemen, I want to welcome you to this event. Every year we honor one our young people who is making a difference in the Blackfoot community."

Bradford pauses for a moment as he looks at his note cards before continuing.

"This year we honor Cynthia Fighting Bull for her extraordinary accomplishments and service to the Blackfoot community. Ms. Fighting Bull not only works tirelessly as a member of Vigil, but she has volunteered countless hours with our alcohol awareness and intervention programs. She is truly a shining star within the Blackfeet nation. Won't you all join me as we recognize this year's Young Leader of Tomorrow, Cynthia Fighting Bull."

Applause engulfs the auditorium. The audience members rise to their feet as Fighting Bull walks to the dais to accept her award. Bradford presents her with a wooden plaque, an engraved gold plate at its center. The two pause momentarily for photographs. Afterwards Bradford takes his seat.

Fighting Bull pulls the dais's malleable microphone stand close to her mouth.

"I am truly honored by this award," she says. "It may sound a bit clichéd but this truly means more to me than most of you will ever know."

She takes a moment to look at the plaque once more, and her eyes tear up.

"Although I was born in Montana, my father got a job with NASA when I was six and we moved to a Cleveland suburb called Euclid. I was the only Native person at my school. It was funny, people would ask me what I was... was I Mexican? Spanish? Maybe biracial? I would try to avoid the topic altogether. I later came to realize that there was no reason to hide or avoid who I really am. And it was when I came to that realization that I decided to change my last name from Sorrell to Fighting Bull. Not because I'm ashamed of my family name but because I am proud to represent the Blackfeet nation wherever I go. Thanks so much."

She departs from the dais and takes her seat with her parents, as once more the auditorium is filled with applause.

* * *

Sunday Worship Service
Mount Zion Baptist Church
Fairfax, Virginia

Mount Zion's senior pastor Rodney Vines, a stout sixty-three year old man, has served his congregation for close to three decades. During his tenure he's been a witness to countless historical events, but he could never have imagined that one of his own congregants would be touted as one of the most powerful men in America. After concluding the day's sermon, Pastor Vines wastes no time in inviting his parishioner and good friend Terrell Morrison up to the podium to speak.

"I know we've been here a long time. Service tends to go over sometimes, and I apologize for that. But if you'd all show up on time instead of thirty minutes *after* the start of service, maybe we could get out at a halfway decent time."

A chorus of "Amens" and "Say it, Pastor" reverberates among the congregation.

Pastor Vines continues, "Instead y'all are having intense fellowship with Sister Sheets and Pastor Pillow."

The congregation breaks into laughter, mostly due to the fact that there is an element of truth to what he is saying.

"In all seriousness though, before we end service, I would like to have Brother Terrell Morrison come up and speak a few words."

Vines turns to Morrison, who is seated behind him. Morrison buttons the top two buttons of his sport coat as he walks to the podium. The pastor gives him a big embrace before taking his seat. Morrison removes the Bible tucked in his armpit and places it on the podium stand, then takes the wireless microphone off from its stand and begins to speak.

"Pastor Vines, thanks so much. Now, if everyone could turn with me to Luke 16 verse 10…"

Members of the congregation turn to the stated verse. The shuffling of pages and beeping of mobile devices are clearly heard throughout the sanctuary. Morrison begins to read.

"'Whoever can be trusted with very little can also be trusted with much, and whoever is dishonest with very little will also be dishonest with much. So if you have not been trustworthy in handling worldly wealth, who will trust you with true riches?' Amen."

The congregation answers with a resounding, "Amen."

"As you can tell from that last verse, I want to talk about stewardship. I'm not talking just about money—although I know Pastor Vines wouldn't mind me reminding you all to pay your tithes," Morrison jokes as he turns to look back at Pastor Vines.

Vines in turn points and smiles at Morrison as if to say, "You got it."

"But, we have to be faithful with what God's given us in terms of our time, talents, and abilities. As you all know, I'm a member of Vigil, and God has blessed me with incredible abilities. Although I use these special abilities to serve my country, my ultimate allegiance is and should be to my Lord and Savior Jesus Christ."

Members of the congregation rise up with applause and shouts of "Amen" and "Say it!"

"So I pray that the Lord can use me and these powers he's blessed me with to help those in need and to let His glory shine. My point is this: whatever you have to give, give it freely, because the gifts we have are from the Lord and not birthed within ourselves. Just as I have been given stewardship of these special abilities, God has also granted each and every one of you stewardship over something in your lives. Therefore, I encourage you to seek God's direction in how you would use the gifts He's given you to glorify Him every day in every way."

* * *

Larry King Special
CNN Headquarters
Atlanta, Georgia

Not too often does a journalistic titan come out of retirement to do a special piece on an individual, but this case is different. On this occasion, Larry King takes the time to interview Captain Alicia Conrad. The venerable King sits facing Conrad in what is intended to be a relaxed atmosphere. The show is about to begin and last-minute makeup prep is applied to both King and Conrad. The producer, a lanky man with thinning hair, starts the countdown to the beginning of the show.

"We are live in… five, four, three, two, one…" The producer points his index finger at King.

"Good evening. Tonight we have an exclusive interview with our guest, Captain Alicia Conrad. Captain Conrad is the leader of Vigil, the US superhuman defense initiative, as well as the daughter of former Assistant Joint

Chiefs of Staff and acclaimed military strategist, John Conrad. Captain, thanks for joining us today."

"It's great to be here," Conrad replies.

"First off, I want to bring up the issue of the rise of the superhuman."

"'Rise of the Superhuman'? That sounds like the title of a bad sci-fi movie," Conrad jokes.

King chuckles briefly before continuing.

"All kidding aside, we've seen a steady increase in their numbers worldwide since the mid to late 1960s. With the steady rise in the superhuman population and the potential hazards they pose, do you see this as the reason behind the formation of Vigil?"

"I'm not a politician, Larry, I'm a soldier. My duty and focus is to protect the United States and her citizens. Part of that duty is to lead a group of highly talented and powerful professionals. Our collective goal is to keep this nation safe from threats both human and superhuman."

"Fair enough," King replies, not at all satisfied with her answer. "Now let's look at it from another angle. Although the superhuman population is growing at a steady rate globally, their numbers amount to about 1 percent of the worldwide population. Given this statistic, do you think that superhumans as a whole represent a credible threat?"

"I look at the formation of this team as a pre-emptive act," Conrad states firmly. "Instead of having a reactionary response, as we've had in the past, I believe our government chose the more prudent course by creating Vigil."

"Coming from someone who claims not to be a politician," King kids, "that sounded like a political punch line to me."

"What can I say? I grew up in Washington, and the stuff kind of rubs off on you," Conrad says.

King shuffles the papers in front of him and pushes his glasses back onto the bridge of his nose. "I want to shift gears here and talk about your father."

"OK," Conrad responds, with a tinge of uneasiness. The topic of her father has always been a sore subject for her. In many ways, she feels as if she is constantly being viewed through the lens of his life and legacy.

"He was one of the most brilliant military minds of this modern era," King says. "He helped David Petraeus shape his counterinsurgency stratagem. Also, he was one of the youngest Assistant Joint Chiefs of Staff. Not to mention, he helped form the security firm CoBALT along with Harold Baltimore. Do you ever feel like you have a lot to live up to?"

"No, I don't," Conrad replies succinctly.

"OK, I know with the unfortunate passing of your parents a while back you've assumed a heavy load of responsibility. Not only have you had to maintain your military career, but you've also had to take care of your siblings at a very young age. Does the strain of this balancing act get to be too much?"

This line of questioning is wholly unexpected. The show's producers submitted pre-selected questions prior to the taping, so as to eliminate any surprises. Mendoza's staff was also responsible for screening the questions, but apparently they did not do a thorough job.

"Larry, I'd rather not comment on my personal life. If we could stick to talking about Vigil, I would appreciate that."

"Yes, yes, I apologize." King turns to his left, picks up copies of *Time*, *Newsweek*, *Essence* and *Rolling Stone* from his desk and reads the cover captions in that order.

"'Vigil: The Super Team of Tomorrow'; 'The Face of the Post-Human race'; 'Captain Conrad: How she keeps her cool with the world on her shoulders'; 'How Vigil will change the world.' Captain, how does it feel to be a pop culture phenomenon?"

Conrad gives him a smile that lights up the room.

"Pretty nice, Larry, pretty nice."

CHAPTER TWELVE

BATTLE READY

July 16th
National Security Agency headquarters
Fort Meade, Maryland

Ramsey and Price pore over the newspaper headlines and magazine articles touting Vigil's success during the National Mall attacks. Price has her laptop propped on the end of Ramsey's desk as she skims through the various online fan posts for Vigil. "It looks like we have a phenomenon on our hands, sir," she says, commenting on the team's newly acquired fame.

"I think you summed it up about right," Ramsey says, peering over the front page of the Washington Post. "Phenomenon, indeed."

She scrolls through an online Zogby opinion poll. "This is amazing. Their favorability score is in the nineties among all demographics. They're scoring higher than the president in approval ratings."

"C'mon, like that's hard to do," Ramsey says sarcastically.

Price turns the laptop's screen in Ramsey's direction. "With these numbers, they can do no wrong."

"And that's exactly what we wanted, remember?"

"Aren't you afraid they're a little bit over-exposed though?"

"No, in order to gain the public trust we have to put them out there."

Ramsey's cell phone rings. He pulls it from his right breast pocket and glances at the caller ID, then flashes a look at Price.

She knows exactly what that look means. Without delay she flips down the laptop screen and retreats from his office.

Once she's gone, he answers the call. A heavily accented voice responds to his greeting. The tone causes Ramsey's countenance to transform from jovial to stern.

"No, don't worry, they're ready." Ramsey nods his head as he listens once more to the other conversant.

"Everything's in place. Just make sure you have everything together on your end."

Ramsey ends the call and presses the intercom button on his desk phone. Price answers.

"Yes, sir."

"Lauren, set up a briefing for the team. They have their first official assignment."

CHAPTER THIRTEEN

HUMANITARIAN AID

July 18th
Vigil Headquarters
Sublevel Two
The Pentagon

The team assembles in their Pentagon headquarters for their first official mission briefing. Ramsey opens the meeting.

"As you all know, you've been given your first assignment. You'll be accompanying Paraguayan deputy foreign minister Emmanuel Vásquez on a UN aid mission to Cuidad Del Este."

Ramsey taps a button on the keyboard of the computer next to him. The center of the table is equipped with a holographic projector. The deputy foreign minister's image, as well as site photos of their Paraguayan destination, appear.

"Mr. Ramsey, with all due respect, why do they need us?" Fighting Bull says. "Couldn't they just as easily have used a military escort?"

"I was just getting to that, Agent Fighting Bull. The destination of the aid shipment is under heavy control by fringe militant factions." He taps on the keyboard again, and images of numerous terrorist cell leaders appear. "Some of these groups have noted ties to organizations such as Hezbollah, and FARC[8].

8 Revolutionary Armed Forces of Colombia

And now with the advent of super-powered terrorism, we don't want to take chances."

"Have you got any actionable intel to back this up?" Blankenchip asks.

"Yes in fact we do." Ramsey taps another button and the image switches to that of a burning caravan of Hummer trucks. "A few days ago a caravan carrying freeze-dried rations to Cuidad del Este was attacked by a contingent of armed robbers; one of them was a pyrokinetic—a fire starter. They looted the caravan and incinerated everyone in it. So you see why it's so important to have superhuman protection on this mission."

"What's our timeframe?" Conrad inquires.

"A plane is being loaded at Andrews Air Force base as we speak. You'll meet with Mr. Vásquez there. Wheels up in an hour."

CHAPTER FOURTEEN

GETTING TO KNOW YOU BETTER

Nine hours later
Paraguayan airspace

The roar of the AC-130H gunship's engines sears through the flawless tropical sky. Flanked by three MH-60 Blackhawks—one on each side and one in front—the gunship cruises smoothly through Paraguayan airspace. The Vigil team members, a detachment of UN marines, and Emmanuel Vásquez's diplomatic entourage are strapped in tight in the gunship's forward cabin. Conrad unbuckles her restrictive seatbelt and walks toward the cockpit.

"What's our ETA?" Her question is posed to the pilot as the co-pilot eyes the flight instrumentation.

"Approximately fourteen minutes, ma'am."

"Good." Conrad walks back to her seat next to Minister Vásquez and she straps herself in.

"We should be arriving shortly Mr. Vásquez."

"Thank you." He then turns his attention toward the view outside the plane. It is clear that his focus is elsewhere and not on the flight details. Conrad tries to recapture his attention.

"Mr. Vásquez, if I could ask a question?"

"Surely." He turns to look at her.

"We were given the Cliff's Notes version at our briefing but I need to know the exact details about what is going on."

Vásquez looks briefly at Conrad before returning his attention to the view outside. "Lately there has been increased tension between the Piñero faction and a splinter group of FARC. The conflict has been so intense that the people living in the surrounding areas starve to death because they cannot access the marketplace."

Vásquez's assertion is correct. Cuidad del Este is a well-known trading center in Paraguay and is the nexus point of three countries—Brazil, Argentina, and Paraguay. Incidentally, it is also well-known for its illicit drug trade.

"What's happened on past attempts?" Conrad inquires.

"Before, we have either had to turn back because of the danger, or our cargo was intercepted. Hopefully this time, with your help, we will finally be successful."

"I'm sure there'll be nothing to worry about," she says in a reassuring tone.

A few seats behind them, Arrowhawk makes a comment to Fighting Bull who is next to him.

"Cynthia, if you wanted to cop a feel all you had to do was ask."

She leans forward and turns to look at him in puzzlement.

"What are you talking about?"

"Our little fiasco on the National Mall."

She smiles and lies back in her chair. "Oh please, stop feeling yourself."

"C'mon now, Cynthia," Arrowhawk protests, "don't tell me you didn't feel the spark when we touched."

"Yeah, I did, but it had nothing whatsoever to do with anything romantic."

She traces her right hand over the fabric of her suit with admiration. "This suit morphs with me when I do a shape change. And when I touch someone…" She grabs Arrowhawk's arm and morphs into him. "It also gives me the ability to copy their abilities for a short period of time."

In a sense the suit is like a second skin, reacting to her metamorphic changes through a brain-computer-interface sensor embedded in the collar. She clearly enjoys it, so much so that she requested that her entire wardrobe be retrofitted with the same material. This allows her the luxury of her clothes morphing with her wherever she goes.

She morphs back to natural form. "That's the spark you felt."

"Oh, and I thought it was me," Arrowhawk says, a hint of dejection in his voice.

She pats him on his shoulder. "You can keep up the illusion, John, if it makes you feel better."

"No illusions, Cynthia. You just can't admit the obvious."

Fighting Bull snickers and changes the subject. "John, do you have any idea how powerful you are? I had your abilities for only a moment, and it was overwhelming."

"That's not the only thing that I've got that's overwhelming."

Fighting Bull ignores the sophomoric comment. "Seriously, how do you control it?"

Arrowhawk looks down, almost embarrassed, but before he can utter a word, their conversation is interrupted by an explosion in the tail of the plane.

Fighting Bull looks out of the side window to see the three flanking helicopters tumbling down into the Paraguayan jungle in burning heaps.

Conrad calls out to the pilot. "Sit rep!"

"We've been hit by some kind of short-range missile, ma'am! We're going down fast," the pilot responds.

With their window of escape getting smaller by the second Conrad immediately initiates evacuation measures.

"All right, everyone, bail out!" She turns to Vásquez in the jump seat. "Mr. Vásquez, you'll parachute down with me."

The plane's passengers comply. One by one they leap out of the gunship's aft door. Their jump packs explode open, unleashing a sea of colorful inflated parachutes. As they descend, a quartet of Apache helicopters surrounds them. The attacking helicopters fire their weapons, piercing the escaping passengers' parachutes. The evacuees begin hurtling down into the Paraguayan jungle.

Through all this chaos Conrad communicates to the team via her radio earpiece. "Arrowhawk, Fighting Bull, and Morrison, I want you to cover our men. Blankenchip and I'll take care of the attackers."

Fighting Bull disengages her parachute and streamlines her body to increase her speed of descent. She radios Arrowhawk.

"John, I'm going to grab the men closest to me. Can you catch us?"

"I'll try," Arrowhawk replies as he continues to tumble through the air at a dizzying speed.

"Try hard," Fighting Bull admonishes, "because here we come." She rushes into the midst of three of the marines, grabbing two of them by their collars. The last one continues to descend faster than she can get to him. She pulls the two other marines close to her and taps a button on her belt buckle, which releases multiple thin titanium filaments that entangle the marines like a spider's web. This particular device was an extra gift, courtesy of Winston Jordan. A small cord extends from Fighting Bull's belt to the entangled marines, allowing her to tow the men in with her as she descends.

The last marine is even further away from her. She pulls a grappling gun from the side compartment of her belt and aims for his midsection. Her shot hits the mark; the grappling hook snags the marine by the top portion of his flak jacket. Fighting Bull attaches the handle of the gun to the left side of her belt, flips the retraction switch on the gun, and reels in the marine as they continue plummeting to the ground.

Arrowhawk has the toughest task of all his teammates. He not only has to contend with the falling marines closest to him, but also the debris from the damaged gunship as it rains down on them. Pieces of the fuselage and rear rotors come close to slicing through the rest of the evacuees, but thankfully Arrowhawk is able to create a solid energy cocoon around this contingent. They tumble to the jungle floor, crashing into the foliage but protected by the cocoon. The marines are unharmed, and Arrowhawk takes a few seconds to gather his bearings. But no sooner does he get his feet under him than Fighting Bull radios him.

"John."

"Yeah," Arrowhawk responds.

"Look up."

As soon as he raises his head he sees Fighting Bull and the three entangled marines tearing through the sky towards him. He has maybe ten seconds before the quartet will hit the ground. He immediately expands the energy cocoon outward for Fighting Bull and her rescued marines to land safely in. The impact of their landing is a strain on Arrowhawk, but he's able to sustain the integrity of his energy cocoon.

As he gently lowers the cocoon with Fighting Bull and her men in it, Morrison disengages his parachute straps and alters his molecular density to iron. He then uses the parachute as a makeshift net to gather in three falling marines. As they continue falling a piece of the gunship's wing rotor slices through the parachute. Morrison grasps the remaining pieces of the parachute and wraps them tightly around two of the marines. He then alters his molecular density to liquid metal and stretches his hand to grab the last marine. Morrison radios Arrowhawk. "Can you grab us too?"

"I guess I can do the impossible twice."

The strain on Arrowhawk's system is almost unbearable, but he nonetheless grits his teeth and does what he's asked. He expands the energy field outward in a concave fashion to provide added cushion for their fall. Morrison and the rest of the marines land safely in Arrowhawk's energy field.

While all this is happening on the ground, there is another conflict playing out in the air. Conrad and Blankenchip trade gunfire with the helicopters.

Conrad—with Vásquez strapped in front of her—fires her pistol repeatedly at the lead helicopter. With her parachute still unopened, she manages to clip the sides of the attacking aircraft. The attackers continue shooting at them with their on-board machine guns. Many of the bullets miss their targets, but some are able to find them.

"AAGCK!" Conrad winces at the sharp pain in her right shoulder.

"You're hit?!" Vásquez says.

"I'm all right," Conrad responds. "They got me in my body armor. On my word I want you to yank the parachute cords as hard as you can."

"A-all right," Vásquez replies.

The Apache helicopter moves in, its propeller blades hovering ever so close to them.

"Now!" Conrad shouts.

Vásquez pulls the cords and the parachute explodes out of the jump pack. The pair is forcefully thrust upward as the parachute inflates, positioning them right above the pursuing helicopter. Conrad then shoots out the rear rotor of the pursuing helicopter. The pilot loses navigational control, and the helicopter begins spiraling down to the jungle floor.

The helicopter to her left fires more rounds in their direction; bullets whiz past her ears. She immediately trains her pistol on the helicopter and fires two bullets into the cockpit, both of which crash through the windshield and hit their target, wounding the pilot in the shoulder. The pilot hits the eject button as his helicopter starts losing altitude, just narrowly avoiding the ensuing crash.

"You OK, Mr. Vásquez?" Conrad asks.

Vásquez can barely comport himself. But somehow he finds the words to answer. "I guess so."

"Bet you never expected so much excitement on a simple humanitarian aid mission."

"No."

The remaining two helicopters fire on Blankenchip relentlessly. Most of the bullets deflect off of his exoskeletal armor. He fires two rounds from his assault rifle at the gas tank of the helicopter to his right. Aiming his weapon is essentially child's play for Blankenchip, thanks in part to the integrated targeting system built into his helmet. So even though he is twisting and turning through the air at a dizzying speed, he has no trouble hitting his target with the highest level of accuracy.

He follows the salvo of bullets with a flare burst released from his right forearm gauntlet. The flare ignites the leaking gas, causing the helicopter to explode. Fortunately for the pilot and the gunner, they bail out before the explosion.

A schematic of the last helicopter's weak points pops up on Blankenchip's heads-up display. The targeting system selects the structural points that will disable the helicopter most effectively. The chopper blades are the broadest and easiest ones for Blankenchip. He fires a round at one of the blades. Immediately the helicopter starts spinning out of control and plunges to the ground. With all of the resistance eliminated, Blankenchip deploys his parachute and has no problem the rest of the way down.

CHAPTER FIFTEEN

THE REAL TRUTH

Two hours later
Paraguayan Jungle

The UN contingent sustains minimal injuries considering that they had a mid-air firefight with multiple Apache helicopters. The UN marines and Vigil do their best to gather and interrogate their prisoners. None of them carry standard identification and they are wearing nondescript army fatigues, making it difficult to identify them. Conrad gets a status report from one of the marines.

"There were no sustained casualties, and about seven wounded or injured. The medics are taking care of them now. We've captured about ten of the combatants. All of the others were either killed, ran off or weren't within our perimeter locus, ma'am."

"Good, keep me up to speed on any new developments."

"Yes, ma'am."

Conrad walks toward Blankenchip, who's trying his best to interrogate one of the opposition force's squad leaders, but there's an obvious language barrier.

"How's it going, Aaron?" she asks.

Blankenchip turns to her. "This is making my ass tired. The guy knows no English and the extent of my Spanish is *'como estas'* and *'muy caliente.'* You handle it."

"Don't you have a translator program built into that thing?" Conrad asks, tapping Blankenchip's armor.

"No, Rosetta Stone wasn't part of the upgrade package." He strokes the chest plate of his armor. "This thing was built for fighting, not a foreign relations summit."

Conrad smiles. "I'll give it a shot."

Blankenchip steps back to give her room. She kneels down to eye level with the captive.

Although her Spanish is a bit rusty, she can still manage decent conversation; well, enough to get what she wants. "Who are you?" she asks.

"My name is Antonio Guillermo Esposito. I am a second lieutenant in the counter-narcotics division of the Paraguayan Naval Marines."

He unbuttons his shirt collar to produce an I.D. tag tucked underneath his Kevlar vest to verify his identity.

After looking at it, she asks, "Why did you attack us?"

"We gathered intelligence from one of our sources that there would be a shipment of powder cocaine smuggled through Cuidad Del Este by way of military convoy."

"Your intelligence was wrong," Conrad protests adamantly.

"Impossible! Our source came directly from within the US government."

"That makes no sense. We are from the US government. This humanitarian aid mission was cleared through the Paraguayan authorities—"

Esposito interrupts her in mid-sentence. "Who is your envoy?"

"Emmanuel Vásquez, why?"

Esposito lets out a boisterous laugh. "You have been severely misinformed. Emmanuel Vásquez is the head of one of the largest drug trafficking cartels in Paraguay. He is probably on his way to meet a buyer right now."

"You can't be serious."

"There's been an ongoing internal investigation of corrupt government officials for the past year and Vásquez has long been suspected of being a high-level drug lord. We've been monitoring him for over a year."

"No," Conrad responds in disbelief.

"Yes," Esposito says bluntly. "He's been trading drugs for weapons with groups such as Hezbollah and the FARC."

"I don't believe you."

Esposito leans in closer to her. "Let me ask you this: have you actually seen what is inside those crates you are escorting?"

Confused and upset, she leaves Esposito. Conrad runs to the remains of the gunship, which is still smoldering from the missile attack. She enters the cargo area, pulls out the Beretta from her flak jacket and shoots the locks off of one of the damaged crates. Upon lifting the lid, she sees standard UN dehydrated food rations on the surface. Digging deeper through the top layer, she finds large quantities of packaged powder cocaine. She slits a bag open with her Swiss army knife, and dips her small finger in to taste the powder. It's exactly as Esposito stated. Looking at the amount of crates, she does the rough math in her head and estimates the amount of cocaine.

Conrad walks out of the cargo bay and heads towards the makeshift camp. Vásquez is sitting around a campfire with some of the marines and members of the team, drinking coffee and telling jokes.

"Would you like to explain this?" Conrad asks angrily.

She throws a bag of the powdered cocaine at Vásquez's feet. He picks up the bag and looks at it intently. His realization of the inevitable starts to sink in.

"Can you explain how an aid mission got turned into a drug-running operation?!" Conrad grabs him up by his shirt collar and slams him into the side of the tree he was sitting under. Those gathered around are shocked at what they hear.

"I want answers, Vásquez," she says, her grip tightening around his neck. "Who are you? What's going on? And why were we carrying over 10,000 kilos of powder cocaine on our plane?!"

Vásquez knows full well that he has no other recourse but to give Conrad what she wants: the truth. Without any hint of hesitation, he responds. "I had hoped that it wouldn't have come down to this. Captain, your mission, your team, your whole entire purpose is a lie!"

PART TWO

DEFIANT

CHAPTER SIXTEEN

FULL DISCLOSURE

Montéz Federal Detention Facility
Asunción, Paraguay

V ásquez sits shackled to a rusted table with only a glass of water on it. He is encircled by an assemblage of Paraguayan law enforcement officers and Vigil. The lighting is poor, casting ominous shadows over Vásquez's interrogators. The cloistered setting makes the atmosphere more intimidating.

Within three hours after Vásquez's capture, the intercepted drug payload is remanded into the custody of Paraguayan authorities, members of Vásquez's entourage are arrested, and Vásquez himself is brought up on federal and international drug and corruption charges. Without question it has been a pretty impressive show of efficiency by the Paraguayan Naval Marines.

"Tell us everything," Conrad says, "starting with how you were able to masquerade a shipment of cocaine as humanitarian aid, to how you funneled UN resources into your operation, and what you mean exactly when you say that the purpose of our team is a lie?"

"Are you sure you want to know everything? Do you think you'll be able to handle the gravity of what I am about to tell you?" Vásquez says this in a tone that just rubs her the wrong way. She responds in kind.

"I'm too old to be coddled, Vásquez. I want full disclosure."

Vásquez looks down, pausing before answering.

"In regard to your first question, I had the shipment packaged and transported from one of my warehouses in Gaithersburg. With my diplomatic status, it wasn't hard to retrieve the proper documents to make everything look official. As for your second question, the UN's Emergency Relief Coordinator is a good friend of mine, so I had no problem getting the aid package approved. Your last question requires a more extensive answer."

Vásquez's hand shakes slightly as he takes a sip of water.

"I am a member of a group called 'The Network.' It's an international alliance—if you want to call it that—of businessmen, government officials, and multibillionaires. Our union was formed out of shared interests. We have been involved in all realms of world affairs from politics and economics to science and even entertainment."

Arrowhawk whispers to himself, "No wonder broadcast television sucks these days." He turns to Vásquez, making air quotation marks with his fingers as he asks, "So what's the 'Network's' end objective-total and utter world domination?"

Vásquez flashes a wry smile. "My friend, we already dominate the world. The world just doesn't know it yet."

Conrad leans in close to Vásquez and jabs her index finger squarely into his chest.

"Prove it."

Beads of sweat form on his forehead. "Do you remember the International Monetary Fund accounting scandal last June wherein billions of dollars were lost due to fraud?"

"It was an economic catastrophe," Fighting Bull interjects. "Dozens of developing nations lost out on financial aid because of it."

Vásquez nods in acknowledgement.

"What about it?" Conrad asks.

"That was actually a scheme arranged by two of our members to force the chairman of the board to step down. One of our members then took over as chairman, giving us unfettered access to all IMF assets. Their planning and execution of the affair was sheer genius," Vásquez replies in a self-congratulatory tone.

"So you sent world stock markets into a tailspin and triggered economic recessions worldwide over the chairman's seat? That's pretty hard to believe," Conrad says.

"You think I'm lying? Check for yourself. I suggest you start with the IMF's internal records. You'll see that what I'm saying is true."

"OK, so what does that have to do with us?"

"Although we have exerted our considerable influence worldwide, there are elements that have sought to eliminate it. So far we have done an excellent job of neutralizing potential threats through internal cooperation." Vásquez looks at each member of Vigil. "Unfortunately, some of our enemies have also realized the benefit of using superhuman operatives. As a result, our power and influence has gradually eroded."

Fighting Bull once more interjects. "If this organization is as powerful as you claim, why not just form your own paramilitary force?"

"The principals were reluctant to dedicate their own resources to such a thing. But there was still the need to strengthen our alliance. It was then that fate stepped in and provided us with an opportunity we couldn't miss."

"Vigil," Conrad says, completing Vásquez's thought.

"Exactly." He points in her direction as if to indicate that the two of them are on the same wavelength. "One of our principals informed us that the United States National Security Council was contemplating creating its own superhuman task force. The proposal was well received and had Congressional support, but lacked the financial wherewithal to achieve it. The suggestion was made that we as a group provide funding for this project, and in turn this task force would deal with our competition, unbeknownst to the former."

"That's top level intel only a member of the NSC's inner circle would know of. There's no way you could have this much detailed knowledge without having someone highly placed," Conrad notes.

Vásquez turns and looks out through the rusty steel-barred window to his right.

"It was Chandler Ramsey."

The team is shocked by this revelation.

"Our operations officer?" Conrad asks, voicing their collective surprise.

"Yes. He's been a principal member of the Network since its inception. He's given us valuable US national security intelligence and federal contracts. He even spearheaded the attack on the National Mall."

"What was the purpose of that?" Fighting Bull asks.

Vásquez leans back in his chair, his fingers touching in a fashion resembling an open pyramid. "It was a field test, to determine the team's combat readiness. If you pay for a product you want to make sure it works properly, right?"

"How come no one in the NSA or the FBI ever caught wind of this?" Arrowhawk asks.

"You would have to ask Chandler. He's well versed in the nuances of subversion. I'm sure that he's figured ways to cover his tracks."

Trying to steer the conversation back on course, Conrad asks, "You were saying about the proposal…"

"Chandler presented to his superiors the idea of making the Vigil project a joint corporate/government venture. It was accepted, and they granted him oversight authority."

"How did you arrange funding for the project?" Conrad asks.

"We set up dummy corporations to serve as fronts for our financial contributions. Our plan worked perfectly. America had its super-squad and we had our 'enforcers'," Vásquez answers with a contemptuous smile.

"That's a pretty elaborate story," Conrad comments. "Why are you so willing to give your friends up so easily?"

"My friends?!" Vásquez laughs. "Those people are not my friends. The Network is simply a means to an end. My allegiance is to myself, and if they can help me get what I want, then that's excellent. If not, then I have no problem selling them out to accomplish my goals."

"How can we be sure that you're not lying?" Fighting Bull asks.

"I'm in federal custody, aren't I? What good would it do for me to lie now?

Plus I've negotiated a deal to reduce my sentence." His point is valid. With numerous charges against him, irrefutable evidence indicating his guilt, and a plea deal, it would have served him no good to lie about these assertions.

"If you want to go further," Vásquez continues, "I suggest you do some digging of your own."

"We'll see," Conrad responds gruffly. She motions to the second lieutenant standing nearby. "We're done here."

The second lieutenant motions to his men to escort Vásquez to his holding cell. Conrad continues speaking to him.

"We need access to all your files on Vásquez."

CHAPTER SEVENTEEN

HONEST OPINIONS

Three hours later
Paraguayan airspace

The Vigil team and their UN entourage fly back to the US in an unmarked 727 plane courtesy of the Paraguayan government. The team secludes itself in the rear cabin while the UN personnel remain in the forward passenger section. The events of the past few hours dominate their discussion.

"So, what do you all think?" Conrad asks.

"He's giving us a load of bull," Blankenchip answers in his inimitable style. "The man's got as much credibility as David Duke at an NAACP rally. And based on their justice minister's files, he's nothing but a two-bit coke dealer with diplomatic immunity."

"I agree," Morrison chimes in.

"But what if there is something to his story?" Arrowhawk counters. "Aren't we obligated to at least check it out?"

"Please, the guy'll say anything to lighten his sentence," Blankenchip snaps back.

"I don't think so," Arrowhawk responds. "He's already done his plea deal with the Paraguayans—there's no real incentive for him to lie. There's got to be something there."

"But a worldwide conspiracy of super rich execs and government bureaucrats out to rule the world?" Morrison interjects. "Get serious."

Arrowhawk turns to look at Morrison. "You know the saying: 'Power corrupts and absolute power corrupts absolutely.'"

"This is priceless; he's quoting Lord Acton now," Blankenchip quips.

Arrowhawk ignores Blankenchip's mocking comment and continues. "Look, abuse of power happens all the time. We have plenty of examples: Nixon and Watergate in the seventies, Iran-Contra in the eighties, the Enron collapse of 2002, and the Wall Street bailouts at the end of the early 2000s."

"Those were totally different situations," Morrison responds. "We're talking about coordinated corruption on an international level. The best course of action is to file a report with the State Department and have them deal with it. We shouldn't even try to get involved."

"Ditto," Blankenchip adds.

Conrad looks to Fighting Bull for input. "Cynthia, do you have anything to say?"

Fighting Bull puts her hand to her chin in a pondering manner. She thinks for a few moments before responding. "On the one hand we've got a man who's a liar and a drug lord. On the other hand, they have records citing Vásquez's ties to a slew of illicit organizations. That can't be totally coincidental." She glances at Arrowhawk. "I hate to admit it but I agree with John; it would be careless of us not to investigate. There's no harm in looking. It'll either discredit or validate Vásquez's claims."

Arrowhawk gives Fighting Bull a flirtatious look. "I knew you really loved me." Then he turns to Conrad. "OK, it looks like we're split evenly. Old school stodgy says do nothing, new school sexy says move forward. You're the deciding vote, Cap."

"You've all made good points," Conrad replies. "True, our job doesn't include conducting criminal investigations, and it'd probably be easier to just hand this off to the State Department or the GAO[9]."

She turns deferentially to the youngest two members of the team. "On

---

9 Government Accountability Office—independent congressional watchdog agency

the other hand, if what Vásquez said is true then we could be involved in one of the greatest acts of treason I've ever seen. He leveled some pretty serious accusations against one of our own. But I don't want to rush blindly into a mole hunt."

"What's our course of action then?" Fighting Bull asks.

"We investigate every contact or associate of Vásquez to determine whether there's a credible link between him and Ramsey."

Conrad turns to Fighting Bull. "Cynthia, I want you to look into Vásquez's international contacts. Everything you can find—his most frequented locales, foreign liaisons, offshore accounts. The whole thing."

She then points to Arrowhawk. "John, I want you to look into the IMF mess he was talking about. If you come across any dirty tricks being played, I want to know. Also, find out why no one on our end had a clue what Vásquez was up to."

"For sure, Cap," he replies, feeling vindicated by the fact that she's agreed with his suggestion.

"Terrell, I need you to check out Vásquez's domestic contacts, as well as his operational funding sources. Aaron, dig up everything on Ramsey's history, not only from his time in the NSA but from his schooling, his employment, and even his family history."

"What'll we tell Ramsey when we get back to DC?" Fighting Bull asks. "We obviously can't tell him everything that's happened."

Blankenchip intercepts the question, a habit of his that was especially common in the past when he was in Conrad's presence. "He'll probably find out anyway. The arrest of a major political figure isn't something that goes unnoticed."

"Thankfully, the Paraguayan authorities are instituting a forty-eight-hour press blackout on the Vásquez arrest," Conrad answers. "That should buy us some time. As for what we tell Ramsey, it's simple: we lie."

Appalled at the thought, Morrison erupts. "What?!"

"Watch out, here comes the Morality Police," Arrowhawk mumbles.

"You're telling us to lie? How does that make us any better than people like Vásquez," Morrison exclaims.

"Relax, Terrell," Conrad says, trying to allay his concerns. "I'm not talking about an out and out lie. Just the truth without all the details."

"What are you suggesting exactly?"

"We explain that we encountered some resistance but eventually delivered the proper goods to the appropriate people."

"And just omit the whole fact that we were aiding and abetting a drug smuggling operation?" Morrison asks.

"What sense would it make if we did tell him?" Arrowhawk asks Morrison. "We have to do this without letting him know that we're on to him."

"I can't believe what I'm hearing," Morrison says in exasperation. "We have an obligation to be upfront and honest. We can't tell half-truths—"

"Look, I understand your concern. I'm as much in disbelief as you are but we have to keep in mind that Ramsey might be involved in a high-level conspiracy," Conrad exhorts. "Like John said, we can't tip him off to the fact that we know this. We have to keep in mind that Ramsey might not be the only one involved. We have to approach this cautiously."

"I still don't agree with it," Morrison says defiantly.

If there is one thing Conrad cannot stand, it's any hint of insubordination from those under her command, so Morrison's tone certainly does not sit well with her. "It doesn't matter, and frankly, I don't care if you agree," she replies firmly. "I am your senior commanding officer, and that's the way we're going to handle the situation."

Morrison gives her a disconcerted look, the kind a man wears when he's been put in his place. As he recovers from the blow to his ego, Fighting Bull brings up another germane issue.

"I'm still curious about who tipped the Paraguayan authorities off about the shipment."

"I wondered the same thing, but unfortunately they said that info was off-limits."

"Interesting..." Fighting Bull says with a quizzical look on her face.

"What's the plan after our data hunt?" Arrowhawk asks.

"We'll have to meet at a neutral location," Conrad answers. "I'm thinking a public place would be the best."

CHAPTER EIGHTEEN

REASONABLE DOUBT

July 29th
International House of Pancakes
West 23rd and Lincoln
Washington, DC

"How many?" the hostess asks with a smile.

"Actually I'm meeting with some people. Thanks," Conrad says.

She makes her way back to the team gathered in a booth in the back corner of the restaurant as they take in a late morning brunch. Although recognized as global icons, they have managed to meld into the crowd quite well. It helps that they are in their civilian clothes and not in their combat uniforms.

"We were wondering when you'd show up, Cap," Arrowhawk says as Conrad takes her seat next to him.

She looks away briefly. "Sorry I'm late, I had some... family issues to deal with."

"Don't you always," Blankenchip says flippantly. He then looks at the forkful of sausage he's about to devour and remarks, "This is a cardiac arrest on a plate."

"Don't worry about it," Arrowhawk says. "I can always use my powers to defib you if you go into arrest."

Blankenchip points his fork in Arrowhawk's direction. "Lay a hand on me, kid, and you'll be the one needing the defibrillator."

"Do you always have to speak in outdated tough-guy clichés?" Arrowhawk replies.

Blankenchip gives him an intent-to-harm glare. Fighting Bull looks at the both of them and shakes her head. She turns to Conrad.

"It seems your hunch to investigate was right." She pulls out a tablet computer from a leather shoulder bag and pulls up a screen detailing Vásquez's travel history. She slides the device over to Conrad who's just given her order to the waiter.

"Vásquez made repeated trips to Afghanistan and the Saudi peninsula within the last ten months. On those trips he traded drugs for arms with Omar el-Basir, one of the top lieutenants in an Al-Qaeda off-shoot. He also met repeatedly with Hasan Haq, a Jordanian oil magnate."

"I see. Does he only deal with extremist organizations?"

"No, he deals with rogue states as well—as if that were any better. He's helped bankroll the development of nuclear weapons for both Iran and North Korea. I've included a list of bank transactions in there as well."

"Thanks, Cynthia." Conrad swipes through the contents on the touch screen. She looks in Arrowhawk's direction.

"Vásquez has been in bed with some of the most notorious crime cartels the FBI's ever faced," Arrowhawk says, "To date he's been involved with over ten known criminal organizations. He's laundered money for the Echevarria cartel and was also involved in the Templeton extortion ring."

"What did you find out about the whole IMF mess?"

"Vásquez was on the money about that. Kevin Dorret, the former British Finance Minister and IMF chairman, stepped down due to allegations brought by two of the board's members: Lawrence Holmes and Lorraine Duvalier. It was alleged that the chair mismanaged billions of dollars from donor nations. Incidentally, Lawrence Holmes was next in line for the position of chairman. With Dorret's resignation, Holmes took over."

"What did the IMF's internal investigation turn up?" Conrad leans forward intently.

"They found the chairman culpable for the loss of funds, but there was something funny going on."

Arrowhawk points to two names on the papers in front of him.

"Holmes and Duvalier were members of both the Development and the International Monetary and Financial Committees. And these were the same subcommittees where the money was lost."

Conrad picks up the papers. "Any connection to Ramsey in all this?"

"Not with IMF, but I did find something else." Arrowhawk pulls out more documents from his shoulder bag. "I looked into how Vásquez was able to fund his operations. He set up phony charities, something similar to a UNICEF or March of Dimes, to launder money. One charity in particular..." He holds up a document with a logo of multi-colored interlocking hands encircling a globe. "Helping Hand Incorporated received over 100 million dollars in donations last year alone. Guess whose name was on that donor list?"

"Ramsey's."

"Bingo." Arrowhawk snaps his fingers. "But it doesn't stop there; Holmes and Duvalier were some of the biggest donors too."

"How come no one on our end picked up on this?"

"Vásquez would usually use his diplomatic status as a shield against scrutiny."

"Good work." Conrad looks to Morrison. "Terrell?"

Morrison pulls out two large manila folders from his briefcase. He opens one of the folders and lays it right next to Conrad's just-arrived plate of French toast.

"Apparently, Vásquez isn't only into money laundering, but also money making—literally. When I was researching Treasury Department archives, I found that an intaglio printing press was stolen from the US Mint four years ago. The press appeared on the black market two months after it was stolen. Vásquez purchased the press and has been using it to produce fake bills."

"Counterfeiting."

"Yes. According to the archives, he's also been involved with a number of casino fronts around the world. He supplied them with counterfeit cash to run their operations. Based on what John said, he's probably diverting money from that scheme into his charity organizations."

Conrad scratches her head. "This is getting more and more interesting."

"It ain't done yet, Alicia," Blankenchip blurts out.

"What've you got?"

Blankenchip removes a small laptop computer from a metal brief case and places it in front of him. He clicks on an icon and begins reading from what he sees onscreen.

"Ramsey's been the model NSA officer. Graduated from Stanford *summa cum laude* with a B.A. in Naval Sciences, spent five years in the Navy and joined the CIA afterwards. He was in the CIA for fifteen years before transferring to the NSA. But there was something curious. He took a six-month leave of absence before his transfer from the CIA to the NSA."

"Any record of what he was doing during that time?"

"I couldn't find anything. Officially he was 'on sabbatical'—whatever that means. Unofficially he virtually fell off the planet during those six months."

"You guess that's when he turned?"

"Maybe, or he's been dirty all along and nobody knew. I also found something else that was suspect. You remember when they were discussing our 'satellite system' during the orientation? Well, come to find out Ramsey was a shareholder in the company that manufactured it."

"What's the name of it?" Conrad asks.

"Hold on..." Blankenchip clicks his mouse.

"Celedane Corporation."

"Never heard of them."

"That's because they're new to the contracting scene. They dealt primarily with industrial manufacturing before branching out into defense contracting."

"Who's the head of that company?" Conrad asks.

"An Italian guy named Victor Angella. Obviously, it's not a coincidence that they got the contract."

"I know. What Vásquez said about the team's charter was true. The language was so ambiguous that it allowed the Network to slip in and fund the project without any suspicion."

"We seem to have enough to start an official investigation," Fighting Bull says.

"I still say we take it to the GAO. We need to steer clear of this or we may end up in a place we don't want to be." Morrison states.

"Even if we were able to get this to the GAO," Arrowhawk says with a mouth half-filled with food, "it would take forever to get an investigation launched."

"What do you say, Alicia?" Fighting Bull asks.

"I still find it hard to believe that one of our own could be involved in something like this," she says contemplatively.

"That's one of the realities we face." Arrowhawk wipes the syrup from around his mouth. "Feds go corrupt just like anybody else."

"Yeah, but I never would've imagined someone this high up in the chain."

"Look, Alicia," Blankenchip starts up. "What do you want to do?"

"We need to find out more. John, see if you can get a sealed warrant to set up wired and wireless surveillance on Ramsey. Try to get it within the week, and I want this done under the radar."

"Yes, ma'am."

Conrad points to Morrison. "You and Cynthia will serve as support on the op."

"Why?" Morrison asks. "Can't surveillance be set up remotely?"

"Don't forget Terrell that this is the NSA we're talking about. It's not like hacking into First National Bank. There are way too many firewalls and channels to get through to surveil remotely. Any surveillance has to be set up on-site, in person."

"I see," Morrison says in a wary fashion.

"Don't worry Terrell, it'll be fun," Arrowhawk says as he pats Morrison's right shoulder.

"Blankenchip and I will head over to the National Reconnaissance Office," Conrad continues. "I have a contact over there. Maybe he can explain what's going on with the satellite system."

CHAPTER NINETEEN

FAVORS

July 30th
Georgetown
Washington, DC

Arrowhawk pulls up to the brick row house of federal judge Keith Parks in Alysande Mendoza's late-model black BMW sports car. Mendoza has let him borrow her BMW since his vehicle is on the opposite coast. *It's nice having friends with benefits*, Arrowhawk thinks as he closes the driver side door. As a matter of fact, he has a knack for making friends with benefits.

As he climbs the worn cement steps leading to Parks' front door, Arrowhawk thinks back to the seminal event that brought him and Parks together. It was Parks who approved his investigation of the former Senior Senator from Kentucky, Francis Kerrington.

Kerrington served as the chairman of the Senate Select Committee on Intelligence. It was during his tenure that he illegally coordinated a CIA assassination attempt on Venezuelan crime lord Desmond Acosta. The CIA funded and armed a rival faction, the Echevarria cartel, which would carry out the assassination attempt. Unfortunately for Kerrington, this organization was also on the FBI terrorist watch list. Arrowhawk was just three years out of training at Quantico when he was assigned to the case. His investigation led to the eventual arrest and conviction of Kerrington. Although this opened the door to Arrowhawk's promotion to ASAC of the L.A. bureau office, it also led to his blacklisting among many of Kerrington's political peers.

He knocks on the judge's door. A raven-haired woman, who looks younger than her fifty-five years, answers the door.

"Hello, Mrs. Parks," Arrowhawk says in a roguish voice as the door opens.

Cassandra Parks smiles. She's been acquainted with Arrowhawk ever since her husband met him. Being a former district attorney herself, she knows that during a time like this, there can be only one thing he's here for.

"What brings you by at this time of night, John?" she asks.

"You know me, just happened to be in the neighborhood and wanted to say hi."

She looks at him askance. "Don't kid a kidder, John. You're here to get a warrant, aren't you?"

Arrowhawk smiles and shrugs.

"John Arrowhawk, you're easier to read than a supermarket tabloid," she jokes.

"But way more interesting," he retorts with a smile.

"Come on in."

As soon as Arrowhawk enters he is greeted—ever so zealously—by the Parks' golden retriever Dolly.

"Hey there, girl." He strokes the canine's fur.

Mrs. Parks walks to the base of the wooden staircase and calls up to her husband.

"Keith, you've got company!"

Judge Parks walks down the wooden stairs with a case brief in his hands, looking as if he were in deep thought before being interrupted. His silver hair is a bit ruffled but somehow still looks presentable, although the deep circular lines under his eyes are evident from many weary years on the bench. Upon seeing who his visitor is, his countenance changes.

"Cass, could you get Agent Arrowhawk here something to drink?"

"Better question to ask is if I want to."

"Ouch!" Arrowhawk blurts out. "I thought we were tighter than that."

"Tighter than that V-neck shirt you're wearing," she says with a wink and nod to him.

"C'mon girl, let's give the boys some time to talk," Mrs. Parks says as she walks back to the kitchen with her hand firmly grasped around Dolly's collar— almost dragging the dog with her.

Judge Parks and Arrowhawk both take a seat on the brown patent leather couch in the corner of the living room. Arrowhawk places his shoulder bag on the marble coffee table in front of them.

"So what brings you to my neck of the woods, John?"

"Got a big favor to ask of you."

Judge Parks smiles. "When are you not asking me for favors?" He reclines slightly in the couch.

Arrowhawk chuckles. "I need authorization to set up surveillance."

"On who?" he says as he sits up to attention.

"Chandler Ramsey."

Judge Parks pauses. "Wait, isn't he NSA?"

"Yup, and Vigil's operations officer."

"But why?"

"Because, although he may be Mr. NSA in the a.m., he's helped personally finance illicit activity across the globe."

Arrowhawk retrieves the documents gathered from the team's previous meeting from his shoulder bag. He takes the binder clip off the documents and lays them in front of the judge.

Parks looks through the items intently. Page after page reveals Ramsey's illegal activities. His eyes widen in disbelief at what he reads. "Is this all true?"

"As far as we've investigated, yes."

He looks up from the documents. "'We'? As in the FBI?"

"No, as in Vigil. This is something we've been investigating outside the auspices of the Bureau."

Judge Parks puts his head in his hands. Mrs. Parks arrives and gives

Arrowhawk a glass of water with lemon. "I didn't have anything stronger like Jack. I figure since you're driving you'd want to stay away from that stuff—even though you have a superhuman metabolism."

"Thanks," he says, looking up at her.

"No problem."

"You know I'm still catching flak from that Kerrington mess?" Judge Parks replies. Indeed, Parks also suffered as a result of his involvement in the Kerrington case. He was on the White House's short list of potential Supreme Court nominees. Once things hit the fan with the Kerrington case—poof! He was inexplicably dropped from contention.

Arrowhawk takes a sip from his glass before responding. "I appreciate you sticking your neck out for me on that. And I understand your concern, but I assure you that this is legit."

"So, no one in the FBI knows about your little investigation?"

"At least none of the details, for now," He says as he hovers his right hand over the documents on the table. "We're trying to keep this close to the vest in case someone in the Bureau is working with Ramsey."

Judge Parks again looks at the evidence in front of him.

"All right, John," Parks relents. "But if this thing goes sideways, it's all going to be on you."

"I assure you, sir, you won't regret it."

CHAPTER TWENTY

TRIALS AND TRUCULENCE

July 31st
Montgomery County Circuit Court
Silver Spring, Maryland

Opening arguments begin in the Conrad custody case. Typically, these hearings are without a jury but due to the high-profile nature of the case and its complexity, the county requested it. The courtroom proceedings are interspersed with the clicking of long-lens cameras and flashing lights.

Conrad's lawyer, Trenton Phillips, sits next to her at the defendant's table. He stood around five foot seven inches—not terribly too imposing. Beneath his well-pressed Sean John suit his heart beats rapidly as the opposition makes its case. Conrad's face is stern as she listens. The county's lawyer, Devin Mayes, stands in the front of the courtroom, facing the jury box. He wore a well-tailored light blue Ralph Lauren suit with a crisp white dress shirt. The cuff links on his shirtsleeve were engraved with his initials. Mayes is one of the best custody lawyers in the DC metro area. By the way he commanded an audience he made everyone aware of this fact. He makes his opening arguments with an adamancy in his voice that grabbed everyone's attention.

"Your Honor, Alicia Conrad has a commendable record as a military officer, but she is a negligent guardian."

Phillips rises to his feet. "Objection! Ms. Conrad's military record has no bearing on this case."

"Sustained," the Judge replies. "Mr. Mayes, please refrain from discussing the defendant's military record." He then looks in Phillips's direction and points. "And Mr. Phillips, may I remind you that you cannot object during counsel's opening arguments."

"I apologize, Your Honor," Mayes answers, knowing full well that this is the furthest thing from the truth. This is his modus operandi. His aim is to project an aura of calm while allowing the opposing party to seem overly emotional. Mayes wanted to push Phillips's buttons, and he was succeeding beautifully.

Mayes readjusts the buttons on his sport coat before beginning again. "As I was saying, Ms. Conrad has been negligent in her duties as the guardian of her siblings, Camille and Cameron." He turns his gaze upon the twins in the gallery. "Over the past ten years she has abandoned the twins to the care of her grandmother, who at the time, I might add, was on a travel visa from Ghana, to travel to Asia for over two years without notifying anyone of her whereabouts." He then leans in over the wooden jury box partition. "Ms. Conrad has even allowed her siblings to live in over five different foster homes. Not to mention, Ms. Conrad has a past history of mental illness…"

Again Mayes touches a nerve, and Phillips responds just as he intended him to. "Objection!" Phillips once more erupts. "Your Honor, Ms. Conrad's medical history is private record. It's inadmissible—"

The judge cuts him of. "Overruled! One more outburst like that, Mr. Phillips, and I will find you in contempt of court. Proceed, Mr. Mayes."

Mayes smiles as he continues. "Thanks again, Your Honor. I'll strike that last comment off the record." He smooths his tie. "In addition, Ms. Conrad's current position as leader of Vigil puts her in constant danger. What happens if she's injured or even killed in the line of duty?" He makes a concerted effort to make eye contact with the women in the jury box. "Despite Ms. Conrad's best intentions, she is unfit to serve as guardian of her siblings."

He again turns to the gallery and points to the twins.

"Please give these children the better lives that they deserve. Thank you."

Touchdown, Mayes thinks. He's accomplished what he set out to do—give off to the jury the perception of absolute calm and control while leaving Phillips looking desperate. He returns to his chair. The judge slams his gavel.

"We will reconvene next week at 10 a.m. Court is adjourned," the judge concludes.

"All rise," the bailiff says.

Those in the courtroom leave with the exception of a few stragglers and the Conrad contingent. Phillips angrily packs his papers away in his briefcase. Despite what just transpired, he tries to reassure Conrad as best he can. By his body language one could wonder if he was the one needing the reassuring.

"Alicia, don't worry," he says with furrowed brow. "We're going to fight this all the way."

"Thanks Trent," Conrad replies in a tone even calmer than her attorney's.

"I'll be in contact."

Phillips leaves, and Conrad turns to her brother and sister. Camille's big brown eyes look anxiously at her big sister.

"Everything's going to be all right, isn't it?" Camille briefly looks up to Cameron on her left. "They aren't going to throw us in another foster home, are they?"

"Stop spazzing, Camille," Cameron says dismissively. "We'll be fine, *right*, Alicia?"

The way he phrases the last part of the question makes it clear that he's actually daring his sister to make things right this time. After years of disappointment from his older sister, he's had low expectations of her. Any inroads she can make in resolving this situation will be a surprise.

"We've been through a lot worse," Conrad says, touching the shoulders of both of her siblings. "We'll make it through like we always have," she says, giving a sad, remorseful look.

Unnoticed by the Conrad family, Maurice Hodges sits in the rear of the gallery with legs folded, intently listening to their conversation. After hearing enough, he walks up to them. "Enjoy this time Ms. Conrad, there may not be many more like it," he says ominously as he smooths out the wrinkles from his cheap polyester sport coat.

Infuriated by his remark, she retorts, "Mr. Hodges, are you trying to make some kind of veiled threat?"

Hodges flinches slightly. "No, Ms. Conrad, there is no double entendre in what I said," he says in a droning voice. "I meant that precious moments with family are few and far between. You should enjoy them while they last." His eyes shift to the twins. "Have a good day."

He flashes a sour smile at Conrad and leaves the courtroom. Conrad gives him a scowl as he leaves. She turns her body to go after him but Cameron grabs her arm and shakes his head as if to say, "No, Alicia." What she wouldn't give to send Hodges through the wall at that very moment—but she convinces herself that he isn't worth it.

CHAPTER TWENTY-ONE

THE STING

August 2nd
National Security Agency headquarters
Fort Meade, Maryland

L auren Price bursts into Ramsey's office. "Sir, have you checked the time?!" Ramsey looks at his wristwatch. "Oh damn!" He hurriedly gathers his briefing reports for his weekly "Stand Up" meeting with the NSA's top level officials. A meeting which he is late for. Price helps Ramsey gather the rest of his belongings, including his sport coat from behind his chair. As she helps him put his arms in the coat sleeves she slips a small circular metallic disc—the size of a thumbtack—into the front right pocket.

"There you go, sir," Price says as she hands him his cup of Starbuck's coffee. Ramsey zooms out of his office on the way to his meeting. The corners of Price's mouth betray a smile. A few moments after Ramsey leaves, Price heads out of Ramsey's office and to the sublevel garage. She takes a measure of her surroundings as she steps off of the elevator. No bystanders are around as she walks calmly to a nondescript tan Econoline van. She knocks on the side door and it creaks as it slides open.

"You ready?" Arrowhawk says as he places the final plastic prostheses on his face. Suddenly, Lauren Price's visage melts away to reveal the image of Chandler Ramsey.

"Wow, Cynthia," Arrowhawk says. "That's just too weird, how you do that."

"Stop staring, John," Fighting Bull responds under the guise of Ramsey. "Is Terrell done?" she says as she cranes her neck to look at the back of the van.

"Yes I am," Morrison shouts from the back as he arranges the fake bald cap prosthesis on his head. The fit is tight, considering that he has a neat mini Afro underneath. Fighting Bull took the luxury of borrowing facial prostheses from the Directorate of Operations' stockroom to help Morrison and Arrowhawk to avoid the NSA's facial recognition software.

Fighting Bull and her teammates make their way from the sublevel parking lot to the first security checkpoint. The security guard carefully scrutinizes Arrowhawk and Morrison's credentials.

"Resolutions IT Solutions," the guard says while flashing his black light over their IDs and scanning their permits.

"Yes," Fighting Bull says. "I've lost a G-1 level document and I need their help to retrieve it."

The guard nods and waves them through. As the trio makes their way to Ramsey's office, a junior analyst runs into them.

"Hello sir. Aren't you headed to your Stand Ups?"

"Aren't you supposed to be filing something?" Fighting Bull responds. The analyst sheepishly slinks away. Arrowhawk leans into Fighting Bull's ear.

"Ouch, Cynthia, why'd you do them like that?"

"They need to remember who's boss." She pulls out the transponder for the tracking device she placed on Chandler Ramsey. "Ramsey's at his meeting, we should be in the clear."

The three of them make their way to Ramsey's office. The outer doorway requires a retinal scan and the last door requires a palm scan, which Fighting Bull provides. They enter Ramsey's office and begin to work. The back wall of his office is lined with floor to ceiling windows that let in the bright Maryland sky. The opposite side walls are adorned with commendations and plaques from his time in the CIA and the Navy. There was just one picture of him and his family on his desk and nothing else in terms of personal items. Fighting Bull walks to the back wall panel and activates the shift-tint blinds for the windows—effectively blocking any outside observers.

"Time check," she says.

Morrison sets the timer on his wristwatch. "We have ten minutes starting…" The timer beeps. "Now!"

Arrowhawk and Morrison unzip their duffle bags and remove their surveillance equipment.

Arrowhawk goes to Ramsey's computer, removes the cover from the side of the computer tower's chassis, and places a small circuit board with four miniature wires extending from it into the hard drive and to some of the fiber-optic cable leading to the device.

Fighting Bull removes small audio surveillance devices from the inner pocket of her sport coat and places the devices into the receiver of the phone, underneath the base of the desk lamp and in the bottom right corner of the frame of his Naval commendation.

Morrison rifles through Ramsey's file cabinet, looking for any evidence of illegal activity, thinking all the while about what he's actually doing: breaking into a high-level NSA official's office. Their method of investigation unnerves him, and he makes this known to his colleagues. "Breaking and entering as a federal agent—I'm really making a vertical career move here."

Arrowhawk gives a short sigh. "This is not the sequel to Watergate, Terrell. Look, this is perfectly legal; we got a sealed warrant from a district judge."

"Just because it's legal doesn't necessarily mean that it's right," Morrison responds. "The way we're going about this does not sit well with me at all."

"You need to relax."

"I'm fine. I'm just surprised that this sort of thing comes so easily to you."

"Terrell, stop being such a whiny girl—"

"Ahem." Fighting Bull clears her throat, reminding Arrowhawk ever so subtly that despite the fact that she has presently taken the form of a male, she is a woman.

"Present company excluded, of course," Arrowhawk says, trying to save face.

"That's what I thought," she retorts.

Arrowhawk counters, "Well, technically you're a man right now, so does that even count?"

She rolls her eyes. Noticing their interplay, Morrison gives both of them an amused look.

"What?" Arrowhawk inquires.

"Nothing."

Looking at her transponder and noting that Ramsey's meeting will be over soon, Fighting Bull interjects, "We've wasted enough time. Let's finish up and get out of here before Ramsey gets back."

The trio goes back to completing their tasks. Arrowhawk tests the connection of the computer tap on his handheld device. The connection is intact. He then turns on Ramsey's computer to insert the malware that will give full access to the team. As he types in the code he comes across something interesting.

"Whoa, what have we got here?"

"What is it?" Fighting Bull asks.

"It looks like our pal Chandler has been double dipping on the NSA's internal LAN."

"Why do you say that?"

"Because he's running hypervisor software on his PC. It's what they use to run a virtual server." The virtual server acts like a unique physical server, able to run its own operating system. It also allows Ramsey to have an independent system outside of the NSA's local area network.

Two floors down, the chief technician in the Information Technology Security Section detects a loss of bandwidth on their network. Suspecting a breach, he pinpoints the anomaly to Chandler Ramsey's workstation.

"This is ITSS; we have a possible breach in section 522. I need a team to check it out," the technician radios to the operator.

"Copy that."

The operator dispatches a security team to investigate the breach.

Within moments, a three-man security team armed with H&K UMP 45 submachine guns emerges from the sublevel two annex. They swiftly make their way up the stairs toward Ramsey's office. All the while, the three members of Vigil are oblivious to the events unfolding just floors beneath them.

"How are we doing on time?" Fighting Bull asks.

Morrison checks his watch.

"We have… three minutes."

"The malware's been inserted and all connections are in place," Arrowhawk says.

Fighting Bull nods.

At that moment, the security team comes through the outer doorway leading to Ramsey's office. They enter a special pass code to open the inner door. The security team's point man flings the door wide open to discover Chandler Ramsey seated at his desk with two technicians in the chairs across from him.

"May I help you, gentlemen?" Fighting Bull asks matter-of-factly.

"Oh, we apologize, sir," the lead security officer says. "The chief tech picked up a network breach on your workstation and we came to see what was wrong."

Fighting Bull leans forward, her forearms pressed against the desk. "ITSS never fails to astound me. You are correct that there was in fact a network breach." She leans back in the chair and points her right forefinger in Morrison and Arrowhawk's direction. "These men here helped me run a network security test to check the response time of ITSS to system attacks."

"But we usually have an in-house team do those security checks, sir," the second security officer says.

"Those lack the spontaneity of an actual attack," Fighting Bull responds. "We can't be complacent; the NSA has to be vigilant at all times."

"We understand sir," the lead security officer answers contritely.

"Now if you would excuse us."

"Oh, yes, sir, sorry again for the interruption."

The security team leaves and the three breathe a collective sigh of relief.

"That was close," Arrowhawk says.

"Tell me about it," Morrison adds.

"'The NSA has to be vigilant at all times?'" Arrowhawk says, impersonating Fighting Bull's speech. "Seriously? Pun intended, right?"

"No, didn't really think about that."

"Where did you learn to—how do I say it—stretch the truth like that, Cynthia?" Morrison asks.

Fighting Bull gives a chuckle.

"You mean lie, Terrell. I'm a spy, remember? Our stock in trade is deceit. After a while it sort of becomes a part of you."

He shakes his head. Just then his watch beeps.

"That's it, time to go, ladies and gents."

CHAPTER TWENTY-TWO

TRUTH BE TOLD

The National Reconnaissance Office
Chantilly, Virginia

"Alicia, it's good to see you," Mark Pendleton says as he welcomes Conrad and Blankenchip into his office. The pair of them are in their green service uniforms as they walk into Pendleton's office.

"So it's not good to see me too?" Blankenchip protests.

"Lieutenant," Pendleton replies succinctly as he shakes Blankenchip's hand. Conrad reaches out her hand to do the same but Pendleton moves it aside and stretches his arms open wide. "Alicia, you know I deserve more than a handshake, c'mere." His arms encircle Conrad like a warm comforter.

Before Pendleton became the NRO's Director of Communications Systems Acquisition and Ops Directorate he was Deputy National Security Advisor when John Conrad served as Vice Chairman of the Joint Chiefs of Staff. He first met Alica when she was just a skinny high school freshman with a facial malar rash. He had seen her grow up through those awkward years and marveled at how that little girl had grown into the confident, powerful woman now in front of him.

"It's good to see you too, sir," Conrad says with a broad smile after hugging Pendleton.

"Come on in, have a seat." He motions over for them to take a load off on the deep-brown leather seats in front of his crescent-moon shaped desk. Pendleton pulls out two bottles of water from his office mini-fridge beside the credenza on the opposite side of his desk. "Here you go."

Conrad and Blankenchip grasp their bottles as they both thank him for their beverages. Pendleton then gets down to business. "So, what've you got for me?"

Blankenchip pulls out his brief case and pulls out a sleek black tablet computer. He presses the on button and hands it to Pendleton. Immediately the screen lights up with scanned images of the evidence that the team has accumulated over the past few days. Pendleton carefully examines the evidence as he swipes the screen left to right. "Is this true?"

"On our first assignment we got into a firefight with the Paraguayan Naval Marines. It was there that we discovered that our UN envoy, the Paraguayan deputy foreign minister, was a reputed drug dealer," Conrad says.

"And he dropped a dime on Ramsey," Blankenchip says. "Come to find out both Ramsey and Vásquez were involved in a group called 'the Network.'" Blankenchip reaches over to the tablet in Pendleton's hands and taps on an icon in the upper right corner of the screen. Instantly a schematic of Ramsey's connections with Vásquez pops up in a spider web orientation. Pendleton then pulls out his reading glasses from his left shirt pocket and places them on the ridge of his nose. He carefully scrutinizes the screen.

"Incredible. Ramsey and Vásquez have had coinciding investment and business dealings over the past several years."

"That's not all." Blankenchip once more reaches over, to Pendleton's annoyance, to tap the tablet screen again. "They both had a considerable minority stake in Celedane Corporation. On top of that, the charitable arm of Celedane made considerable donations to one of Vásquez's front charities, 'Helping Hand Incorporated'."

"Celedane. That name should sound familiar to you Mark," Conrad says quietly.

"Yes, it is. They won the bid for the Vigil project," Pendleton remarks as his eyes dart back and forth on the screen.

"So, it has to either be an unbelievable coincidence or else something shady is going on with Ramsey," Blankenchip mentions. "How can the company that designed the Vigil satellite system just so happen to have Ramsey as a shareholder? And that same company donates cash to a phony charity run by a corrupt politician. Something's not right."

"That's why we came, Mark," Conrad says. "We were hoping you could tell us more about the satellite system."

"Hold on a second."

Pendleton pulls his top desk drawer open, retrieves a pen-like device, and places it on the top of the desk. He presses a rectangular button on the side, and the device emits a small sound. Pendleton explains, "It's a surveillance scrambler. Just in case someone has the office wired."

The scrambler emits white noise to counter any audio intake from their conversation. Although it's inaudible to them, it causes havoc to any listening device within range.

Blankenchip smiles with the widest of grins. "I gotta get me one of those things."

"What you've just said confirms my suspicions about the Vigil satellite defense system…" Pendleton says.

This statement catches Conrad and Blankenchip by surprise.

She leans forward. "'Defense system?' We were told they were just reconnaissance and tactical satellites that take photos and run video feeds."

Pendleton leans back just slightly in his swivel armchair and looks directly at Conrad.

"Alicia—and I'm saying this as your friend—you've been played."

Blankenchip looks at Conrad and then at Pendleton with irritation. "How exactly have we been 'played'?"

"Vigil was never just a team; it's a system."

Pendleton removes a disk from the bookshelf behind him and inserts it into his computer. He turns on the attached holographic projector and presses a button on his keyboard. A blue-tinted translucent three-dimensional schematic of numerous geosynchronous satellites appears.

"Vigil was envisioned to be the most comprehensive global surveillance and tactical system since ECHELON. Its reach extends from the expanse of space to the depths of the Atlantic. Vigil has monitoring posts on every continent and major ocean body. On top of that, the SDS is equipped with a space-based laser accompaniment designed as the ultimate deterrent to any ICBM threats."

"Star Wars for the twenty-first century, huh?" Conrad says.

"Exactly."

Blankenchip is unimpressed. "Great; nice picture show. What does it have to do with us?"

"Back in 2003, President Bush signed National Security Presidential Directive 27," Pendleton says.

"I read about that in a briefing," Blankenchip says. "It had another name though, didn't it? It's on the tip of my tongue…"

"The Commercial Remote Sensing Space Policy," Pendleton responds.

"I knew that."

"Right. Anyway, that directive placed the National Imagery and Mapping Agency in charge of attaining all commercial imagery for the national security community. The belief at that time was that commercial imagery was good enough for national security needs. That paved the way for commercial entities to develop highly sensitive satellite systems for the US government. When the Vigil satellite project came around, NIMA opened up the bid to a number of contractors. Initially, it seemed like Lockheed had the best offer, but at the last minute Celedane came in with a lower bid."

"Was Ramsey involved in the negotiating process?" Conrad asks.

"Not directly but one of his staff members was. I think her name was… was it…" He pauses for a moment to remember. "Lauren Price?"

"Yeah, that's his chief aid," Blankenchip says.

"She pushed hard for Celedane. At that time we had no clue that Ramsey was a shareholder in Celedane because he had his holdings through a shell company."

"Doesn't that go against conflict of interest?" Blankenchip asks.

"If Ramsey were a part of the direct process, yes, but since he was working through his proxy, we technically couldn't do anything about it."

"What happened after Celedane got the contract?" Conrad asks.

"The production process went along smoothly. All the deliverables were even ahead of schedule. We launched the system about a month and a half ago. Operationally, things looked good, but then something funny happened. We temporarily lost navigational control of the system. At first we thought it was just a glitch, but it kept happening. The dwell times over target locations would get shorter and shorter, and we couldn't track moving targets as easily. Last week we lost all navigational control of the system."

"What happened?" Conrad asks.

"We think that Celedane installed a backdoor override into the navigational avionics."

"Can you repair the problem remotely?"

"No, it has to be done manually. The suckers had it hard-wired into the system. We're sending up a team to fix the problem in three days."

Conrad and Blankenchip look at each other with devious grins and turn toward Pendleton. He eyes them, confused.

"Why are you looking at me like that?"

It takes a brief moment for Pendleton to pick up on what the two of them were thinking.

"What? Oh! Oh no, you are not going up there."

"C'mon, Pendleton, stop being such a spineless bureaucrat," Blankenchip says.

"I can't approve that. You have no training and it's too dangerous."

Conrad tries to allay his fears somewhat. "Mark, remember who you're talking to here."

She smiles at Pendleton, and he smiles back.

"Alicia, you'll be the end of me."

CHAPTER TWENTY-THREE

SPACE IS THE PLACE

August 5th
Twenty thousand miles above Earth

The feeling of weightlessness takes some getting used to for Morrison. They had only a few days to prepare for the mission, and he doesn't feel at all ready. A one-day crash course—courtesy of Pendleton—on navigating in a weightless environment does not make one an astronaut by any stretch of the imagination. *At least Alicia seems like she knows what she's doing, even though the rest us don't,* he thinks to himself before being snapped back into reality by the sudden jolt of the external fuel tank detaching from their shuttle.

Their shuttle, the Eaglet One, cruises toward their destination. The shuttle's captain, Alvin Dailey, radios the rest of the team over the intercom system.

"The orbiter is independent. We'll be coming up on the satellite array within the next few minutes."

The Eaglet One's Orbital Maneuvering System engines kick in as the team and crew are propelled into geostationary orbit. As the Eaglet One makes its way closer to the Satellite Defense System array, they come upon another shuttle docked to the SDS command module. The Space Based Laser is housed on the command module. Dailey stares in awe of the structure when his telemetry alarms go haywire. Proximity alerts warn of an energy surge building up within the command module.

"Can you pinpoint where that surge is coming from?" Dailey asks his co-pilot, Della Rogers.

"No, I can't tell, Al," Rogers replies while tapping away on the telemetry controls.

Suddenly a high-intensity focused band of red energy is released from the SBL. The laser beam slices through the Eaglet One's tail and sears through part of the OMS engines on the shuttle's aft section. Eaglet One begins to twist off course and lose attitude. Dailey and Rogers frantically try to regain navigational control.

Conrad radios to the upper deck cockpit. "Captain Dailey, status report now!"

"The shuttle tail wing's been destroyed and the number one OMS engine has been damaged!"

"Can you still get us to the command module?"

Daily looks at his instrumentation. "With the other two engines still on line, I can maybe get us close."

"Good, then do it," Conrad says.

"You don't understand, Captain, with the tail wing gone, we can't reenter Earth's atmosphere. We'll be stuck up here."

Conrad looks out of the mid-deck side-port window. She sees the hostile shuttle docked on the command module.

"Captain Dailey, the shuttle that's docked out there, do you think you can fly it?"

Dailey quickly looks at the telemetry scanner to see that it's of the same design as the Eaglet One.

"Yes, I think I can."

"Good. Just get us close, and we'll take care of the rest."

Conrad unstraps herself from her chair, floats a short distance, and angles her body to face the rest of the team seated in rows of two in front of her.

"We need to get our people over to that command module so we can hitch a ride back on that ship," Conrad says as she points to the hostile shuttle just within view through the port window.

As she speaks the SBL cannon aperture begins to glow. Once more the Eaglet One's telemetry warns of the impending surge.

"The laser's charging up to fire again," Dailey says, warning the rest of the crew.

Conrad's eyes widen as she sees the ominous glow coming of the SBL aperture. "John, I need a force field up now!" she shouts.

"What?! I can't..."

"Just do it!"

Another energy beam rips across space in the Eaglet One's direction. Just before the beam hits its target, an alternating hot and cold force field deflects it—causing the beam to diffuse around the field. Arrowhawk grimaces slightly at the effect of the beam slamming against his energy rampart. Surprisingly the strain on him wasn't as bad as when he put up the force field in Washington. Out here in space it seemed he was able to recover faster. Maybe due to the fact that he was absorbing solar energy more efficiently without the inhibition of the ozone layer. But before he can gain his bearings, the hostile shuttle's mid-deck airlock opens. One by one, seven men armed with laser rifles and equipped with Manual Maneuvering Units exit the shuttle.

"Captain, my team will engage the hostiles to clear a path to the command module," Conrad says. "Once there, you're going to have to open up the mid-fuselage hatch for repairs."

The three mission specialists, Anita Chatterjee, Jeff Choi, and Christopher McShane have been assigned to the task of repairing the command module. Blankenchip is to assist. Having a dual degree in computer and mechanical engineering has made him invaluable in assisting the NRO mission specialists. Conrad needs him in place to assure that the team will have complete control of the SDS.

The Eaglet One's dual airlock allows multiple astronauts to exit the ship simultaneously. Each team member enters the pressurized airlock individually and proceed through the unpressurized payload bay. Conrad is first to exit, followed closely by Fighting Bull, Morrison and Arrowhawk. They each wear a Z-Millennium biosuit based on the NASA Z-1 spacesuit design. The suits have bearings in the joints that provide them with more mobility than the clunky Extravehicular Mobility Units (EMUs) utilized by previous space explorers.

The hostiles begin firing their weapons on the team as Dailey fires the remaining OMS engines to maneuver the Eaglet One to within close range of the SDS command module. The team members return fire with their own laser rifles.

"Stay in tight formation," Conrad says over the comm-link. "Don't let them pick you off."

The laser fire of one of the hostiles hits Fighting Bull in the torso. The force of the blast slams her into the remnants of the Eaglet One's tail wing. Her suit sustains a six-inch tear to the left flank region. Conrad sees this.

"Cynthia!" she shouts over the radio.

Fighting Bull looks down at the hole in her suit—almost immediately the tear closes up as the microencapsulated polymers that line her suit are released, producing a foam composite that seals off the tear. "I think I'm OK, Alicia." She then looks up to see her attacker closing in for the kill. Before he can pull his rifle trigger, Morrison rushes in to tackle him. Using his biosuit's assist control mini-boosters, he propels himself into the hostile like a ruthless rugby player. The two men struggle. The hostile tries to pull the trigger of his rifle but Morrison wedges his left forefinger between the back part of the trigger and the trigger guard, keeping his opponent from firing. He then comes around with his right elbow and delivers a blow to hostiles neck which temporarily disorients him. Now that the rifle is freed from the hostile's grip, Morrison reaches for it as it starts to float away. The hostile toggles his MMU joystick to maneuver his way out for an escape. Morrison aims the laser rifle in the hostile's direction and fires, hitting the MMU's propellant tank. The hostile loses navigational control and sputters out of control into the atmosphere.

"What's your sit rep, Morrison?" Conrad asks while combating a slew of hostiles.

"We're good here, Captain. You think they're just mad at us for exceeding the quota of black people in space at one time?" Morrison asks flippantly over their radio comm-link.

"Classic," Arrowhawk says before directing his attention elsewhere. "Cynthia, you OK?"

"Yeah, I'm fine," she responds. She turns to look at Morrison. "Thanks Terrell."

"Anytime, that's what I'm here for."

"If you guys are done complimenting each other," Conrad says, as she fends off the remaining hostiles, "I could use a little help here."

Arrowhawk turns in Conrad's direction and raises his arms with hands widespread. Bioelectric energy surges from his arms and flows into his fingertips to coalesce into beams of pure yellow energy that blast away Conrad's two attackers.

"Thanks, John, but all this fighting won't mean anything if we don't get our guys safely to the command module. I need you to chaperone our ship over there while we take care of the remaining resistance. Can you do that?"

"I guess, Cap."

He clicks his boots together to activate the assist control mini-boosters. He's propelled to the front of the Eaglet One. As he gets closer to the command module, he blasts open the hostile shuttle's airlock.

Meanwhile the four remaining hostiles fire upon the team as the Eaglet One closes in on the command module. Fighting Bull trains her laser rifle at the midsection of one of the hostiles. The shot pierces through the hostile's suit, exposing them to the cold atmosphere of space. Within moments the hostile turns into a frozen corpse. Another pair of hostiles shoot at Morrison—the weapon's fire grazes his biosuit. Morrison immediately returns fire on the hostiles, hitting one in the chest and another in his faceplate. As they progress, another of the hostiles fires his MMU and propels into Conrad. He slams into her and removes an energy dagger from his supply pack and slashes at her. Her biosuit sustains tears to her mid-section which quickly close up. She is able to grab the hostile's arm to keep him from striking her again. She pulls her rifle on her attacker but he is able to swat it away. She then elbows him chest and goes after her rifle. The pursuing attacker goes after her with his energy dagger but Conrad grabs her rifle and blasts him away and into the side of Eaglet One.

After dispatching the remaining attacking hostiles, the trio quickly enters the hostile shuttle through the opened airlock. They move rapidly from the mid-deck to the upper deck cockpit. One of the hostiles in the cockpit fires his weapon at Conrad but misses the mark. Conrad's mini-boosters ignite to quickly propel her into her attacker. She slams him against the wall. Meanwhile, Morrison and Fighting Bull point their weapons at the remaining crew members. Being all the wiser, they all raise their hands in surrender.

Conrad radios to the Eaglet One over the comm-link. "We've secured the hostile shuttle. You can begin the repairs."

"Copy that, Captain," Dailey says in acknowledgment. He starts flipping on the hatch control switches. Immediately the mid-fuselage cargo bay door opens and the shuttle's Remote Manipulator Arm is released. The RMA latches onto the SDS command module to stabilize it. The mission specialists deploy from the airlocks with Blankenchip following closely behind.

They locate the command module's avionics system and carefully rewire the system to close the back-door override. Blankenchip hands a circuit board to Chatterjee, who places it into the command and control subsystem panel. After completing their task, the mission specialists, along with Blankenchip, board the hostile shuttle.

Dailey releases the RMA from the SDS command module. Then he and Rogers disembark from the damaged Eaglet One and board the hostile shuttle. Arrowhawk follows behind them and seals the airlock. Before Dailey takes the controls of the hostile shuttle, the original crew is ushered into the shuttle's escape pods and jettisoned into Earth's atmosphere. Dailey then releases the hostile ship from the SDS command module's docking unit and activates the shuttle's Reaction Control System to change the shuttle's attitude. The RCS thrusters turn the shuttle tail first. Then the OMS engines fire, slowing the shuttle down in preparation for reentry.

Twenty long minutes pass before Dailey activates the RCS thrusters to pitch the shuttle so it's upside down, with the shuttle's bottom facing the atmosphere. Many of the team members are caught off guard by this sudden movement. As the ship reenters the Earth's atmosphere, the crew is jostled around a bit, but it's nothing compared to what they have just faced down.

CHAPTER TWENTY-FOUR

TRANSITION STATES

August 12th
NSA Headquarters
Fort Meade, Maryland

Ramsey looks intently out of his floor to ceiling windows and he paces. It's a look of concern and anger. Nearly a week has passed since Ramsey has heard anything from the members of the team. Emails and phone calls have gone unanswered. As far as staffs at their various agencies of employment are concerned, they've taken vacation time. Ramsey understands what is going on. The team has suddenly vanished off the face of the Earth and cut off communication. He knows that they aren't fools. He and Hanahan made sure they recruited the best of the best, not just hacks who happen to have super powers. Ramsey knows they are deliberately marginalizing him. He walks over to the window's side paneling and activates the shift-tint blinds. The blinds were not real blinds but instead, a layer of photochromic molecules imbedded into the window glass—allowing Ramsey to shut out the ambient sunlight while providing him the privacy he needed for his phone call.

He pulls his cell phone from his blazer's inner pocket and dials. A tempered female voice answers.

"It's me, we got an issue," Ramsey says as he takes a seat in front of his computer.

"What kind of issue, Chandler?" the female voice says, emphasizing the word issue.

"Vigil's gone off the reservation."

"The team or the satellite system?"

"Both. About a week ago we lost operational control over the SDS." He pulls up a schematic of the satellite defense system onscreen. "Now it's in God knows whose hands. And to top it off, the team's completely cut off all communication."

"What do you need?"

"A little help getting their attention."

"What exactly do you want done?"

"You're a clever girl. I'm sure you can think of something."

"Clever woman you mean," she says, correcting him.

"Yes, that's what I meant. Why don't you use our most powerful weapon?"

"And what's that?"

"Fear."

"With the way they look, that shouldn't be a problem. What means would you prefer? Subterfuge, character assassination, or scandal?" the woman asks, a smile traced across her lips.

"How about all of the above and then some," Ramsey answers happily.

"I'll need access."

"Already done. I've sent you all their files over the INTERLINC server. Check your Inbox."

The woman clicks on the email icon on the desktop screen in front of her. "Got it. Give me a few days."

"Sounds good."

Ramsey presses "End Call" on his cell phone touch screen and pauses to reflect on what he's set into motion. If he's right, then he's gotten the upper hand on Vigil. If he's wrong, he'll have to do some major damage control to repair his relationship with the team. Neither of these two possibilities upsets him. Given that he's set things in motion on one front, he knows more has to be done on his end.

Ramsey taps the intercom button on his office phone and summons Lauren Price. Within moments, the attractive brunette appears.

"I have an assignment for you. Remember our sleeper assets?"

"Yes," she says enthusiastically.

"I want them activated. Now."

* * *

August 14th
Bruegger's Bagels
Brooklyn, New York

The Flatbush area of Brooklyn is where Blankenchip got his start. His parents emigrated there from Eastern Germany at the end of the Second World War. Throughout his travels he's always found his way back home. It's only fitting that he reconnect with his two children here.

Blankenchip's relationship with Jack and Charity has been somewhat strained, to use the politest of terms. For most of their lives, he wasn't home. Various CCI assignments took him all over the globe and as a result kept family time to a minimum. Career took precedence over family and that's the main reason his marriage didn't last. It was a sacrifice he made that cost him more than he let show. Despite not having their father around, his children have done pretty well for themselves. Jack is wrapping up his last semester at SUNY-Queens and plans to start an MBA program at NYU with the hope of eventually joining an investment firm. Charity, on the other hand, is heading into her last year at PS 103 and is in the midst of selecting between Columbia and Brown for college. When their father contacted them to tell them he wanted to meet, it was a shock to both of them, but welcomed nonetheless even though you could barely tell. After his harrowing experience in space, Blankenchip knows he has to speak to his kids, because he cannot take anything for granted.

"So..." he says, starting the conversation ever so awkwardly

Jack and Charity respond to his conversation opener with disaffected stares. Undeterred, Blankenchip muddles through.

"How's it going?"

"Are you honestly asking us this?" Charity responds.

"Well, I thought—"

Before Blankenchip can complete his sentence his son interrupts him. "Maybe, if you would return—let's see, pick your media type," he lifts up his phone to emphasize his point, "text message, phone call, email; then you'd know."

"I've been kind of busy," Blankenchip flatly responds.

"No kidding," Charity says. She pulls out her smartphone from her purse and taps the touchscreen and a video decrying Vigil's actions and absence appears onscreen. "They have you guys plastered all over the news every day."

Blankenchip eyes zero in on the screen. "Well, it's not as straightforward as it seems, Char."

"Dad, why did you call us here?" Jack asks.

Blankenchip takes a moment before answering. Even though he usually doesn't allow himself to be emotional, especially in front of his children, he can feel the beginnings of tears welling up in his eyes. These two children, even though they don't know it fully, are Blankenchip's pride and joy. Expressing this to them is a task.

"The reason I called you here was to let you know how much I…" The words seem to escape him.

He tries again. "How proud I am of you guys."

Both Jack and Charity pause, seeing that the tone their father is using isn't just fluff. Something else is behind it.

"What's going on, Dad?" Jack asks. "You're usually not this deathly serious when you talk to us."

"It's nothing, I…"

Charity interjects. "Spill it, Dad."

Indeed, Blankenchip isn't being forthright with his children.

"With all that's going down in DC, I wanted to get away to see you guys. That's all."

Charity pushes her glass of organic orange juice to the side and leans forward. "What's going down in DC?"

Blankenchip tries his best not to get into the details. "I mean that with all that I've been up to with Vigil, we've made some new enemies. Enemies that don't necessarily play nice. And I honestly don't know when's the next time I'll see you."

"So what's this, our good-bye meeting?" Charity asks.

"Oh hell no, it's not," Blankenchip responds bluntly. "I just wanted to see you guys before things started heading down the pisser, which I know they will."

"So what's next?" Jack asks.

"I don't know, but I do know that I wanted to tell you both that I still care for you. And that you two are always on my mind." It is this assurance that allows his children's attitudes to lighten up a bit.

"And to tell us that you love us?" Charity asks, half in jest and half in seriousness.

"You said it, I didn't," Blankenchip responds with a smile.

Just a few booths behind them, two men with barely noticeable earpieces observe the cheerful gathering as they sip black coffee.

* * *

August 16th
Barnes and Noble Bookstore
Fairfax, Virginia

Morrison sits at a table in the Starbuck's section of the store, reading the latest issue of *Christianity Today*. The chair next to him is littered with a bunch of newspapers and magazines detailing Vigil's plummeting public image. He takes a few sips of his black coffee while he waits for his soon-to-be ex-wife Danielle. With all of the chaos going on with his team, it only seemed fitting that his divorce would add on to it all.

The pair have known each other since their college days at Yale. They met in Political Science 101. Morrison was a Criminology major taking the class as an elective, and she was a Biology student, with plans to attend medical school, just trying to get her general education requirements out of the way. Danielle caught his eye during a study session, and after that the two were inseparable.

Things had started off well; the two were in love and no one could tell them otherwise. After two years of dating, they married. Danielle was later admitted to George Washington University School of Medicine while Morrison eventually got into the non-uniformed Secret Service program after completing his master's degree in criminal justice. It was during his early years in the service that he had what he would call his moment of clarity.

While serving on diplomatic detail, Morrison had been protecting Portuguese ambassador Alberto de Silva on his goodwill US tour. One of the stops was the Houghton Biomedical Research Lab. The facility was well known for its extensive use of animal test subjects. A member of the Pangaea Consortium, an extremist environmental action organization, breached the perimeter with aims of disrupting the event. The man, armed with a metallic flask of hydrochloric acid, lunged toward the ambassador. Morrison quickly intercepted the attacker, but in the process of wrangling the flask away, he toppled over the edge of a protective side railing and crashed into a containment unit of an unrefined Duritium-based proteolytic enzyme.

Morrison had not only suffered multiple severe lacerations from the shattered containment glass but he was awash in the chemical enzyme that was contained within. He sustained subdermal burns to eighty percent of his body and some third-degree burns on his forearms down to the bone. Upon his arrival at the George Washington Medical Center, the trauma team had little hope that he would survive, and even if he did, he would need extensive reconstructive surgery. Oddly enough, Danielle was on her trauma surgery elective when he was brought in. It was almost unbearable for her to see her husband in this state. But within minutes after he was brought into the trauma bay, the team noticed something unexpected—Morrison's skin was knitting itself back together. Instead of muscle fibers and skin cells, strands of metallic fibers began to cover areas of exposed skin and muscle tissue. Interestingly, the muscle strands were of the same composition as the metal gurney he was lying in. The enzyme had an intercalative effect on Morrison's DNA, interrupting segments of DNA strands and allowing for insertion of the organic components into his own DNA. In essence, the chemical bonded to his DNA, allowing him to alter his molecular structure into whatever he came into physical contact with.

This trauma had more than a physiologic effect on Morrison. To him what happened was no accident. He believed it was divine intervention that saved him and blessed him with these new abilities. Seeing this as a gift from God, he decided to commit himself fully to his faith. Unfortunately, while Morrison's faith was renewed his relationship with Danielle began to sour. She had never been the religious type, but his newfound zealousness was a bit off-putting to her. Their differing views, among other things, began to cause conflict in their marriage. Even after months of counseling, they eventually found themselves going down the road of divorce.

Morrison was devastated; divorce is the last thing he ever wanted. Despite his multiple pleas to her to reconsider, the inevitable couldn't be avoided. Now, he's waiting for the woman he expected to spend the rest of his life with to serve him with divorce papers.

Danielle walks in from a side door by the Starbuck's counter. She wears a nice yellow and blue floral dress that caresses her smooth caramel skin. Her dark curly hair is pulled back into a ponytail. Even after twelve years together, Morrison's heart still leaps whenever he sees her. He ominously eyes the gray folder containing the divorce papers neatly tucked under her left arm. She greets him with a half-hug and a kiss on the cheek.

"Hey," Danielle says.

"How's it going, Dani?"

"Same old. And you?"

"Well, you know." He pulls out a copy of the latest issue of USA Today and points to a pie chart that ranks America's greatest national threats. The highest percentage is given to Vigil.

"Yeah, so how's that working for you?"

"Obviously not too well. It's like I'm constantly on edge having to watch my back all the time."

"I've been getting calls asking about where you've been. They even were bugging me when I was doing consults in the MICU." Danielle was just two years out after completing her Infectious Disease fellowship at NIH.

"And what do you say?"

"I generally deflect the question. I tell them I don't know where you are and that they should move on and ask someone else. And if that doesn't work I tell them that I'm a doctor and that they should stop bugging me or else people will die," she says with a sense of deadpan humor.

"Thanks, I appreciate it."

Even though they're going through all this, Morrison can still rely on the fact that she would always keep his confidence.

"Before I forget, I need you to sign these." She slides the folder over to Morrison.

At first he glares at the folder then looks up at her. She turns her gaze away. He then removes the documents and thoroughly scrutinizes them. He once more looks up at Danielle.

"What?" she asks. This time she has the confidence to look at him eye to eye.

"Did you ever think we'd get to this point?"

She doesn't answer right away. Instead she looks away and fumbles with the charm bracelet on her left wrist that Morrison bought her for their tenth anniversary. Her voice is soft as she replies. "No."

Morrison tries to make eye contact with her, but she avoids it. This speaks volumes to him.

"Look at me, Dani," he pleads.

Danielle lifts her head to catch Morrison's gaze.

"Do you want this?" he asks softly.

She pauses before answering, "Yes." She quickly turns her head away again.

He slowly reaches for the black pen in the left breast pocket of his sport coat. Morrison makes broad strokes of with his pen as he lays his signature on the papers. This whole process doesn't feel right in his heart.

Throughout all this, Morrison has failed to notice two men sitting three tables over listening to their conversation through the wireless audio receiver that was placed under his table. The conversation is not only being transmitted to these men through their earpieces, but also to a listening outpost in Fort Meade, Maryland.

* * *

Lisner Auditorium
George Washington University
Washington, DC

The cavernous auditorium is empty with the exception of two souls. A reunion of sorts is going on in the Terrace Right section of the facility.

"Thanks for meeting me, Tom," Fighting Bull says to Tom Danforth.

"Any time, Cynthia."

Fighting Bull grasps the hand of her former mentor. She thinks back to the first handshake she had with Danforth. It was back 10 years ago while she was in her sophomore English class at Euclid High School when her journey started. Two girls seated two rows behind her would not stop hurling insults at her under their breaths. Despite informing her teacher of the incessant insults, it was of little use. Time after time she could hear their insults, "There goes little Ms. Perfect," "Cynthia thinks she's all that, she ain't nothing!" "I hate that stuck up little whore." Fighting Bull did her best to ignore them but her antagonists were relentless. Eventually verbal insults turned to physical bullying. The height of the bullying came between the second and third period. She was boxed into a row of lockers by four girls. Two of them grabbed her and pushed her to the ground. In fear and anger, Fighting Bull's adrenaline kicked in—thoughts of the strongest person that she knew, her father, rushed through her mind. Suddenly her body was transformed into that of her father. The girls that attacked her were horrified. Not only did she scare those girls but also the kids in the hall as well. Fighting Bull ran out of the building with tattered clothes and tears in her eyes.

The following day, Fighting Bull was called into the principal's office. She was mortified. She was exposed as a Variant. Would she be suspended? Expelled? Her heart was beating a million miles an hour as she walked down the long hallway to the principal's office. Her hands shook as she reached for the principal's door handle. After her principal invited her to have a seat in the worn brown leather chair she was introduced to Danforth. At the time he portrayed himself as a recruiter for what he termed, "those with abilities." At the time he could not formally recruit her as an agent because she was underage but he could develop her as an asset.

With her unique power set, she was the perfect candidate for the Directorate of Operations' superhuman recruitment initiative. When she turned eighteen he arranged for her post-secondary education through a CIA black fund and shepherded her through the process of becoming a top-rated field agent. Now, after serving over thirty years as an analyst, field agent, and operations officer, Danforth had taken on a new role, that of CIA station chief at the US embassy in Jordan.

"Is this what you were looking for?" Danforth removes a sheet of paper from his leather attaché and hands it to her. Detailed on the sheet is a list of visa filings over the past three months.

"Yeah, this is what I needed." Fighting Bull scans the list to see that of the 120 filed applications, fifty of them were filed by Ascension Staffing Services on behalf of Omani Oil and Gas Incorporated—which is owned by Hassan

Haq. It was during her investigation of Emmanuel Vásquez's recent travels that Fighting Bull found he had made a number of trips to Jordan to meet with Haq. There was a long paper trail linking the two over the course of two years.

"Ascension Staffing Services?" Fighting Bull asks.

"Yeah, they're an international staffing agency. The funny thing is that on average we get maybe ten or fifteen applications max from them. Then when we got hit with fifty applications on behalf of one company in such close proximity to each other, something didn't feel right."

"You figured something was up."

"Exactly. Haq isn't clean by any stretch. He's been linked to human trafficking rings across the globe, from the Saudi Peninsula to the Philippines. A lot of the 'employees' they file for who are supposed to be seasonal oil rig workers are in fact human traffickers. We've never gotten anything concrete on him. Hopefully, you and your new friends can help with this."

Fighting Bull reviews the paper once more before folding it and placing it in her suit jacket pocket.

"Thanks, Tom."

"So, how is it going with your new friends? You playing nice?"

Fighting Bull smiles. "Always."

"Yeah, right. Are you at least trying to follow orders."

"Well…"

"I knew it!"

"Look, Tom, I get the job done, no matter what it takes. Sometimes that means bucking the rules a little bit."

"It's not worth it if you're constantly tempting fate because of it."

Fighting Bull nods in acknowledgement.

"You've got nothing to prove, Cynthia."

Something awakens in her as she looks up at him, "No, I have *everything* to prove," she says in a resolute voice. She leans back in the uncomfortable auditorium seat. "You know I'm the youngest on the team? I just don't want them to discount me because of that."

"Believe me, they all know that you're the best."

"Why's that?"

"Because I trained you."

Fighting Bull smiles at the remark.

Danforth checks his watch. "Look, I've got another meeting to get to. I'll see you when I see you."

Danforth gives her a hug before departing. "Just don't do something stupid and get yourself killed."

He leaves. She's walking out of one of the auditorium's side exit doors when her phone rings. Pulling the phone from her coat pocket, she sees her younger sister Amaya's photo on the screen.

"Hey," Fighting Bull answers.

"Hey, where are you?"

"Oh, just out and about."

"What's going on?"

"Nothing, just worried about you."

As the two women continue their conversation, two men linger a few feet behind Fighting Bull. One wears a Washington Nationals baseball cap, a hooded sweatshirt, and jeans. The other is in dress casual attire: slacks, a light blue button down shirt, and a jacket with no tie. Pretty normal looking men except that they're wearing barely visible earpieces and carrying concealed sidearms. A few blocks away on the corner of Twenty-fourth and I Street, a gray Econoline van sits parked with its sole occupant recording Fighting Bull's conversation.

"There's no need to worry, I'm fine," Fighting Bull assures her sister as she ventures down the escalator to the Foggy Bottom Metro station. The two men follow. The one with the ball cap makes sure he goes unnoticed as he takes the same escalator down. The man in the slacks goes through the opposite entrance.

"Well, I heard you guys went AWOL," Amaya continues.

"Not exactly," Fighting Bull responds. "We've just taken a temporary leave of absence."

"That's not what they're saying online. Cynthia, they're calling you guys traitors. Some are even saying you're terrorists."

"You can't believe everything you see or read, 'Maya, you know that."

"What about the space shuttle thing? They're saying you guys hijacked it. Is that true?"

"No, what we did was legit."

"Then you guys need to clarify that with the press because they're treating you like Public Enemy number one."

Fighting Bull weaves her way through the crowd on the waiting platform as she continues talking. The man with the baseball cap inches closer, staying just a few feet behind.

"Public Enemy number one, huh?" Fighting Bull chuckles. "Well, we'll see about that. Look, 'Maya, everything's fine with us. Don't worry."

"OK," Amaya says begrudgingly.

"So, how about you guys? How are thing's going?"

"All right, I guess. Fall semester classes are starting up again soon," Amaya says as she scrolls through her schedule on her laptop screen. She was about to begin her sophomore year at Ohio State majoring in Political Science, just like her older sister.

"And how's Larry doing?"

"Fine."

"He still going to his AA meetings?"

"Yeah. Considering that you're not around to twist his arm, he's doing well."

"Well I am his co-sponsor."

"A slave driver is more like it," Amaya kids.

Larry was the eldest of the four siblings and the only boy. After being introduced to beer at fourteen, it wasn't long before he graduated to liquor, and he eventually became a full-fledged alcoholic.

"Well, I do it because I love him," Fighting Bull says as she reflects on her close uncle, who died of liver failure because of his alcohol abuse, and she was determined that the same fate wouldn't befall her older brother.

"That's good to hear. Anyway, I gotta run. I'll give you a call when I get the chance," Fighting Bull says. "Love you."

She tucks her cell phone in her right pants pocket and steps to the edge of the platform for the Orange Line train to take her back towards Virginia. Across the train track, the man in the button-down shirt sees Fighting Bull and taps his earpiece. Reflexively, the man in the ball cap, who is just feet behind her, paces toward Fighting Bull. A bystander briefly gets in his line of sight. The ball capped man quickly moves around the bystander but is astonished to discover that she's vanished. He calls out to his partner over the earpiece.

"I've lost visual. Do you have eyes on her?"

His partner scans the crowd but comes up empty.

"I got nothing. Cade, you got anything on the security cams?"

The two men's associate, Louis Cade, sits in the gray van a few blocks away, frantically typing on the black keyboard in front of him. He taps into the Metro station's security camera feed. Footage from the array of cameras flashes on his flat-screen monitor.

"I'm coming up empty, guys," he responds.

"Dammit!" the man in the ball cap screams. He runs up the flight of stairs that bridges both sides of the waiting platform. As he darts past a utility room, he's grabbed from behind. He instinctively pulls out a Beretta M92F from his shoulder holster and trains it on his assailant. Just as he's about to pull the trigger, he sees that it's his partner in the button-down shirt.

The man lifts up his hands in surrender. "Whoa, it's me!"

"Shockey, don't scare me like that," the man in the ball cap says as he places his weapon back in its holster. "Did you see her?"

"Nope."

"I've never lost a tail before. This girl is good," the man in the ball cap says as he turns his back to Shockey.

"You have no idea."

Suddenly Shockey puts the man in the ball cap in a choke hold. He grasps at Shockey's arms, but loses consciousness before he can break free. The man slumps to the ground, breathing shallowly. Over the ball-capped man's earpiece comes the squawk of the real Shockey's voice. Morphing from Shockey to the personage of the man with the ball cap, Fighting Bull grabs his earpiece and places it in her ear.

"Yeah," she responds.

"Hamrick, did you catch her?"

"Nah, she got away."

"He's gonna be pissed. All right, I'll meet you at the van."

"I forgot, where did Cade park it?"

"You gettin' old on me, Hamrick? On the corner of I and Twenty-fourth."

"Gotcha."

A few minutes later the two of them rendezvous at the gray Econoline van, which is parked in a secluded alley way. As Cade pulls open the noisy sliding door, Fighting Bull grabs Shockey from behind and pulls his silencer-tipped Taurus 709 pistol from its holster. She thrusts the barrel of the gun to his right temple.

"What the hell?" Cade shouts as he hurriedly rushes for his Walther & Mather PPK pistol.

"Don't even!" Fighting Bull warns as she trains her weapon on Cade.

"What's wrong with you Hamrick, have you gone insane?" Cade protests as he lifts up his hands.

"It's not Hamrick! It's her," Shockey shouts. "It was in her file, she's a shape shifter!" Before he can utter another word, she twirls the pistol by its trigger guard and hits him in the temple with the pistol grip. Shockey's head cocks to the left as his body slumps to the ground unconscious.

"Two points for being literate. Too bad it's too late to matter," she says.

Cade immediately reaches for his weapon. As soon as he grasps the pistol grip, a bullet pierces his right shoulder.

"Aaagh," he screams.

"The next one will be through your brain if I don't get some answers. Who sent you?"

"Go to hell," Cade says in defiance.

Fighting Bull pins his wounded shoulder to the wall of the van.

"Aaagh, dammit!" Cade screams.

"Tell me now," she says as she plants the barrel of the gun squarely against his forehead.

"It's Ramsey, all right!"

"How long have you been following us?"

"Since you guys fell off the grid."

"Taps, tails, and surveil?" Fighting Bull inquires, referring to the modes by which they are possibly being pursued.

"Yes."

"Thanks." Fighting Bull elbows him in the left temple, knocking him to the van floor unconscious.

She reaches into Cade's left pants pocket to retrieve his cell phone and scans the call history. The last four calls are from area codes coming from the Fort Meade region, confirming what Cade said. Fighting Bull morphs back to her original form. She dials Conrad's home phone number from Cade's phone.

"Hello," Conrad answers.

"Alicia, get off the phone and call me back on a secure line," Fighting Bull says, and abruptly hangs up.

A few moments later, Conrad calls back from her father's old encrypted satellite phone.

"Cynthia, what's going on?"

"We're being tailed. Looks like Ramsey's let loose some of his old CIA contacts. They've been on us for the past week or so."

"Can't say that I'm surprised."

"What's the plan?"

"We do the right thing," Conrad says with calm assuredness. "You'll be hearing from me in the next couple of days."

"What's brewing in that head of yours, Alicia?"

"Don't worry, you'll see."

* * *

August 19th
L.A. Fitness
10921 Wilshire Boulevard
Los Angeles, California

Arrowhawk packs his street clothes into his green and black Adidas gym bag before shutting the locker door closed. He had to find a way to blow off some steam during this time and the best way he knew how was through a lengthy cardio session with weightlifting interspersed between. His mind reflects on his current situation with the team and whether he should cut his losses. It had been over two weeks since the team returned from space and Conrad had been silent. Maybe it was time for him to move on.

He exits the men's locker room and as the door behind him begins to close one of the men behind him holds the door open. As Arrowhawk walks to the front exit doors he meets the eyes of an attractive blonde woman in a pink sports bra and tight yoga pants with curved stripes on the side. He gives her a flirtatious look. The woman gives one back.

"I'm sorry," a muscular young man says as he accidentally bumps into Arrowhawk. The impacts jostles Arrowhawk slightly due to the other man's mass, but he recovers nicely.

"It's OK, just be careful," Arrowhawk says as he pulls up on the dislodged shoulder strap of his gym bag.

Arrowhawk looks up and searches around for the attractive blonde but she has disappeared into the gym crowd. He laments that he couldn't talk to the woman, but there would be others; there are *always* others. The sunshine almost blinds Arrowhawk as he walks outside of the building and heads west on Wilshire boulevard. As he makes his way to his car he hears an unfamiliar cellphone ring tone. He reaches into the right pocket of his nylon jogging pants for his phone; he sees that the screen is not on. The ringing continues. He fervently searches his things and pulls out a plain black flip phone from the side pocket of his duffle bag. The phone's screen reads "Restricted." Arrowhawk presses the "Answer" button to accept the call.

"Hello."

"I thought you were gonna burn a hole through that blonde chick's sports bra with how hard you were staring."

"Cynthia?"

"In the flesh, Casanova."

"How did you...?"

"C'mon, remember who you're talking to. Jacked beefcake guy with the tight Under Armour shirt."

"That was you who bumped into me. Should have figured, my bag felt a little heavy after I knocked into you."

"It's called good spycraft."

"Get over yourself, Cynthia."

"Just say it, 'Cynthia, you are the best spy on the planet.'"

"When hell freezes over."

"Hah. So, as much I would like to continue this lovely conversation I hate to tell you that you're being tailed."

Arrowhawk looks over his shoulder briefly. "How many?"

"I ran a quick surveillance detection route and I counted four."

"What's the play?"

"They're running a standard surveillance package. Two in the rear, one across the street and one ahead. I'll take care of the two to the rear. You try and shake the other two."

"Got it." Arrowhawk bypasses his car that's parked on the side of the street and continues down Wilshire. The two agents trailing behind him look at each other and one wearing a nondescript brown leather jacket whispers something into his sleeve. His partner, clothed in an L.A. Clippers jersey and jeans, picks up the pace in pursuit of Arrowhawk. The leather jacketed agent begins briskly walking in the same direction when he bumps into an elderly woman with a severe hunched back.

"My goodness son, I didn't see you there," the woman says, pardoning herself.

"Just watch where you're going next time," the agent says as he tries to maneuver around the old woman. He gets halfway past her when he feels a sharp pain behind his knee cap. The agent bends to the ground in pain when he turns to see the elderly woman over him with a smile on her face. She swiftly reaches into the agent's right jacket pocket as he struggles to recover and removes his own Taser and places it firmly against his neck. The jolt of the shock makes him go into convulsive spasms.

"Oh my God he's having a seizure!" the elderly woman screams. The intensity of her scream alerts the bystanders around them. "Someone call an ambulance." A crowd of people begin to huddle around the agent as the old woman slips into the crowd and changes form into a large African American man. Fighting Bull thinks to herself, *I love the old lady gag, it gets them every time.*

The other agent in the Clipper's jersey turns back to see his compatriot having convulsions on the sidewalk with others around. He taps his earpiece to let the other agents know what's going on before heading back to help his spastic colleague. As he makes his way he is grabbed by the collar of his jersey by the large African American man and is thrown into an adjacent alleyway. Those around are so transfixed with the seizing agent that they fail to notice what has just happened.

The other agent lands to the ground with a huge thud. He's woozy as he tries to recover. He can see the African American man in front of him but his image is out of focus. Field training kicks in and he reaches for his holstered H&K pistol strapped to the small of his back. The African American man leaps toward him and in midair his features melt away to reveal Fighting Bull in her original form. She kicks the pistol out of his hand. As his right hand flails back from the blow, the agent comes around with his left and punches Fighting Bull in her right flank region. She tumbles to the ground. The agent reaches for his weapon on the ground but Fighting Bull grabs an empty glass bottle by her and hurls it at the agent's occiput. The impact of the blow takes him to the ground. Fighting Bull quickly gets up and puts the agent in a choke hold. The agent violently fights back, punching behind him while Fighting Bull is on his back. A few blows land but despite all this she hangs on. Her grip is unrelenting and the agent eventually loses consciousness.

She lets go and the agent slumps to the ground. She breathes heavily as she leans over to pick up the agent's gun. Fighting Bull wipes the blood off her lip and pulls out her cell phone from her pants pocket.

Meanwhile, Arrowhawk continues making his way down Wilshire Boulevard and toward the Hammer Museum. As he walks up the museum steps, he receives a text message from Fighting Bull alerting him that two of the agents were taken out. That meant that he still had to contend with his other two pursuers. He pushes the glass entry door open and greets the front entrance attendant who warmly smiles back. Arrowhawk makes his way to the Contemporary Art exhibit. The other two agents trail behind but out of view of Arrowhawk. After lingering in front of a Mark Bradford piece for a few minutes, Arrowhawk eventually walks up the stairwell to the third-floor exhibit hall. The agents follow closely behind.

The crowds thin out the closer they get to the third floor. Arrowhawk quickly ducks into the men's bathroom. The two agents draw their weapons and lean against the wall of the men's bathroom entrance. They reach into their pockets to pull silencers out and place them on their weapons. The two agents make hand gestures for the one to take point and the other to trail. The leading agent carefully pushes the door open with his pistol raised. The two agents swiftly scan the expanse of the men's bathroom to see that the urinals are empty and no one is at the row of sinks on the opposite side. The lead agent crouches to get closer to the ground to look for any feet poking out from underneath the stalls. There are none to be found.

They carefully open the stall doors one by one, working their way from the outside stalls in. Once they reach the middle stall they brace themselves and point their weapons at the stall door. As the first agent begins to squeeze the trigger a bioelectric energy beam rips open the stall door and hurtles the first agent into the mirrors above the bank of sinks. His body bounces ungracefully off the sink counter and to the ground. The second agent immediately unloads rounds of bullets on Arrowhawk as he emerges from the stall. Arrowhawk erects an energy forcefield that melts each bullet as it's fired on him. After running out of bullets the agent reaches for the tactical knife in his left side pocket. The agent parries forward with his knife but Arrowhawk blocks him with the outside of his right forearm and counters with a roundhouse punch with his left fist. The knife falls out of the agent's hand as he's hit. The agent then recovers and delivers a knee to Arrowhawk's groin. He doubles over and the agent grabs Arrowhawk and slams his head into the wall and begins punching him in multiple succession, in his back. Arrowhawk then swivels around and delivers a sharp elbow to the agent's right temple. The impact of the blow takes the agent to the ground. The agent then reaches for his felled knife but Arrowhawk delivers a focused laser blast from his right index and forefingers that singes the weapon. Not giving up, the agent clips Arrowhawk's ankles with his left leg, causing Arrowhawk to tumble back to the ground as well. The agent leaps on top of Arrowhawk but he's able to use the agent's momentum to flip him over to the other side. The agent bangs his head on the sink counter just above them. Arrowhawk then grabs the agent by the back of the head and slams it once more into edge of the counter, smashing the agent's nose and knocking him unconscious. Arrowhawk then falls back down to the ground breathing heavily.

The men's bathroom doors burst open. Arrowhawk points his energized hand to the door, ready to blast whoever comes in next. He is relieved to see that it is Fighting Bull with her gun raised.

"What took you so long?" He asks.

"I was kind of busy," she says as she rubs the side of her bruised face. She holsters the weapon in the back of her slim-cut trousers and reaches down to give Arrowhawk a hand up.

"Are they alive?" Fighting Bull asks, looking at the grounded agents.

"I think so."

"Geez, John, you made a mess. Couldn't you have just blasted them both and gotten it over with?"

"Too easy and too dangerous," he says as he looks away from her. "So, these were Ramsey's men?"

"Yup," Fighting Bull says as she helps Arrowhawk steady himself. "They've been tracking us since we got back from space."

"I should've figured this would happen. Has Alicia contacted you yet?"

She nods. "Alicia has a plan but we have to head back to DC to gather a few things."

* * *

August 20th
Pier 1
Brooklyn Bridge Park
Brooklyn, New York

Blankenchip walks along the pier in Brooklyn Bridge Park. He climbs the steps of Granite Prospect into a throng of people taking in the sights along the East River overlooking the Manhattan skyline. A groundskeeper buzzes by in his golf cart before Blankenchip eyes Conrad atop the steps. He takes a seat next to her.

"A flip phone is kind of retro, don't you think?" Blankenchip says pulling out a black and red flip phone from the inner pocket of his hooded jacket.

"The disposable phones were the only way I could make sure that I could get through to you on a secure line."

"I was kind of surprised when the courier delivered it to my apartment," he says as he flips open the phone. "So, I counted three on my tail coming here."

"Yeah, I picked up on that as well."

He looks over Conrad's shoulder. "How did you shake yours?"

She gives a roguish grin. "I have my ways."

He looks down briefly. "Have you spoken to Terrell?"

"Yes, I sent him a couriered phone as well. He intercepted two agents a few days ago. As far as he can tell there were no others sent for him. He'll meet us in DC on the way to the Pentagon."

"What's the plan on this one, Alicia?"

"I've been compiling all the info that we have on Ramsey and cross referencing it with the data from the surveillance intercepts and we've just scratched the surface." Her eye catches one of Ramsey's agents in the southwest corner of the walkway leading up to Granite Prospect. "We have to get our gear and go dark. If we are going to get down to the bottom of all this, we need to get Ramsey's flying henchmonkeys off of our backs."

"You already have a location in mind?"

"Yeah, Tempe. There's an old decommissioned base where we can set up temporary base ops."

Blankenchip looks over his shoulder. "There are a lot of civilians around. How do you want to work this thing?"

"I have a car parked at Fulton Park Landing. I'll meet you there in ten minutes." Conrad quietly gets up and leaves. One of Ramsey's agents trails her as she walks along the cement pathway to her vehicle. Blankenchip sees the other two agents that stick out from the crowd with their tinted eyeglasses and supposedly conspicuous earpieces, and waits a few minutes before getting up to leave. As Blankenchip gets up from his seat, he heads over to the carousels just behind the steps of Granite Prospect. The two agents follow about twenty meters behind, ever so slowly. As they move in closer to the throng of parents and children around the carousel they lose track of Blankenchip. The lead agent circles back around the carousel but still no sign of Blankenchip. A row of carousel horses mounted with gleeful children passes around next to the lead agent. Just as the agent turns around to meet back with his partner, he's greeted by a quick fist to the face by Blankenchip, who's mounted on top of one of the carousel horses. Stunned, the agent reaches for his gun tucked within his shoulder holster. But Blankenchip grabs the agent's hand before he can unholster the weapon. The agent tries to headbutt Blankenchip as the carousel continues circling around but instead hits the carousel pole of the Blankenchip's horse, effectively knocking him unconscious. Blankenchip then props up his body atop an adjacent carousel horse.

Meanwhile the second agent radios his partner but gets no response. The agent once more scans the crowd around the carousel but comes up with nothing. He then taps his earpiece to contact the third agent that was dispatched to Conrad but again gets no response. Getting worried, the second agent puts his hand underneath his coat to handle the pistol grip of his weapon but does not unholster it. He starts heading toward Fulton Ferry Landing. On his way past the Vale he is cut off by what appears to be the groundskeeper in the golf cart. Looking closer, the agent sees that its actually Blankenchip in the cart. Instantly, the agent draws his weapon but Blankenchip pulls his arm into the car and bangs the agent's wrist against the cart's canopy beam; dislodging the weapon. The agent punches Blankenchip in the right cheek with his free hand. A spattering of blood comes out of Blankenchip's mouth. He then recovers and counters with a blow to the agent's stomach and groin. The agent doubles over briefly. He then has the presence of mind to reach for the tactical knife in the side slot of his left boot. The agent slices up at Blankenchip's head but instead makes contact with Blankenchip's shirt.

Blankenchip grabs the agent's wrist and violently wrenches it clockwise, causing the agent to drop the weapon. Blankenchip then follows through by grabbing the back of the agent's neck and drilling his face into the hub of the golf cart's steering wheel. The ensuing honk draws the attention of bystanders and the park police. Mounted on horses, the park police start coming after Blankenchip. He then quickly moves aside the unconscious agent and slams on the golf cart's accelerator. As the police begin gaining on him a red SUV screeches in front of him, blocking off the chasing police. The horses begin to nay as they are brought back to their hind legs. Conrad flings open the passenger side door.

"Get in!" she yells at Blankenchip. Without hesitation, he quickly leaps from the golf cart into the SUV's passenger seat.

"The hell are you now, Sarah Connor?" Blankenchip yells after barely making it inside the vehicle. Conrad smiles and spins the SUV around and speeds them away.

* * *

August 21st
Sublevel Two
The Pentagon
Arlington, Virginia

"Training exercise, ma'am?" the Flight Supervisor asks while scrutinizing Conrad's credentials.

'That's right, lieutenant."

He reaches over to his clipboard. "But there are no flight assignments listed on the schedule for the Avian today."

"It's not going to be listed on there." She reaches into the right side pocket of her BDU pants and pulls out a piece of paper. "We have a direct order from SecDef to engage in tactical flight exercises at Andrews."

The Flight Supervisior reviews the order with Hanahan's plagiarized signature, courtesy of Fighting Bull.

"This is highly unusual, since you still haven't been assigned an official pilot yet."

"And whose fault is that, lieutenant?"

He nods in acknowledgement.

"OK, ma'am, you're clear to go." He looks behind her. "Where is the rest of your team?"

"Oh, they're coming, they're just packing equipment for the exercise." She keeps her gaze focused on the Flight Supervisor as she reaches into the right pant pocket and taps her cellphone screen, which sends a signal immediately to Blankenchip.

Blankenchip along with the rest of the team is about fifty feet down the hall in the rotunda. He's been busy deactivating the tracking devices in each team member's uniform. His phone beeps as he's putting the finishing touches on Morrison's uniform.

"All right that's the signal, we gotta get out of here."

"Are you done?' Morrison asks as he's patiently standing still while Blankenchip uses his phased electromagnetic scalpel on his uniform.

"Yep."

"You got everything packed up, John?" Fighting Bull asks.

Arrowhawk lifts up a large plastic composite suitcase. "All right here."

"Good, I'm all squared away as well," Fighting Bull says as she lifts up her smaller compact suitcase. She eyes the large metallic locker box that's by Morrison's feet. "Terrell, you need help carrying that?

"Ha. Ha," Morrison says dryly as he easily hoists the box over his right shoulder.

They gather their things and walk calmly through the rotunda doors and to the flight bay, past the gaze of Lieutenant Rider. As they board the Avian they settle in to their seats. Conrad takes the pilot seat and types in the coordinates for Davis Army Base into the flight computer. Blankenchip takes the seat next to her.

"You ready for this, Alicia?"

"As ready as I'll ever be."

CHAPTER TWENTY-FIVE

GETTING TO KNOW YOU... AGAIN

August 23rd
Davis Army Base
Tempe, Arizona

A few days pass as Conrad strategizes the teams next steps. They settle in and pass the time by engaging in leisure various activities including playing a game of Spades, which they are in the midst of now.

Fighting Bull deals the cards. "All right gentlemen, John and I are up two games to one. Do you really want to continue embarrassing yourselves?"

"Just deal the cards, Tiger Lilly," Blankenchip utters. "We'll worry about winning."

Without even looking up from the cards Fighting Bull responds, "That's really creative, Aaron; did you pull that one from out of your phylactery?"

"The girl has balls," he laughingly says. "Look, Cynthia, I use nicknames with people I like. Nothing personal."

"How else am I supposed to take it?" she answers with shoulders shrugged and arms open. "Every time you talk to me you use outdated, racist epithets," she points in his direction. "How else am I supposed to take it?""

"I'm just making conversation."

"You want to have a civil conversation," she flops Blankenchip's last dealt card on the table, "start by using my name."

Arrowhawk interjects, "Whoa there, firecracker, do I sense a bit of tension?"

Fighting Bull gives a stare that burrows into Arrowhawk. "You should be angry too. But I shouldn't be surprised, you're only half Lakota."

The tone of her remark stings him, but he quickly tries to shift the topic of conversation.

"Look, I know we're all on edge because our popularity dropped from A-list to former reality-TV-star status, but I honestly expected this."

Blankenchip looks over in his direction. "What kind of nonsense are you talking?"

"I'm talking about the fact that our government has a record of abandoning those most loyal to it."

"Don't you think you're being a bit cynical?" Morrison intones as he shuffles through his cards.

"It's true," Arrowhawk says. "Look at the Bay of Pigs in the sixties, Ollie North with Iran-Contra in the 1980s and even the Abu Ghraib fiasco during the Second Gulf War."

"I knew a couple of those guys and what happened there wasn't OKed by any of the top brass. Those kids were the sole ones responsible," Blankenchip counters.

"So you're telling me that *no one* in the Pentagon condoned the systematic abuses going on there?" Arrowhawk shoves his right index finger onto the table to emphasize his point. "Not only there, but at Guantanamo too?"

"There was nothing systematic about it, kid." Blankenchip lifts up his arms in exasperation. "Those were isolated cases, and later investigations proved that."

"Whatever," Arrowhawk says dismissively. "What I'm saying is that whenever we go into conflicts we make alliances, whether it's with Cuban rebels or Kurdish Bushmen. We promise them food, money, medical aid, military training, all in exchange for their help in overthrowing some tyrannical regime. After we get what we want we leave them high and dry. They get pissed and in turn, yesterday's allies become tomorrow's enemies."

"Do you realize that your little pontification makes no sense?" Fighting Bull chimes in. "It's not some sort of grand government-wide conspiracy. It's textbook blame-shifting. Ramsey played us, pure and simple. He used his contacts within the Network to paint us as traitors and shift attention from what's really going on."

"That's what I'm saying. We work in a system that's fundamentally flawed, where those in power can manipulate it any way they see fit."

"Globally or nationally?" Fighting Bull asks.

"Both, but ours in particular," Arrowhawk responds.

"Whoa, hold on now," Morrison says raising his right hand in objection. "I agree, our system isn't perfect, but honestly, which one is? I mean, it's probably the best in the world, and it's worked pretty well for over 200 years. Sure, there are people who abuse their power; but that's why we have checks and balances."

"I don't need a civics lesson, Terrell," Arrowhawk says with a glare. "You can believe that rhetoric your flag-waving buddies spit, but you'll be shocked when you find out your American dream is really a nightmare."

"I'd rather live the dream than fear a nightmare," Morrison answers confidently.

Arrowhawk shrugs as he lays down his cards. "How long has she been in there?" he nods in the direction of the communications room where Conrad is secluding herself. "I want to know what our next move is going to be."

"Chill out." Blankenchip gets up from his chair. "I'll go see what's taking her so long."

"I can't believe it; he *finally* uses jargon that's semi-current. You've been watching YouTube videos behind my back, haven't you?"

Blankenchip gives him a menacing stare.

"Jeez, man, I was just kidding," Arrowhawk says. "You don't have to give me the look of death."

Blankenchip gives Arrowhawk an obscene gesture with his middle finger as he walks toward the communications room.

CHAPTER TWENTY-SIX

HARD TRUTHS

Communications Room
Davis Army Base

Conrad sits alone in the dimly lit room at a large, oval table littered with an array of documents and photos. The photos are a mix of images of Network members and of significant moments in her life. It's a unique intersection of her life on display right on the table. Among the pictures is one of her and her siblings. There's also one of her Special Forces unit.

She sits still, gazing over all the information before her. A cheerless look sits on her face as she leans over the mass of documents before her. Major James's dog tag clinks against her own as it dangles around her neck. She reaches over the table to pick up a picture of herself and James and pats her abdomen while gazing at it.

A hard knock on the door breaks her attention, and she quickly drops the photo.

"Yeah."

Blankenchip peaks his head through the doorway.

"Got a minute, Alicia?"

"Yeah, come in."

He pulls up a slightly rusted folding chair. As he sits, he picks up the picture of Camille and Cameron. Blankenchip smiles. "How old are the twins now?"

"Sixteen."

"Damn, these kids grow up so fast."

"No kidding."

Blankenchip reaches over and picks up the old worn picture of their Special Forces Unit.

"When did we take this?"

"About ten years ago, sometime before the Afghan op."

"I remember now. You had just come on board."

"And you were mad when I did. I remember you damn near killed me during an aquatic exercise." She gently takes the photo from his hand.

"I was just trying to toughen you up."

"Depriving someone of air for ten minutes is not toughening them up." Her eyes go up from the photo to Blankenchip. "It's attempted homicide."

"Heh heh, I know. It was fun though," he says with a Cheshire-cat-like smile.

"Yeah, for *you*, you sick bastard."

Blankenchip smiles at the remark, clasps his fingers behind his head and leans back in his chair.

"Those were the days though. Man, if PJ were still around, who knows what would have happened. You'd probably be married with kids by now, and Camille and Cameron would be an aunt and an uncle," he says as he shifts his body and leans forward. "Probably wouldn't have even volunteered for the SHARP initiative, and I'd finally be in charge of my own CCI unit..."

"Aaron..."

"You know it's true, Alicia," he says as he straightens up in his chair, his voice more intense. "PJ's death pushed you over the edge. Afterwards, you didn't care what happened to you, let alone your family!"

"That's not true..."

"What did you tell Dr. Cornelius in pre-op before you began the process?"

She lowers her head and says softly, "Make me unstoppable."

"Does that sound like someone who's got it all together? You let those R&D pinheads experiment on you like some glorified guinea pig—"

"A glorified guinea pig that you gladly would've been if you hadn't had that shrapnel injury," Conrad counters.

"Well, if I had Hanahan in my back pocket," he snaps back, "I probably would've been chosen too. As a matter of fact, I probably would've been leading this team!"

"Shut up! You don't know me! You have no idea what I've been through or any idea how much Paul meant to me! To you he was an old Army buddy." She looks down at James's picture. "But to me he was the world. Yes, I was distraught after he was killed." She points her right index finger at Blankenchip. "But don't you even dare insinuate that I stopped caring about my brother and sister because of it."

Blankenchip tries to soften his tone. "I'm saying—"

She cuts him off. "I've lost everything that meant anything to me: Paul, my parents, and now, they're trying to take away the twins."

"Look I'm sorry. I didn't mean it," he says unconvincingly.

"Yes, you did. Get out. Now."

Blankenchip leaves the room and quietly closes the door behind him. After he's gone, Conrad's emotions overwhelm her and her eyes start welling up with tears. She looks at the ceiling and then back down at the papers in front of her. She pauses for a moment, wipes away the tears, and gets back to work.

CHAPTER TWENTY-SEVEN

DECISION POINT

Blankenchip walks back to join the rest of the group, thinking about what he just said. Not too often does he take thought, or even care, about the impact of what he says on others. *But maybe this time,* he thinks, *I should've kept my mouth shut.*

The mood at the table is much more jovial, as the rest of the team is engrossed in a riveting conversation about the best American TV families of the past century.

"*The Cosby Show,* to me, portrayed the perfect American family," Morrison says.

"Except for the whole sexual assault part," Fighting Bull notes.

"Yeah. That's true."

"But I did have an affinity for those Coogi sweaters he used to wear."

"Dude, you're smoking crack; *The Brady Bunch* was by far the best," Arrowhawk says emphatically.

"You were old enough to watch that show?" Fighting Bull asks.

"Old enough to pop the DVDs into the Blu-Ray player," he responds. "I mean, everything was perfect. Even their grass was perfect."

"They had Astroturf," Blankenchip says, returning to his chair just in time to burst Arrowhawk's bubble.

"You're ruining my moment here, you know that, right?"

Fighting Bull offers her opinion. "Guys… the Bundys, from 'Married With Children'."

All three men let out a collective, "AAAAAAWWWWWWWW!!!"

Fighting Bull laughs as her teammates pelt her with potato chips and playing cards.

Conrad emerges from the communications room unnoticed and plops a stack of manila folders onto the table. The sudden thud of the folders gets the team's attention.

"What's this?" Morrison asks.

"Those are your assignments."

"Come again?" This from Arrowhawk.

"Thanks to our surveillance on Ramsey, we were able to find out the main players in the Network," Conrad says. "The information inside these files includes details on them, or the Principals, as they call themselves."

"What did you find?" Fighting Bull asks.

"More than I had imagined: records of blackmail, corporate and international espionage, assassinations, human trafficking, and that's just the tip of the iceberg."

"So what's our move?" Blankenchip wants to know.

"Over the past week there's been a lot of communications chatter among the Principals about something called 'Hegemony,'" Conrad answers.

"Any clue as to what that is?" Fighting Bull asks.

"No, but we're about to find out. Getting evidence on Ramsey is our first priority, but if we take the rest of them down in the process, that's an added bonus."

"It's going to be kind of hard to operate as public enemy number one," Arrowhawk adds.

"Ramsey may have stripped us of a lot of things, but we still have our respective positions. That's legitimacy enough."

"You're asking a lot out of us," Morrison contends.

"I know, Terrell, but these people have caused a lot of death and chaos, all for personal gain." She looks all around the table at her teammates. "I believe we have a personal responsibility to stop them and I'm asking you to see this thing through with me."

The team members glance at each other, not exactly sure what to say. It's only a few seconds but it feels like an eternity before anyone speaks.

Arrowhawk is the first to respond. "Heck, I'm in. I just want to see what comes out of this whole convoluted mess."

"I'm in," Fighting Bull says.

"Ditto," Blankenchip says in agreement.

Conrad turns to the last holdout. "Terrell?"

Morrison looks down at his folder as he takes a few deep breaths in. Despite his reservations about the course of action they've been taking, he can't deny the insurmountable evidence in front of him.

Morrison looks up. "I'm in if we do this the right way. We can't resort to the same methods as our enemies."

"Understood. We begin tomorrow."

PART THREE

WORLD TOUR

CHAPTER TWENTY-EIGHT

CASH CHASE

August 25th
Credite Suisse
Bern, Switzerland

"Mr. Cernik? Mr. Birchler will see you now," the bank attendant says to Arrowhawk.

Arrowhawk nods. "Wish me luck," he whispers as he folds his sunglass shades and tucks them in the left breast packet of his blazer.

"Copy that John, going radio silent. Good luck," Conrad replies over his earpiece.

Arrowhawk was assuming the guise of Antonin Cernik, a wealthy Czech oligarch with ties to the Russian government. His meeting with Florian Birchler was aimed at helping him set up accounts through which he can funnel bribes to various Russian officials in exchange for lucrative government contracts.

The attendant walks Arrowhawk down a long hallway with marble floors. They arrive at an office with dark wood-finished doors. Birchler flings the doors open. He nods to the attendant, who quickly leaves.

"A pleasure to meet you Mr. Cernik," Birchler says, firmly shaking Arrowhawk's hand. "Please have a seat."

Arrowhawk nods and makes himself comfortable on the plush Corinthian leather chair across from Birchler's desk.

"Care for a drink?"

Arrowhawk initially pauses, then replies. "No, thanks."

Birchler takes a seat in his chair.

"Now I understand that you're interested in setting up some trusts?"

"Yes, I have some business dealings that I would like to keep confidential—especially from the Czech National Bank."

Birchler smiles. "That shouldn't be a problem." He taps on his laptop screen which immediately comes to life. "Before we get started, I want to know what kind of products you're interested in."

"Anything that will keep the CNB in the dark and off of my back," Arrowhawk replies in a halfway decent Czech accent.

"Excellent. I will present you with a couple of options," he says as he types away on his keyboard.

Arrowhawk leans forward in his chair. "Lorraine told me you were good."

Birchler stops typing.

"Lorraine Duvalier?"

"Yes, she's a good friend of mine."

"I see," Birchler says. "Let me check on something for you."

Birchler hastily turns to get up from his chair.

"Hold it," Arrowhawk says, dropping the fake accent.

Birchler turns to see the barrel of a Beretta pointed at him.

"I can't let you run off on me like that."

"You must be insane," Birchler says disdainfully. "Do you plan on robbing me? There's no cash here."

"You're right. All the money I need is right on that computer of yours."

"This won't work. You know that this office is video-monitored twenty-four hours a day. Security is but moments away, you simpleton."

"That's why I let off a low-level electromagnetic pulse as soon as I walked into the room."

Arrowhawk's electromagnetic pulse is graded to disrupt the monitoring equipment in Birchler's office but keep other electronics—namely Birchler's computer—intact. It requires a focus that temporarily keeps him from using his powers offensively.

"Who are you?"

Arrowhawk carefully removes his facial prosthetics.

"Agent Arrowhawk. So Vigil has gotten wise to their masters."

"Shut up." Arrowhawk grabs him by the shirt collar and sits him back down in his chair. "Now, I need you to open up the transaction history of all these accounts."

He places a sheet of paper with the names of various Network Principals next to Birchler's computer.

"But I can't—" Birchler protests before the barrel of Arrowhawk's gun is thrust deeper into his cheek. He places his hand on the computer screen and types in a few keys. Immediately, the transaction history of the Network Principals streams across the screen.

As the information flows across Birchler's computer screen, Arrowhawk notices wire transfers from multiple accounts to the same shell company, "Lorian Logistics."

"Hold on—what's 'Lorian Logistics'?"

"I don't know."

"Click on the account detail history!"

Birchler complies. Arrowhawk sees that across all these transactions a singular name pops up consistently, Erosin Analaise.

"Who's that?" he says pointing to Analaise's name onscreen.

"I don't know."

Arrowhawk thrusts the gun deeper into Birchler's cheek.

"Honestly, I don't know!" he screams.

He eases the gun off Birchler's cheek and pushes him aside. Arrowhawk removes an external drive from his blazer and inserts it into Birchler's computer. The drive releases a botnet program that systematically drains all of the Principals' accounts. While he does this, Birchler presses the silent alarm button underneath his desk. Just then Arrowhawk glances over to see him quickly pull his hand back.

"What are you doing?!" Arrowhawk points the gun at his head.

"The sane thing. I called security you dolt."

Arrowhawk pistol-whips Birchler so badly that it leaves a gash across his forehead. As Birchler loses consciousness, Arrowhawk turns his attention back to the computer screen.

"C'mon c'mon!" he yells as the botnet completes its task. He taps his earpiece as he yanks the external drive out of the computer.

"Cap, I've been made. I need an exit!"

Conrad taps on the touchscreen monitor in front of her. A schematic of the Birchler's office pops up.

"There's a panic room right behind Birchler's desk with a service elevator."

"Got it."

Arrowhawk turns his attention to the wall behind him and sees a Monet painting. He eyes the edge of painting's frame which obscures a metal panel. He moves the painting to see a biometric hand scanner. He grabs Birchler slumped over body and places his hand on the scanner. Instantly a sliding door opens revealing a cloistered room with metallic walls.

"Hurry up," Conrad says over his earpiece. "I see a security team coming right up on you."

He drops Birchler's body and hurriedly rushes inside. Arrowhawk catches a brief glimpse of security guards flooding the office as he enters the panic room. Weapons fire from the oncoming guards ricochets off the sliding door as it closes behind him.

Arrowhawk rushes to the service elevator and presses the down button. He turns to his right to see one of Birchler's snowboards on a rack and grabs it. He quickly puts on his shades as well. The service elevator doors finally open and he takes it down to the lower level supply cellar where Credite Suisse's staff keeps their vehicles and maintenance equipment. This is where Credite Suisse's staff keeps their vehicles and maintenance equipment. Arrowhawk is greeted by more guards with weapons drawn. He emits a broad energy blast which incapacitates the guards. Eying the exit doors which lead directly to the mountain side slope, he rushes for it.

A handful of the guards recover. They hop on the snowmobiles in the supply cellar and follow after him.

"I thought you said that the bank job was supposed to be easy!" Arrowhawk yells.

"I never said that," Conrad says as she continues monitoring him via real-time video feed. "John, you're going to have to veer about forty-five degrees to the right to avoid the skiers down the mountain."

"Are you serious?"

"There's a chalet at the base of the mountain!"

"Great. Is there any chance I can get a little help?"

"I'm en route, but I still can't get to you in time."

"So, shooting them down from the sky isn't an option?"

"No. Can you blast them?"

"Going this fast my accuracy would be off."

"How about a force field?"

"It takes more concentration than I can give it right now."

As he speeds down the mountainside, he eyes a snow mound.

"Cap, I'm gonna try something."

After passing the mound, he emits a focused beam of thermal energy from his hand, which shatters it. The plume of snow inundates his pursuers.

One of the guards loses control of his snowmobile and gets caught in a thicket of snow, causing the front end of the vehicle to flip forward. The guard is jettisoned off of his snowmobile and into the trunk of a nearby Evergreen tree—the impact cracks several vertebrae in the guard's spine. In trying to avoid the fallen guard, a second guard veers his vehicle around him but loses traction, causing the snowmobile to skid uncontrollably and flip over, pinning him underneath.

Arrowhawk looks back contentedly and continues down the mountainside. Unbeknownst to him, a wave of snow cascades towards him.

Conrad sees the impending danger on screen. "Oh damn."

"What?"

"Your blast set off an avalanche!"

Arrowhawk turns his head to see an alluvion of snow heading towards him.

"What am I supposed to do now?"

"You don't have a choice. You'll have to put up a force field."

"Cap, I told you I can't."

"John, look, it's the only way to keep the avalanche from killing those people down below."

"I don't know if I can do that…"

"Listen—you can. You put up a force field around a whole space shuttle, for God's sake. I know what you're capable of. You just have to know what you're capable of."

Arrowhawk reluctantly nods in agreement. He crouches, streamlining his body to increase his speed of descent, and swiftly makes his way to the chalet. Many of the patrons notice the oncoming avalanche and run. He has just seconds before the avalanche comes crashing down on the building.

As he swings down in front of the chalet he fires pulsed thermal beams into the snow-laden ground—creating a trench. He takes a couple of deep breaths to psyche himself up.

"Come on, Johnny. This is no sweat, you got this," he says to himself.

With that, he raises his hands and generates a concave force field about four stories high and almost as wide to intercept the avalanche.

The wall of snow slams into the energy construct. Arrowhawk stumbles backward as the snow continues to batter his force field. Despite the strain, he endures; the force field holds. Most of the excess snow lands in the trench. In a few moments the avalanche subsides and he's able to let the field down. He puts his hands on his knees and breathes heavily as he recovers. Some of the ski patrons clap and cheer at what they've just witnessed.

"You all right, John?" Conrad asks over his earpiece.

"Oh, just peachy."

"Nice work, stud. I knew you had it in you."

"I would not recommend doing that again. Ever."

"I'm certain."

"How's everybody else doing?"

Conrad slides her chair over to an adjacent set of monitors. She taps one of the screens, and it displays a split-image satellite feed from Paris and Accra. She double taps the Paris screen, zooming in on Fighting Bull as she climbs the side of the Louvre's executive office building. She double taps the second image, zooming in on the hood of Blankenchip and Morrison's cab.

"Cynthia is at the Louvre right now and Terrell and Aaron have just entered Accra."

"I wish I had gotten further past Credite Suisse's firewalls. Those Network jerks would have had bank penalties in the millions, but Birchler tipped off security before I could go deeper."

"You've done more than enough. With over half of their private accounts wiped out, they're already in bad enough shape."

"No doubt. The transfers to the holding accounts went off without a hitch, by the way. But I noticed something: a lot of the Network Principals made multiple fifty-million-dollar wire transfers to the account of the same shell company."

"What's the common denominator between them?"

"These funds were all accessed by a guy named Erosin Analaise."

"Did Birchler say who that was?"

"No, he didn't know. Even if he was lying he wouldn't have helped much anyway."

"It doesn't matter. We're still monitoring all the Principals' communications. That name's bound to show up sooner or later."

"Gotcha. So, when are you picking me up? I'm freezing my *tuchas* out here."

A rush of wind blows over Arrowhawk. He looks up to see the Avian's gleaming undercarriage overhead.

"You were saying?" Conrad responds through the ship's loudspeaker.

"Did I tell you how much I love having you as my boss?"

CHAPTER TWENTY-NINE

FLASHBACK

The Previous Day
Davis Army base
Tempe, Arizona

Conrad clutches a holographic tablet computer, or holo-tab for short, displaying a three-dimensional holographic image of the Network's members in a family-tree style format.

"The Network consists of…"

Each member's face enlarges as she uses her Tactile Holographic Interface Gloves, or THIGs, to point to their pictures.

"Victor Angella, Italian billionaire and CEO of Celedane Corporation; Lorraine Duvalier from France, CEO and founder of the computer firm Binary Technologies; Lawrence Holmes from the UK, former British finance minister and owner of Bioquest Industries, a multimillion-dollar biotech firm; Hassan Haq, Jordanian oil baron; Codai Harada, a well-known Yakuza crime lord; Weiping Pei, Chinese intelligence minister and director of the Ministry of State Security; Abner Chase, renowned US museum mogul and philanthropist; Taryn Marunowski, CEO and president of US multimedia giant, Halcyon Incorporated; Nicolai Popov, Russian nuclear scientist formerly with the International Atomic Energy Agency; Akwesi Dankwah, five-star general in the Ghanaian army; Emanuel Vásquez, and our own Chandler Ramsey."

Conrad taps the holo-tab's screen, a numeric graphic pops up.

"Just to give you the scope of their wealth, their combined net worth is estimated at 950 billion dollars."

"That's amazing. Combined worth of close to a trillion dollars?" Fighting Bull shakes her head in astonishment.

"Not chump change, that's for sure," Blankenchip comments.

Conrad continues, "Their operations span the globe."

She presses another button on the touch screen and the schematic changes again to a detailed view of the planet. The schematic is littered with icons delineating Network business interests and financial holdings.

"The main arteries of Network activity are outlined in your folders. Does anybody have any questions so far?"

"Get to the point, Alicia," Blankenchip admonishes.

Conrad flashes Blankenchip an annoyed look. She taps the hologram and images of four members of the Network pop up.

"Over the past two weeks, Ramsey's been in frequent contact with four members in particular: Dankwah, Duvalier, Chase, and Harada. They've been sending email and phone messages back and forth on a daily basis about something called 'Hegemony.' We need to find out what 'Hegemony' is and Ramsey's connection to it."

She turns to Arrowhawk. "John, you're heading to Switzerland. The funding stream for their illicit activities starts there."

Conrad taps the screen once more and the image of a fit middle-aged man with gun-metal gray hair appears. "Florian Birchler is the Network's main banker. He's the Chief Fund Manager for Credite Suisse, and he also has his hands in all sorts of dirty money."

"Dude looks pretty young to be a top-tier exec."

"Don't let his looks fool you. He's actually 55 years old. He's an avid snow boarder and outdoor enthusiast. That's how he keeps in shape."

"I see. So, he's our only in to the Network's financial dealings?"

"Exactly. Besides the Network Principals themselves, he's the only one with direct access to their accounts. All transactions require a biometric passkey and Birchler's our access point."

"We can't just hack in remotely?"

"No, they have one of the most sophisticated firewall defenses seen this century. If we hack in, we have to do it on-site."

He nods in acknowledgment. "Got it."

"Cynthia, you're heading to the Louvre. As board trustees, Chase and Duvalier have satellite offices there. I want you to get all the intel you can on their activities with Ramsey and the Network."

"Stealth op?" Fighting Bull inquires.

"Yes. I want you in and out of there without a soul knowing you were there. Aaron and Terrell, you'll be heading to Ghana. General Dankwah is the point man for all of the Network's military operations. Find out as much as you can about his involvement with Ramsey as well as 'Hegemony'."

"What about you?" Blankenchip asks.

"I'll be monitoring operations until someone can relieve me," Conrad answers. "After that, I'm off to Japan to look into Harada's connection to Ramsey."

"After we get all that information, then what?"

"I have a contact on the Joint Committee on National Security who would be interested in what we've found. And John can use his connections with the Justice Department to convict Ramsey on federal charges."

"Even if we do gather enough evidence to convict Ramsey on federal charges," Morrison asks, "how do we know he won't just flee to a country without an extradition agreement with the U.S? You even said that the Network is worldwide. Who's to say that one of his buddies wouldn't just put him up in the meantime?"

"The Network is an alliance of convenience," Conrad answers. "When it all boils down, they're all out for themselves. None of them will want to deal with the heat that Ramsey is about to bring on them."

CHAPTER THIRTY

FRAMEWORK, PART ONE

August 25th
The Louvre Museum
Paris, France

Fighting Bull makes her way sinuously through the Louvre's ventilation system. She finds her way to the vent just above the adjoining offices of Duvalier and Chase. The two were extremely close, such that there was no partition between their offices; it was an open floor arrangement. As members of the board of trustees, the pair has offices on the top floor of the Denon Wing, located in the museum's southern section. She removes a multi-use screwdriver from the duffle bag slung over her shoulder and carefully unscrews the vent cover, making sure it doesn't fall to the ground in the process. After removing the cover, she places a small telescopic camera just through the vent opening.

She adjusts the optics of the lens to see the expanse of the office space. She pans the camera and locates the paired motion detector and security camera mounted on the ceiling. Fighting Bull has to be particularly careful because the motion detector is wired to the main security system, which, once activated, will immediately alert security. She removes a canister filled with gelatin foam from her bag and lowers the nozzle just through the vent opening but above the sightline of the motion detector. She sprays the paired motion sensor and camera. They short circuit as a result.

Fighting Bull attaches a rappelling rope to the inside of the vent system walls and secures it to her belt harness. She lowers herself into the office. As soon as her feet touch the floor, she radios Conrad.

"I've just entered their office suite. I'll be uploading the files to the server in a few minutes."

"Copy that," Conrad replies over the radio link.

Fighting Bull lays her bag under Duvalier's desk and takes a seat in the French leather chair. After pushing up her night vision goggles, she turns on the desk lamp and wastes no time hacking Duvalier's computer.

As she uploads the data to the Avian's server she opens up a few files. Information streams across the screen, detailing Ramsey's relationship with both Chase and Duvalier. There is evidence that Ramsey is a majority shareholder in both of their companies. In another file she finds information on a front charity set up by Chase and Duvalier that was used to funnel money to terrorist-linked organizations. The charity is called "L'Avantage Pour Les Enfants". Within yet another file is evidence that Ramsey facilitated the creation of the organization and contributed over ten million dollars over the course of five years to the charity. In reality, Ramsey redirected funds from the NSA's Combined Federal Campaign to APLE.

"Ramsey, you are so done once we get through with you," she says.

After downloading the files off of Duvalier's computer, she moves to Chase's computer. Above it is an arrangement of closed-circuit security video monitors that audit all activity occurring in the Louvre at all times.

As she begins downloading information from the computer she notices something on the security monitors—a five-man team standing over two bleeding security guards in the foyer area leading up to the office entrance. The men start walking in her direction.

Fighting Bull immediately turns off Chase's computer screen, slips into Duvalier's office and takes cover in the closet next to her desk. The men unlock the door and enter the office area. Each man is outfitted in all black, with ski masks, leather gloves, cargo pants, and military issue boots.

Their sidearm of choice is a holstered Beretta M92F.

One of the men walks over to Duvalier's computer. Another infiltrator makes his way to a mounted painting just behind Chase's chair. He carefully removes the painting and gently taps the wall looking for a hollow spot. Then he presses his hand on a particular spot, and a panel slides back to reveal a wall safe. He goes to work opening the safe.

The remaining two men rummage through Duvalier and Chase's desk drawers and file cabinets. Fighting Bull observes all this through the slits in the closet door. In a very quiet voice, she radios Conrad.

"I've encountered four hostiles."

"Are they in your line of sight?" Conrad asks.

"No, I ducked into the office closet. But they are taking evidence that we need. I am going to intercept," she says as she cocks her gun.

"No, I want you to abort the mission," Conrad shouts vehemently.

"Not after coming this far, Captain; I can handle this."

"Don't be stupid, Cynthia," Arrowhawk retorts. "Get out of there now!"

"Nice to see that you care, John, but it's not your call," Fighting Bull replies in an assured tone.

"But it is *mine*," Conrad asserts. "I repeat, abort the mission. That is an order!"

At that moment, another one of the men notices something.

"We got a rappelling rope coming out of the vent opening sir."

As the others take a look, another man sees the duffle bag under Duvalier's desk. The group's leader comments, "Looks like we're not alone here—Tyson, check the closets. Smith, check the vents."

Tyson heads in Fighting Bull's direction. She radios back to the Avian.

"I've been compromised!"

"Cynthia!"

The door knob turns ever so slightly as Conrad's voice is heard over Fighting Bull's earpiece, but there's no response in return.

CHAPTER THIRTY-ONE

THE METHOD MEN

Quarishi Street
Accra, Ghana

As Morrison and Blankenchip ride in the back of a cab in downtown Accra, they look over floor plans for Dankwah's facility. Dankwah has an office space in the middle of Accra from which he runs his operations. It formerly served as the main headquarters of Kyerewaa Cocoa International.

Blankenchip points to the floor plan. "The perimeter security is pretty light, so it should be easy to get inside. He uses solid-state holographics to mask the exterior of his office so he doesn't attract any unwanted attention. What better place to hide than in plain sight, right?"

"Yeah, right," Morrison responds.

Blankenchip notices that Morrison seems distracted. "You've been acting pissy all day. What's the problem?"

"I just don't like how we're sneaking around like this. This covert stuff is just not my thing."

Morrison was well accustomed to resorting to cloak and dagger techniques when protecting the president, but not while conducting a criminal investigation.

"What is your 'thing'?"

"Being more forthright."

"There goes that righteous talk again"

"Look, I'm not so Pollyannaish as to think this whole thing can be solved with a wave of a wand; but there's a right way to do things."

"Let me ask you a question—why are things so black and white with you?"

"Because there's right and there's wrong."

"And it's because of your religious beliefs that you think that way?"

"Yes, I would say that."

"And I guess you've been this way for quite some time?"

"Not really. I'd say ever since about three years ago when I got serious about my faith. A little bit before my wife decided she wanted a divorce."

"You're married?"

"Have been for what would be twelve years this coming December."

"What happened?"

"Well, she had a different vision of where our relationship should be heading. We were going in two different directions, and it just wasn't what she wanted, I guess."

"And religion got you through it?"

"I wouldn't say religion, but my personal relationship with Christ."

"Hmmph, I see," Blankenchip grunts, unimpressed. "How are things now?"

"My wife... or soon to be ex-wife... and I still talk from time to time."

"You're a better man than me. I haven't talked to my ex-wife in seven years. After the divorce I dropped that broad like a two-ton load."

Morrison chuckles at the comment. "I felt that way at first. But all that resentment was a burden until I decided to forgive her. After I did that, a load was lifted off of my shoulders. You should try it."

"Spoken like a true evangelical. Look, sometimes things aren't as black and white as you'd like to think, Terrell. You have to make compromises at times."

"But when does it stop? Till you've compromised your morals?"

"I don't have all the answers, but we're in a whole different ball game now. You do whatever it takes to win. No matter what the cost."

Blankenchip turns to the driver. "We'll get off here."

He pulls out a wad of dollars and hands them to the driver, who gladly accepts the compensation.

Blankenchip and Morrison enter the modest apartment building directly across from Dankwah's office. The two men estimate that the best location to set up visual surveillance is the third floor. They climb the wooden steps to an apartment they surmise overlooks Dankwah's office. Blankenchip knocks on the door, and the tenant opens it. He offers the man three hundred dollars to walk a few hours in the city in exchange for the use of his apartment. The tenant bargains for more. Blankenchip grudgingly ups the amount to four hundred before the tenant gladly obliges. It takes a few moments for Blankenchip and Morrison to set up a thermal imaging camera to observe Dankwah and his assistants in his office. A half an hour later Dankwah leaves his office and enters a black Toyota 4-Runner with his entourage. Blankenchip and Morrison quickly make their way across the street and into Dankwah's office, where they get to work.

"I'll take his computer; you go through his paper files," Blankenchip orders, more than asks.

Morrison gives him a disaffected look.

"Please?"

"Much better."

Within Dankwah's filing cabinets Morrison finds memoranda of agreement between him and a number of Network Principals. He also discovers evidence that Dankwah granted illegal gold-mining and logging rights to various members of the Network. And there are records of Dankwah's utilization of military personnel and vehicles to coordinate the transport of weapons to groups such as Al-Aqsa Brigade and members of the Pakistani Intelligence agency, the ISI. As Morrison continues searching through the files, Blankenchip yells. "What the hell!"

"What is it?"

"Come over here."

Morrison goes to Blankenchip and leans over his shoulder.

"What've you got?"

Blankenchip clicks on a file labeled "C.A.T. Transport."

"Does this look familiar to you?"

A schematic of an altered version of the Battle C.A.T. armor appears onscreen. The design is much bulkier than Blankenchip's. It appears more durable, but less sleek, making mobility for any potential user a challenge. It more closely resembled a tank than a combat suit.

"They stole your armor designs," Morrison says.

"Yep."

"And improved on them too."

Blankenchip gives him a mean scowl.

"I'm just saying." Morrison shrugs.

"Don't."

"But how did they get a hold of the armor designs anyway?"

"It was classified Top Secret. Not even Ramsey had clearance for it. Someone from DARPA must have given it to him."

"DARPA?"

"Defense Advanced Research Projects Agency," Blankenchip explains. "They do all the high-end R&D stuff for Defense. I worked with a group of design engineers there to create the armor. Let me see something…"

Blankenchip clicks on an onscreen icon.

"Improved on it, huh? They left out the EMP shielding in the power-centric core. One electromagnetic blast and those things are useless."

Blankenchip clicks on another file, and a window opens up with a listing of numbers.

"It looks like they produced about two hundred units of the armor and shipped them to Doriana, off the coast of Lemalia, about a week ago. There's no record of the recipient on the electronic shipping manifest."

"So Ramsey steals the Battle C.A.T. designs and sends them to Dankwah, who in turn manufactures them and sends them to Lemalia for…?"

"Dankwah doesn't have the capacity to manufacture the armor. My guess is that Victor Angella's company, Celedane, or one of its subsidiaries, manufactured and sent them here. Made it look like a simple military contract purchase so it would all seemed legit. Dankwah in turn sends them off to Lemalia. It serves as a convenient transit stop and no one suspects a thing."

"And here I thought John was the detective on this team," Morrison comments. "But the question is: Who did they ship the armor to?"

"It could be anybody. Terrorists, dictators, Ronald McDonald, take your pick."

CHAPTER THIRTY-TWO

FRAMEWORK, PART TWO

The Louvre
Paris, France

Fighting Bull crashes through the office window as she's shot in her right flank. She skids down the side of the building, frantically grabbing for something to break her fall. She fortunately latches on to a lower floor window sill and hangs on with a vise grip. She quickly checks her side and sees that there's barely a scratch on the fabric. An electrostatic charge on the finger pad adherens points on her gloves activates. She carefully plants her hands and feet on to the side of the building. The electrostatic charge allows her to adhere to the building's surface like an insect.

One of the hostiles points his pistol out of the broken window—looking to finish the job, just in case gravity hadn't done it for him. He sees nothing. Just as he turns to go back, a bullet pierces his neck. As he crashes back into the office space, his team members are momentarily surprised. They quickly reach for their weapons as their teammate's lifeless body hits the ground.

Fighting Bull hurls herself through the window while unleashing a salvo of bullets. She hits a hostile in the chest and another in the left shoulder. Using the adherens points on her boots, she runs across the side of the office wall to avoid getting shot while returning fire on her assailants. She tags one of the hostiles in the chest as she sprints across the office wall. She quickly eyes a chocolate brown credenza in Duvalier's corner of the office to take cover behind. As she moves into position, she's hit point blank in the right shoulder. Fighting Bull lets out a low groan at the impact of the bullet. She lands awkwardly behind the credenza, right next to the hostile with the bullet hole in his chest.

The last two hostiles continue firing at her until their clips are empty. As they move in, closing for the kill, they reload their weapons.

Thinking fast, Fighting Bull props the dead hostile on a nearby rolling leg rest. As the other men inch closer, sweat beads up on her forehead. She pushes the dead infiltrator out from behind the credenza. Instinctively, both men fire at the corpse, but realize too late that it's not their target.

Fighting Bull does a front roll in the opposite direction and trains her Sig Sauer P-225 pistols on the last two hostiles. Without hesitation she hits one in the chest and another in the head. Not a breath comes out of them as they collapse to the ground. Fighting Bull turns to pick up her earpiece, which fell out during the firefight. She places it into her right ear and radios back to the Avian.

"I've neutralized the hostiles," she says calmly, without an inkling in her voice that she was almost killed. "It's all clear."

"Any casualties?" Conrad asks.

"Four. One of them is wounded and barely conscious."

Noting Fighting Bull's impressive body count, Arrowhawk makes a comment to Conrad away from the microphone.

"Four out of five casualties? The chick plays for keeps, doesn't she?"

Conrad nods her head in acknowledgement. "Yeah, but she doesn't listen."

She again speaks to Fighting Bull. "You're lucky you didn't get killed."

"Well, they hit me dead on twice. But there isn't even a mark on my uniform. The tech guys said our uniforms are made out of a mesh of biosteel and what again?"

"'Peripheral particles,'" Arrowhawk chimes in. "They're derived from pulverized Duritium. It makes conventional Kevlar look like wet tissue paper. Not only does it stop the bullet, but it also absorbs the impact."

"I love it," Fighting Bull says gleefully.

"I don't have time for it now, but we're going to have to have a little chat after I get back from Tokyo, Cynthia," Conrad says over the microphone.

In a contrite tone, she answers, "I understand."

"Where did those men come from?" Conrad asks, shifting the topic back to the assignment.

"I don't know."

Fighting Bull picks up the folder next to the wounded hostile. She flips through it briefly. She then smacks him in the face. He struggles to regain consciousness.

"Huh? Wh-What?" the man responds sluggishly.

"Who sent you?" Fighting Bull asks.

The man gives her a smirk, and contorts his jaw as if he's chewing something. His lips begin to twitch, and he grimaces. Suddenly, his eyes roll back and his head flops backward.

Momentarily stunned by the event, Fighting Bull steps back before regaining her bearings and checking for a carotid pulse. The rise and fall of the chest associated with normal breathing are also absent, and the status of the man is no longer in doubt. She reaches into his mouth to find the remnants of something in his right back molar.

"Damn."

"What is it?" Conrad asks over the radio link.

"The idiot killed himself with a cyanide pill."

"Any identifying information on him?"

Fighting Bull checks the man's pockets, but finds them empty with the exception of a cell phone. "Just a phone. Hold on, there's a tattoo on his forearm."

"What does it look like?"

"It's an eagle with arrows in one talon, lightning in the other, and a globe in the background. Sound familiar to you?"

"Probably a Special Forces tat. Did you bring your camera with you?"

"Never leave home without it," Fighting Bull replies.

"OK, take a picture of it and upload it to the Avian's server," Conrad orders.

"Copy that, Captain."

Fighting Bull removes a small digital camera from her duffle bag and snaps multiple photos of the tattoo as well as of the dead infiltrators. Within moments the image is uploaded to the Avian's on-board server, and Arrowhawk pulls up the image onscreen. It takes just a brief glance at the photo for Conrad to get the confirmation she needed.

"Yeah, that's definitely Spec Forces. Maybe 81st Airborne or Berets. Cynthia, get out of there. We will rendezvous with you at the extraction point."

CHAPTER THIRTY-THREE

THE NEW DANGER

Halcyon Studios
New York, New York

At age thirty, Pat Tanaka was one of the youngest solo news anchors to headline a prime-time news journal for HM News. Her youth and passion for her craft more than make up for her lack of journalistic experience. She developed a reputation for getting to the bottom of an issue without worrying about all the niceties. Her producer counts down to air time as the lights turn to her.

"Good evening. My name is Pat Tanaka and welcome to 'Flash Point.' This segment's discussion will address the rise of the superhuman and its effects on US national security. I am joined this evening by Doctor Donald Swanson, a senior fellow at the Center for Strategic and International Studies. Doctor Swanson is an expert on superhuman policy. Thank you for joining us this evening, Doctor Swanson."

"It's good to be here, Pat," Swanson replies.

"First off, Doctor, for those in the audience unfamiliar with the superhuman community, could you give a general overview?"

"Sure, Pat." Swanson slides the tablet computer next to him in full view of the camera. He taps the screen and a multi-colored pie chart appears.

"Superhumans are divided into three groups: Augments, Variants, and

Contingents." He points to each section of the divided pie chart as he speaks.

"Could you break that down for our audience, please?"

"Of course." Swanson taps on the section of the chart labeled "Augments." It enlarges to reveal multiple bullet points under the title. "Augments are those who were intentionally enhanced through biological or technological experimentation. Variants, on the other hand…" he taps the section with the corresponding title heading, "…are individuals born with superhuman abilities—we don't understand why at this point, but we are still looking into it. And Contingents are those who acquire their special abilities through pure accident and coincidence."

"Thank you for the summary," Tanaka says, wasting no time in getting to her next point. "Now let's talk about Vigil. As we know, they have gone AWOL. I want to ask you, what effect does their apparent abandonment have on our national security?"

"It has a tremendous impact on our national security," Swanson replies bluntly. "Vigil was intended as the first-line deterrent against major threats to our national security, especially superhuman ones."

"But what about our conventional military? Couldn't they defend us from attacks from potential enemies, even superhumans?"

"That's the problem. All of the resources that would have gone into superhuman defense were channeled into Vigil. With Vigil out as a defensive option, we would be in bad shape against a singular superhuman threat, let alone an army of them."

Tanaka looks down at the notes she's written. "I want to touch on something you just said. You stated that we would be vulnerable to attack from a group of superhumans. If in fact Vigil has gone rogue, do you think they have the potential to turn around and attack us?"

"I don't like to talk in hypotheticals," Swanson replies.

Not one to let up on an issue, she continues to press him. "In your expert opinion then. Based on all of the research you've done, could Vigil become a threat to this country?"

"Based on my research, Vigil could, and I stress *could*, pose a threat to this country."

This is exactly what she's been looking for—the element of reasonable doubt. With that, Tanaka abruptly ends the segment.

"Thanks for spending time with us, Doctor Swanson."

"It's been my pleasure."

"Stay tuned, we'll be right back with more 'Flash Point.'"

CHAPTER THIRTY-FOUR

PUBLIC OPINION

Aboard the Avian
Outskirts of Accra, Ghana

As Arrowhawk and Fighting Bull watch the end of the now concluded segment on "Flashpoint," Arrowhawk uploads Fighting Bull's photos to the Avian's server. He also attaches the photo to an encrypted email to one of his FBI colleagues in L.A.

"Nice," Fighting Bull comments acerbically regarding the segment.

"Yeah, but she's not quite my type," Arrowhawk retorts smartly, referring to Tanaka's looks.

Fighting Bull glares at him.

"Of course. You like the girls who treat their vaginas like *In-N-Out Burger.*"

Arrowhawk looks up at her with a mix of surprise and anger. "What is your damn problem?!" he demands as he gets up from his chair. "You've been on my case from day one."

"Forget it."

"No, I want to hear it. Did I do something to you? Piss you off somehow?!"

"That's not it."

"Then what is it?"

Fighting Bull looks him in the eye and asks, "What are you so afraid of?"

"What?"

"Whenever you're out in the field, you act like a scared little punk. It's like you're tiptoeing through daisies when you use your powers." She points to him. "The things you can do and what you are—you should be proud of that. I know I am."

He pauses for a moment. "Let me ask you a question, when did your powers manifest?"

"When I was a sophomore in high school," Fighting Bull responds.

"How did they manifest?"

"It was in a fight. It was so stupid. Some girls were picking on me and I tried to stop it. When they started hitting me, I felt a rush of adrenaline, and then changed. I morphed into my dad. It was so embarrassing. My clothes were torn up, and I ran home in tears."

"Really? Ew."

"Shut up."

"Well, when I manifested I was fourteen, on my first real date with a girl, Mallory Richmond." He smiles as he thinks about her.

"What, you lost your virginity to her?" Fighting Bull asks smartly.

"Hmmph, I wish. More like in between first and second base." He takes a moment before continuing. "When I kissed her, like you, my adrenaline was pumping and I felt... I felt really hot. My whole body felt like it was burning." Arrowhawk pauses to look at his hands. "I let off an energy blast that set the girl on fire. She survived, but with third degree burns. The poor girl had to undergo multiple plastic surgeries and lost an arm. Every time she looks at her amputated arm she'll remember me. Can you imagine that being someone's lasting memory of you? That you maimed them?" He puts his head down and gently places his right hand on his swivel chair. "That's why I hold back."

Wow, how awful, Fighting Bull thinks to herself. "I understand John. It's painful, I know. We've all done screwed up things with these powers we've been given, but you can't live like you're fourteen anymore. We all mature and get better. This is now; you've learned how to control your powers. You don't need to hold back."

She gently places her hand on his chest as she says this. He looks at it and then at her.

"Hey, anybody home? Can we get in now?" Blankenchip's voice comes on over the Avian's radio, interrupting their conversation.

Fighting Bull turns her attention to the exterior monitors, where she sees Blankenchip and Morrison waiting entrance onto the ship. She walks over to open the Avian's main hatch to let them onboard. Arrowhawk goes back to dividing his attention between monitoring Conrad's status and viewing the rest of "Flash Point."

"Did Alicia leave already?" Morrison asks Fighting Bull as he enters the ship's main cabin.

"Yeah, John dropped her off after picking me up."

Blankenchip goes to the central console where Arrowhawk is seated and leans over his shoulder.

"What were you watchin', kid?"

Arrowhawk turns and looks at him with an arched eyebrow with an expression of annoyance and frustration.

"Do I look like your son?"

"Stop being such a sensitive priss."

Arrowhawk shakes his head and responds to the question. "Just some egghead on T.V. talking about how we pose a 'potential threat.' It's a total load of trash."

Fighting Bull chimes. "Isn't HM News owned by Taryn Marunowski's company?"

"Yep," Arrowhawk mutters.

"Fair and balanced news coverage, hungh?" she says mockingly.

Picking up on the sarcasm, Arrowhawk adds, "Tell me about it. Can we say, 'Rupert Murdoch' anyone?"

"Hey! I watch that channel," Morrison protests.

"Figures," Arrowhawk retorts in a monotone voice.

"Seriously, though, our reputation is taking a beating," Fighting Bull says. "I was talking to my sister the other day, and she thought we'd become terrorists or something."

"Yeah, I was reading the newspaper, and a poll said that we're the biggest threat to America," Morrison adds. "Can you believe it? We beat out perennial favorites al-Qaeda and Li'l Kim Jong Junior."

"That's the power of the media for you," Arrowhawk says.

"It's more than that," Blankenchip states. "It's textbook psychological warfare. The Network makes us out to be the enemy to distract from the real threat."

Turning to Arrowhawk, he asks, "How's Alicia doing?"

Still ruminating on Blankenchip's statement, he's slow to respond.

Blankenchip snaps his fingers in Arrowhawk's face. "Hello?"

"Yeah, yeah I heard you," Arrowhawk finally says. "You know, Aaron, there are moments when you actually make sense."

"The moment's gone. Get over it," Blankenchip says bluntly. "Alicia's status, now."

Arrowhawk taps the screen to enlarge a satellite image of the top of the Kinazawa building. A thermal mirror image lines up right beside it. Conrad's thermal signature is displayed on-screen with her vital signs data listed beside it.

"She just entered through the skylight window and should be starting the download now."

CHAPTER THIRTY-FIVE

FAMILY MATTERS

Kinazawa Office Tower
Tokyo, Japan

The top floor of the Kinazawa office tower served as the main headquarters of Shatoshi IT Solution, which also doubled as one of the fronts for Harada's racketeering operations. Codai Harada stores most of her high profile information on an isolated server that can be accessed by only one computer. That computer is located within the CEO's main office. The office is relatively inconspicuous, which serves well to conceal its true purpose.

Conrad enters through the skylight above the main foyer, where she makes her way to the CEO's office and picks the lock. Inside, she takes a seat in front of the main computer and begins hacking into the stored files.

Arrowhawk radios her.

"How's it going, Cap?"

"I've just accessed Harada's hard drive." Conrad's eyes dart across the screen. "I'll start the download in a few seconds. I'm going radio silent in the meantime."

"Copy that, Cap."

Conrad taps her earpiece, disconnecting her communication with Arrowhawk. As she begins downloading the information, the specially designed botnet virus searches for the term *Hegemony* on the computer's shadow drive.

Multiple data files pop on-screen and she opens one of them.

"Oh my God," she mutters aloud.

After the files are downloaded she packs up all of her equipment and proceeds to her exit. She goes back to the rappelling line attached to the base of the skylight opening and reattaches the carabiner to her belt harness.

Just as she's about to ascend, her cell phone vibrates. Conrad glances at the caller ID and answers.

Her sister's voice comes over the line. "Alicia, it's me. Where are you?

"I'm working. Are you OK?"

"Yeah, I'm fine," Camille says, but it's clear in her voice that the opposite is true.

"No, you're not. What's going on?"

"Well, they made us testify today."

"How'd it go?"

"OK, I guess. They were asking us stuff like, 'Do you think your sister is a good guardian?' and 'Did you ever feel abandoned by her?' Mr. Phillips objected a couple times when they were getting too personal."

"What did you say?" Conrad asks, somewhat wary of her sister's forthcoming response.

"I answered as best as I could."

"What about when they asked if you'd ever felt abandoned?" Conrad asks, her voice cracking.

"Well, I told the truth," Camille responds. "I told them that I *have* felt abandoned—especially after you left us for a while; but I understood that your work sometimes makes it hard for you to be with us."

"Oh, Camille," Conrad replies in a sad tone.

"But it's true. We needed you then, and even though Cam won't admit it, we still need you."

"You know I'm always there for you and Cam."

"Then come home," Camille says, as if it were truly that simple.

"I can't right now. I'm working on something really important."

"More important than us?" Camille asks plainly.

Conrad can hear the disappointment in her sister's voice.

"No, definitely not more important than you. When this is over I'll be home, I promise."

"Are you sure?"

"Yes."

At that moment Conrad's earpiece buzzes. She taps on it and Arrowhawk's voice comes over the line.

"Cap?"

Conrad adjusts her earpiece. "Hold on a sec, Camille…" She puts her cell phone down and switches over to Arrowhawk. "Go ahead, John."

"Hate to break protocol, but I think you might've tripped a silent alarm because the satellite's picking up ten warm bodies on the roof of the building."

"Do they have guns?"

"Not as far as I can tell," Arrowhawk says as he magnifies the satellite image onscreen.

"Thanks for the heads-up."

"You want backup? We can be there in two minutes."

"No."

Conrad puts her cell phone back to her left ear.

"Camille, I have to go, but we'll talk soon."

"OK."

"Remember that I love you both very much."

"Un-huh," Camille responds, sounding less than convinced.

Conrad looks at her cell phone after her sister hangs up. *This has to stop,* she thinks. *They deserve better and I have to be better.* After tucking her phone into her thigh pocket, she grabs on the rappelling rope and begins her climb up through the skylight. Once she reaches the roof, she is confronted by ten men in black and grey outfits equipped with traditional Japanese weapons. Conrad attempts to break the tension with a bit of levity.

"Halloween is still a few months away, boys. Aren't you a little early?"

Her joke elicits no response.

"OK, tough crowd."

Conrad pulls out two Glock 17 pistols from the holsters tucked within the small of her back. As she trains her guns on the men, two of them hurl their chain whips at her and knock the weapons out of her hands.

Another assassin lunges at her with his sword, but Conrad twists her body to the left, just barely avoiding decapitation, although sustaining a deep gash to her right cheek. As she turns around, the wound closes just as quickly as it was formed, without any evidence of trauma. The assassins look on in bewilderment at what they've witnessed. She wipes the remaining blood off her face.

"Bet you didn't see that coming," she remarks flippantly.

She tightens her brown head wrap, strikes a Pi Qua Q'an kung fu fighting stance, and motions to the assassins to come forward.

CHAPTER THIRTY-SIX

REVELATIONS

Aboard the Avian

The team is transfixed by what they see on the screen. Arrowhawk voices their collective curiosity.

"Is it just me, or did she just shrug off a sword to the face?"

"It's not just you," Morrison confirms.

"What's with the Kurasawa homage?" Arrowhawk asks, referring to the assassins' attire and weapons.

"They're called Gijō-hei, or Honor Guard," Fighting Bull replies. "Codai Harada fashions herself as a modern-day Japanese feudal lord. All of her elite assassins are trained in the use of both traditional and conventional weaponry."

"And how did you find that out?" Arrowhawk asks.

"Easy, I actually read her file."

"I've never seen anyone move like that in my life," Morrison says as Conrad engages the assassins on-screen.

"Yeah, it's like watching a kung fu movie but without the bad dubbing and lack of a plot," Arrowhawk says.

"She moves so effortlessly," Morrison comments, as Conrad ducks an attack from behind by a chain whip, and counters with a reverse kick to the assassin's abdomen. "It's almost as if she can predict what their next moves will be."

Blankenchip chimes in. "That's because she can, sort of."

The other three look at him confused.

"You lost us," Arrowhawk utters.

"Alicia isn't exactly normal," Blankenchip explains.

"That kind of goes without saying," Arrowhawk says. "She's making those guys look like washed-up Mixed Martial Artists."

"What do you mean?" Fighting Bull asks.

"Alicia is an enhanced human."

"Was she a SHARP participant?"

"One of the few who survived."

"SHARP?" Arrowhawk interjects.

"The Super Human Actualization Research Program," Fighting Bull begins explaining, "was a classified government initiative to develop the first superhuman operatives among all the military and intelligence agencies. Everyone from the CIA to the Air Force was scrambling to create their own superhumans. The problem was that most of the experiments were unsuccessful and almost all of the volunteers died in the process. It was scrapped shortly afterwards, and instead they started recruiting people that were born superhuman."

"Affirmative Action for superhumans, huh?"

"More like leveling the playing field," Fighting Bull retorts. "Why do you think the FBI was after you so bad to join?"

"Because of my urbane wit, of course."

She smiles and shakes her head.

"Our SHARP program was run through DARPA," Blankenchip says. "The project aimed to develop the optimum field soldier—more durable, stronger, faster, and smarter. As a result, her strength, speed, agility and reflexes were all enhanced. And thanks to the nanites in her blood, she can heal from any wound or poison almost instantaneously. The weirdest ability she developed was something the R&D guys call 'Enhanced Mental Perception.' The way she describes it, it's like having a 360-degree camera in your brain. She can mentally 'see' everything in her immediate environment up to a couple yards."

"Man, the ultimate fighting machine, that's a nice bullet point on your résumé," Arrowhawk exclaims.

"Yeah, but she paid the price for it," Blankenchip says.

"What do you mean?" Fighting Bull asks.

"She went through a lot… everything from nanite infusions, genetic engineering, to bionetic and neural implants. One of the side effects was that it caused severe mental instability. Simply put, the broad went crazy."

"Why didn't they just put her in an asylum or dose her up with some Haldol?" Arrowhawk asks.

"They weren't going to throw away millions of dollars in research and development because she went a little loco. They tried medicating her, but her physiology was so screwed up that normal meds didn't work. She decided to turn to eastern medicine and went to northern China to live with a bunch of Shaolin monks for two years." He points to the screen, where Conrad is pummeling an assassin in the face. "And that's where she learned that kung fu crap that she's using on those idiots down there."

"So the monks helped her overcome her mental instabilities?" Fighting Bull asks.

"She wouldn't be leader if she was still crazy, right?" Blankenchip responds matter-of-factly.

"What about her family in all this, where were they?" Morrison asks.

"Alicia's parents were killed in a car accident when she was eighteen, and she ended up being stuck with their toddler twins. She's raised them since then."

"What about extended family? Couldn't they have helped?"

"You have no idea how hard-headed that broad is," Blankenchip chuckles. "She refused to let them be broken up and instead decided to take sole custody. As a matter of fact, she's in a fight to keep custody of them now."

"Because of what happened to her?"

"That, and she hasn't exactly been the best parent."

"How does she do it? To go through all that and stay strong?" Morrison comments.

"She's definitely one of a kind," Blankenchip says as he stares at the screen. "The first woman to serve in active combat on an elite Special Forces unit and the first enhanced soldier in the world. She's probably one of the top five deadliest people on the planet."

There is a hint of admiration in his voice as he said this, something he would never admit to if anyone were to ask.

"And I bet you're number one on that list?" Arrowhawk says sarcastically.

Blankenchip smiles. "Now we're seeing eye to eye, kid."

CHAPTER THIRTY-SEVEN

BATTLE

Kinazawa Office Tower rooftop
Tokyo, Japan

Conrad narrowly dodges the katana blade of one of the assassins as it comes down to slice her in two. She evades the assault with a sideways somersault. Before he recovers to attack her again, Conrad connects with a concussive roundhouse kick to the jaw.

Two assassins attack in unison. One of them swipes at her with the end of one of his nunchukas, the other tries to sweep her off her feet with a Bo staff. She arches her back and extends her neck to avoid the nunchuka strike while kicking her legs out from underneath her to avoid the Bo staff. She lands on the palms of her hands. Then in one fluid movement, she grabs the nunchuka away from the assassin in front of her and swings it across her chest, striking the assassin with the Bo staff in his head, momentarily stunning him.

Next, Conrad wraps the neck of the assassin in front of her with the chain of the nunchuka. She flips him over her back, and slams him headfirst into the ground.

The other one tries to attack her from behind with his staff, but with the aid of her Enhanced Mental Perception, she ducks the attack. She crouches, tucks her knees to her chest, rolls back, and forcefully kicks the assassin in the stomach with both legs like a spring-loaded projectile. The impact of the blow is so powerful that it flips him backward, causing him to land on the back of his head. This fractures his skull and knocks him unconscious.

Another assassin attacks with a Yari—a long wooden staff with a double-pronged blade at the end, one part curved and the other straight. He swipes at Conrad in an upward arc. She leans her head to the left to dodge the attack. He bears down to strike another blow, but before he can, she delivers a three-punch combination to his abdomen and chest. She completes the combination with a roundhouse kick to the face, which flings the assassin high into the air. He crashes to the ground.

When she turns to face the next assassin, he punches her in the bridge of her nose. She rolls backward with the blow. Another assassin, poised behind her, reaches for her neck as she falls back. She flip kicks him in the jaw with her right foot. Then she uses this assassin's chest as a spring board, pushing off of him to give her momentum to arch her body backward and kick another assassin in the face with both feet. And in a matter of seconds, two highly trained killers are taken out of the fight.

She recovers, but tenuously, her feet near the edge of the roof. At that moment another assassin's chain whip entangles her legs. He yanks the chain back, pulling Conrad off balance. She starts to tumble backward off the edge of the building.

As she falls, she twists and reorients her body to complete a reverse somersault off the Kinazawa Office Tower. She lands on to the next building perfectly. The C-leg micro-implants in her calf-muscles help absorb most of the impact of the landing. Not only that, but they allowed her to leap distances of over one hundred and fifty feet due to their spring release mechanism.

The remaining four assassins fire grappling hooks into the rooftop that she lands on. The assassins zip-line the twenty-foot distance to get to her.

One of the quartet lunges at Conrad wielding a staff with a small spiked metal ball chained to the end. He whips the metal ball around haphazardly, trying desperately to hit her, but fails to connect every time. Conrad finally grabs the end of the staff and flips the assassin over her back. Then she slams the spiked ball into the assassin's midsection, eliminating him from combat.

The assassin with the chain whip decides to hurl it in Conrad's direction once more, but this time she grabs the end of it with her right hand, she then uses her left hand to yank the chain *and* the assassin toward her. When he's within inches of her, she kicks him in the neck. The impact of the blow hyperflexes his neck and crushes his trachea. He falls to the ground gasping for breath.

The last two assassins double-team Conrad, with one attacking from the rear and the other from the front.

The first attacks with two Sai blades and the other with Escrim sticks, weapons similar to police batons. Conrad ducks the first strike of the Sai blades and leans back to block the downward strike from the Escrim sticks. As she leans back her head wrap falls off. The assassin strikes at Conrad again with the Sai blades, but she spins to the left to dodge the attack. The assassin behind her just barely dodges the Sai blades as well.

She sweeps the feet of the assassin in front of her, and with one sinuous motion, pirouettes on the ball of her left foot and delivers a roundhouse kick to the face of the assassin behind her. One of the Escrim sticks falls out of his hand, and Conrad grabs it in midair. Moving with élan, she introduces the stick to the bridge of the nose of the assassin in front of her, breaking his nose, and completes the combination with a blow to his temple, which knocks him out.

The last assassin recovers from Conrad's roundhouse blow and comes across his back with the other Escrim stick. She blocks it with her left forearm. He continues to attack. She counters his every attempt as if it's child's play. She grabs the final Escrim stick from the assassin as he aims for her forehead, twirls the two sticks like majorette batons, and delivers bruising blows to the assassin's temples. She follows up with kicks to the chest and face. As the assassin stumbles backward, Conrad finishes the combination with a forceful uppercut to the jaw that lifts him off the ground. The assassin lands forcefully, unconscious.

Conrad dusts off her clothes and walks over to a fallen assassin to pick up her head wrap, which came off during the fight. She cleans it off. Her earpiece was stuck inside her head wrap. She places it back in her ear.

Arrowhawk's voice crackles over her earpiece. "Did you even break a sweat?"

Conrad smiles. "Just a little."

"You gotta teach me those moves sometime," he says. "Did you find anything good?"

"'Hegemony.' It's a lot bigger than we imagined."

CHAPTER THIRTY-EIGHT

REASON TO WORRY

August 26th
Network Headquarters
Rome, Italy

Just fifty feet below the streets of Rome lies the Network's meeting place. The Principals frequently assemble within the second-century-era Catacombs of Raphael. The catacombs are retrofitted with all of the creature comforts the Principals demanded. Around an ornate oval marble table the members sit, their attention focused on one member in particular, Chandler Ramsey. He can feel their staring eyes boring into him as he sits uncomfortably in his auburn leather chair. Within the span of a few days, Vigil has dealt a significant blow to the Network. The Principals are extremely disappointed in Ramsey's inability to keep Vigil under tight rein, and they hold nothing back.

"Chandler, what is this foolishness?" General Akwesi Dankwah shouts in his thick Ashanti accent. "Can't you get your little soldiers under control?"

"I'm trying the best I can," Ramsey replies.

"Obviously, your best isn't good enough," Taryn Marunowski chimes in. "If you don't do something soon, everything we've planned will go all to hell."

From their very first meeting, French billionaire Lorraine Duvalier was never fond of Ramsey. So it's no surprise that she doesn't hesitate to take the opportunity to emasculate her rival.

"I've already lost over two million euros in personal assets because of Vigil's exploits. Aren't you the one who was supposed to keep them on a short leash?"

"I have a plan to get them off our backs, Lorraine. Believe me, they will no longer be a problem," Ramsey says assuredly.

"I hope so, for your sake," Duvalier retorts.

Unsettled by her comment, Ramsey blasts back. "Excuse me, Lorraine, is that supposed to be some sort of threat?"

"Small women make threats; I make promises."

During the initial interchange, Network chairman Victor Angella has remained quiet. He's always been the most level-headed among the members. Seeing that the situation is quickly devolving, he steps in.

"Calm down." Angella motions with both hands like a referee. "Chandler, Lorraine is just expressing, in her own inimitable way, concerns we've been having about your ability to continue as a Principal member of this alliance."

"What kind of idiocy is this?" Ramsey exclaims as he rises up out of his seat. "Victor, I am a founding member of this group. I've been here longer than Lorraine and half the people at this table."

"We aren't discounting your history with this alliance, but your recent performance has been less than optimal." Angella glances over at the empty seat once occupied by Vásquez. "We would hate to see what happened to Emmanuel happen to you."

"Don't worry, as I said, I have contingencies."

"Contingencies, such as?" Weiping Pei asks.

"I've already stripped Vigil of their security clearances, and with Taryn's help, turned them into social pariahs. There are also secrets that they—and especially Alicia Conrad—wouldn't want revealed."

"And how do you plan on hurting the indestructible woman?" Duvalier asks.

Ramsey looks her in the eye and says with a wry smile, "The same way you hurt any other woman. You go after her heart."

Duvalier visibly bristles at the remark, but Angella steps in before the conversation can turn sour again.

"I'm glad to see that you have initiatives in place." He turns his gaze on the rest of the table. "See, Hegemony is still salvageable. We can move forward despite our loses."

Angella turns to Pei. "Weiping, do you still hold sway with your UN Security Council representative?"

The Chinese minister with thinning hair and bifocal glasses looks in Angella's direction. "Yes. I've told him to block any attempts at a military intervention."

"Good." Angella looks down the table to Nicolai Popov. "Is the launching site online?"

"Yes, all systems are running at peak efficiency," Popov answers. "We should be at full launching capability within the week."

"Excellent." Angella turns to Codai Harada, seated three chairs away from him.

"Codai, are your agents in play?"

"My men are in place," Harada responds succinctly.

Angella looks to the right of Harada, where Lawrence Holmes is seated.

"Any new developments concerning Aldessa's murder?"

"My sources say that it might have been a state-sponsored assassination, but nothing has been ruled out," Holmes responds.

"Keep us apprised." Angella looks in Ramsey's direction. "And Chandler, we have your assurance that Vigil's interference will no longer be a problem?"

"Yes," Ramsey answers confidently. "Once I'm through with them, they'll wish they'd never challenged us."

PART FOUR

PURSUIT

CHAPTER THIRTY-NINE

THE GAME IS ON

Davis Army Base
Tempe, Arizona

Over the course of forty-eight hours, Vigil's mission objectives have drastically changed. Conrad's trip to Japan revealed much more concerning the Network's plan. On the initial plane ride back, Conrad provided the team with a truncated version of what she found. The information that she has is still fragmented. It took roughly a day to put the pieces together into a discernable picture. She re-assembles the team for a formal briefing.

"When we started out we had no idea what Hegemony was. For all we knew it could have been a weapon of mass destruction, an attack plan, or a business strategy. Well, it's all of those rolled into one."

"What do you mean?" Arrowhawk asks.

She places folders in front of each member before continuing. "'Hegemony' is a multilateral offensive aimed at destabilizing the Legaud administration and establishing complete economic and political control of Lemalia."

"Why Lemalia?" Morrison flips carefully through the pages in his folder.

"The Network virtually owns their economy." Conrad pulls out a sheet from her folder to show the rest of the team. "About ninety percent of the country's GDP is generated from businesses controlled by the Network Principals. President Legaud's nationalization plan stripped away their control and placed it into the hands of the government. As a result, the Principals have lost billions. Now, they've decided to take it all back by whatever means necessary."

Once more Arrowhawk raises his hand to interject. "I know I'm playing devil's advocate here," he says, "but so what?"

"Are you deaf?" Blankenchip barks back. "Didn't you hear what she just said?"

Arrowhawk shifts from the reclining position in his chair to sit up attentively. He pulls a page from an S&P internal report in his folder that details the financial damage caused by Legaud's nationalization plan.

"Look, Legaud basically set up a quasi-socialist system overnight." He points to a line graph on the report detailing Lemalia's economic decline. "He's devalued his country's currency and even the NYSE, the S&P, and the Nikkei are all in a slump because of this idiotic move."

Without missing a beat, Fighting Bull, who is seated to his left, responds in kind.

"What should we do instead, give the Network a free pass because we're the champions of capitalist ideals?"

"No. I'm just saying that what Legaud did was wrong. How he got into power was wrong. It wouldn't surprise me if he had something to do with Aldessa's assassination."

"Cue Mulder; here we go with the conspiracies again," Morrison says, taking a playful jab at Arrowhawk.

"Hear me out," Arrowhawk pleads. "Hasn't anybody wondered why investigations into Mohann Aldessa's assassination have come up with nothing?"

"We'll deal with that later," Conrad says, taking control of the conversation once more. "Right now we have to focus on our immediate problem."

"What are the specs on Hegemony?" Blankenchip asks.

"It's a multistage plan involving the G-20 and the Lemalian insurgency. They've already begun funding radicals within the People's National Democratic Party."

"Aldessa's party?"

"Correct. Their plan calls for radicals in his party to destabilize the country in order to upset Legaud's transition to power."

"What are these radicals called?" Morrison asks.

"The United People's Front."

"So they operate kind of like Hamas, with a political arm as well as a militant one?" Fighting Bull asks.

"In a sense."

"My question, though, is why the PNDP?" Fighting Bull continues, "Couldn't the Network have just tasked one of the groups they usually do business with?"

"Because Aldessa's been the Network's boy for the better part of a decade," Conrad responds. "In fact, his entire political career was funded by the Network."

"Do you have proof?" Morrison asks bluntly.

Conrad turns to the holo-tab next to her and gently taps the screen twice. A holographic schematic of various documents appears in front of them.

"Harada's computer has phone conversation transcripts, emails, and letters outlining Aldessa's deal with the Network. The agreement called for them to back Aldessa's campaign. With their resources, he was virtually guaranteed a win. In return, Aldessa would dissolve parliament and consolidate power onto himself."

"Essentially turning him into a puppet dictator," Fighting Bull says, finishing the thought.

"Exactly."

"Who's the Network's point man in the PNDP?" Blankenchip asks.

"Aldessa's military advisor, Erosin Analaise."

"The guy they sent the money to?" Arrowhawk asks.

"Yes. Analaise has been funneling Network monies into the UPF. They've also received training, weapons, and equipment from General Dankwah's personnel."

Morrison adds support to Conrad's assertion. "We found records on

Dankwah's computer of training and materiel transactions over the last month and a half with an unnamed source. Best bet is Analaise was that source."

"On top of that, they ripped off my armor designs and shipped two hundred units from Dankwah's headquarters," Blankenchip says angrily. "Dankwah provided them with the gold for the power centric core's circuit boards. Based on what you're saying they must have been sent to Analaise's people."

"How would they get your armor designs?" Conrad asks.

"I worked with a Ph.D. named Raines. He's the only one who could've given Ramsey access to them."

Fighting Bull gets back to one of Conrad's earlier statements. "You said something about there being multiple stages…?"

"Yeah."

Conrad taps on the holo-tab's screen once more. Instantly an image of the G-20 logo pops.

"The second stage involves using nuclear weapons on four G-20 nations: Japan, the US, Russia, and Germany."

"How were they going to do that?" Arrowhawk asks.

"Nicolai Popov, the former IAEA scientist, was given access to Soviet era nukes. Popov modified the weapons to have a more concentrated lethal effect. The blast radius would decrease but the radioactivity levels would increase tenfold. Their aim is to bomb these countries and force them into the conflict. With the US being attacked, this would have forced Vigil to be directly involved in any strike against Lemalia."

"How did Popov get access to Soviet nuclear weapons?" Fighting Bull asks.

"Several years ago Ramsey headed a joint NSA/SVR task force to retrieve unsecured nuclear weapons from former Soviet bloc nations. All of the recovered weapons were stored in a facility in Kazakhstan. It was decommissioned two years ago and Ramsey provided Popov access to it."

"Why would they blame Lemalia?" Morrison asks. "Satellite feeds would clearly trace an attack to the Network's launching site."

"That gets me to my next point." Conrad once more taps the screen, and the holographic image changes to a schematic of the Vigil satellite defense system. "Our satellite system has a signal modifier that can intercept and alter relay signals to produce false feeds."

"The thing those men we fought in space were trying to take over," Morrison mentions.

"Since we stopped that, how do they plan on carrying out their ploy?" Arrowhawk asks.

"Through false intelligence and media deception, courtesy of Ramsey and Marunowski."

"What else do they have planned?" Fighting Bull asks.

"The assassination of President Legaud," Conrad responds calmly.

"It just keeps getting better and better," Arrowhawk says to himself in a mordant tone.

"The hit is planned for the Mediterranean Economic Summit in Greece in three days."

"Which is ironic since the country went bankrupt not too long ago," Fighting Bull says as an aside.

"Popov's launching site is online and set to initiate the assault within the week," Conrad continues, "so we've got our work cut out for us."

"What's the plan?" Morrison asks.

"You and John are heading to Greece. Aaron and I will be going to Kazakhstan."

"Not before I talk to Raines," Blankenchip interjects. "I need to find out why he sold out to Ramsey."

"What about me?" Fighting Bull asks.

Conrad turns and looks Fighting Bull directly in eye. "You're sitting this one out."

"Excuse me, Captain?"

"You heard what I said."

"Why?"

"Because your cavalier actions in France showed me that you can't take orders in the field."

"But—"

"Besides, we'll need logistical support," Conrad says before Fighting Bull can complete her sentence.

"I've been your best asset in the field."

"You're overestimating your value, Cynthia. The fact is that you were insubordinate when I ordered you to abort the mission in Paris—that proved to me you're a liability we can't afford."

"That's ridiculous."

Conrad turns to the rest of the team. "Can you excuse us please?"

She takes Fighting Bull to the communications room while the three men begin conversing.

"Oooo, someone's in trouble," Arrowhawk teases playfully as the women walk off.

"I had a feeling this thing would snowball out of control," Morrison says.

"Yeah, bad enough we have to stop Ramsey, now we have to stop freakin' World War Three," Arrowhawk adds.

"Stop being such a drama queen, John," Blankenchip grumbles. "That's why we're here—to stop the bad guys and protect the civilians."

"I'm not sure what's more shocking, you finally calling me something other than 'kid,' or the fact that you said something that I actually agree with."

"If we get involved in some sort of war, what would our stance be?" Morrison says.

"What do you mean?" Arrowhawk asks.

"Since Legaud took over, the US no longer formally recognizes Lemalia. How are we supposed to respond since we're technically supposed to uphold national policy?"

"If you hadn't noticed, we haven't been on Uncle Sam's good side the past few weeks," Blankenchip interjects.

"But stop to think, Terrell. Who helped formulate that policy?"

"You're thinking Ramsey had something to do with this?"

"I wouldn't be surprised," Arrowhawk says. "He's high enough on the NSA totem pole to have an impact."

"Shut up," Blankenchip blurts out. "You civilian types always worry about the little stuff. Spend so much time deliberating and not enough on executing. Like I just said, stop the bad guys and protect the civilians. Simple."

"Sorry, but things are never that simple," Arrowhawk counters.

"Sure they are."

"How so?" Morrison asks.

"Whoever has the biggest gun wins," Blankenchip says with a grin.

CHAPTER FORTY

STRATEGIC ALLIANCES

August 29th
Halcyon Incorporated headquarters
Los Angeles, California

Taryn Marunowski waits impatiently for the elevator. Typically she has one of her assistants pick up lunch, but they always seem to find an ingenious way to mess up her order. Her mentality is, "If you want something done right, you have to do it yourself." The delayed elevator, especially, doesn't help, considering the fact that she's on a tight schedule with about a twenty-minute window to grab lunch before meeting with the director of news programming. All but fed up, Marunowski decides to take the stairs down to the ground level.

She pulls up on her Louis Vuitton purse, which is sliding over her left shoulder, as she exits the building to walk across the street. Marunowski quickly pulls her cell phone from the purse to check the time and slips it back into the purse's front pocket. She quickly walks to the Potbelly Sandwich Shop to pick up a roast beef sandwich with all the toppings. She may be a multi-media mogul, but deep down she'll always be a girl from Parma, Ohio, who loves to eat.

In the middle of the crosswalk, unnoticed by Marunowski, a young woman wearing a Cleveland Browns ball cap and an Enyce track suit brushes against her. In less than a second the young woman is able to tap a small credit-card-sized device against the side of Marunowski's purse. The young woman inserts the device into a nondescript cell phone and makes her way across the street in the opposite direction.

* * *

NSA Headquarters
Fort Mead, Maryland

Chandler Ramsey works on his desktop computer when he receives a call on his secured line, which was installed by Duvalier's personnel.

"Chandler, it's Taryn," Marunowski says.

"Hey, Taryn, what's up?"

"My blood pressure, for one thing. What do you plan to do about Vigil?"

"Listen, I've already set things in motion. Vigil will hardly be an inconvenience once I'm through with them."

"That's cold comfort for somebody who's lost a million in personal assets overnight."

"You're a multimillionaire, Taryn. What's one million to you?"

"A shopping spree on Rodeo Drive and a weekend on the French Riviera," Marunowski answers without hesitation.

"You're that much of a tight wad?" Ramsey asks incredulously.

"No, I just like to have my money close at hand."

"Anyway," Ramsey says, clearly not at all sympathetic to the woes of his associate, "do you have your reporters embedded with the UPF yet?"

"Don't worry, Chandler; I have my best foreign correspondents on the job."

"Don't forget that we're trying to paint them in the most sympathetic light. We need public opinion on their side."

"Chandler, in my thirty years in this business I've learned one thing: all reality is media reality. We shape the public's perception of what is real. We tell them how to feel, think, and act. Without us there wouldn't be such a thing as 'public opinion.' So don't talk to me about 'swaying public opinion'; I create it."

"Thanks for the enlightening speech," Ramsey responds in an uninspired voice.

"Just taking advantage of my constitutional rights."

"Reminds me of something Kierkegaard said: 'People demand freedom of speech as a compensation for the freedom of thought which they seldom use'."

"Is that an indirect insult, Chandler?"

"No, just making a comment. By the way, nice piece you guys did with that Swanson guy the other day."

"Yeah. Chandler, I'm inundated today, so if you could just run through the plan again for me?"

"You weren't paying attention at our last meeting?"

"Yeah but you know how Victor's voice lulls me right to sleep."

"Don't remind me. Anyway, Analaise received the shipment of armor yesterday. It's going to be distributed to the unit making the strike at Kalaran. Akwesi's outfitted the remaining units with weapons, tanks, and artillery. Victor's supplying the communications and tactical support."

"How's the equipment getting to the secondary and tertiary units?"

"A supply train from the eastern coast to the Desian region will be making hourly trips to resupply the units."

"How about our intelligence capabilities?" Marunowski inquires intently.

"Codai's got sleeper agents on presidential security detail, as well as the military operations command center. Once they launch their counter-offensive, we'll be updated on their status in real time."

Noticing the glee in Ramsey's voice, Marunowski comments, "You seem to be having fun with this, Chandler."

"I'm just anxious. Lemalia's a strategic asset not just to us but also to this country."

"America's basically cut off all ties to Lemalia. How do you see that as a plus?"

"Once Legaud is out and Analaise is in, we'll normalize relations and reestablish trade talks. All of Lemalia's natural resources will be under our control. The US market will get exclusive access to Duritium, and we'll make a killing on the sales."

"You're a hypocrite, Chandler. You'd be willing to profit off the country you claim to love in order to accomplish your own agenda?"

Ramsey hardens his voice as he answers. "I wouldn't be the first one. Look, the idiots on the Hill are only interested in getting votes. The bureaucrats in Washington are masters in the exercise of futility. They've allowed America to fall behind both economically and militarily. None of them is willing to make the hard sacrifices it takes to bring this nation back to preeminence. If it takes starting a war to do that, then I'm willing to make that sacrifice."

"You're delusional. What sacrifices are you really making if you're not the one fighting the war?"

Ramsey responds with cold determination in his voice. "We're all patriots in our own little ways, Taryn. Some show it by fighting on the front lines, others do it by destabilizing mineral-rich countries."

"I didn't know you could be so cutthroat," Marunowski responds.

"I'll take that as a compliment, coming from you."

CHAPTER FORTY-ONE

CONFESSION

Outside the Natick Research Facility
Natick, Massachusetts

Philip Raines is the principal investigator for the Cybernetic Armor Technology Initiative, which is run through DARPA's Future Force Warrior Program. He and Blankenchip were the first to successfully develop a fully functioning cybernetic combat armor for field use. The two were extremely close for the two years they worked together. Besides Blankenchip, no one else knows the intricacies of the C.A.T. as intimately as Raines. This fact leaves little doubt as to the source of the leak to the Network.

Raines likes to jog to clear his head from the arduous task of his research, and this day is no different. He runs along the winding trail by the research facility, then takes a detour on one of the unpaved paths that diverge from the main trail. As he makes his way, he trips over an exposed tree root and lands less than gracefully with outstretched hands. He wipes the mud off his shorts and knees. After recovering, he readies himself to rise and looks up to see Blankenchip standing over him. Blankenchip extends his hand.

"Need a hand up, Phil?"

Raines grabs Blankenchip's hand.

"What are you doing here, Aaron?"

"Wanted to clear my head, take a break."

"Here... in the middle of Massachusetts... now?" Raines asks incredulously.

"Let's take a walk, Phil."

The pair stroll down to the side of a stream at the end of the unpaved path. Raines gets right to the point.

"What do you want, Aaron? I know this isn't a social visit. Especially when you and your team are public enemy number one."

Blankenchip removes his cell phone from his coat pocket and taps the screen. Immediately a schematic of the stolen C.A.T. armor designs pops up onscreen. He lifts the phone to show Raines. He looks at it and then turns to Blankenchip.

"Why?" Blankenchip asks.

"Why not?" Raines responds reflexively. "I'm so hamstrung with funding cuts that I can't get any research off the ground."

"That's a lame-ass excuse!" Blankenchip retorts. "You don't betray your country to some wannabe Illuminati because you can't get your pet projects paid for."

Blankenchip's anger rises at Raines' duplicity. After suffering a shrapnel injury to his spine, he was disqualified as a candidate for SHARP. After developing a post-operative infection in his spine and months of physical rehabilitation, he used his engineering skill to develop the C.A.T. with the help of Raines. To Blankenchip, this was his ticket back into active duty. So for him, this is personal. Raines was one of the few people he trusted, and his betrayal cuts Blankenchip to his very core.

"You don't understand, Aaron, I've worked for over thirty-five years in Defense R&D and I've had some of my best ideas shot down due to funding cuts and lack of vision," Raines responds.

"Who came to you first? Was it Ramsey, or his henchwench Price?"

"Before I say anything, I want immunity."

"From who? I'm not the feds, sunshine."

"I need some guarantees Aaron."

"I guarantee I won't shove my foot up your ass crack if you tell me what I want to hear."

Raines hesitates before responding. "Ramsey came to me a few months back requesting the armor designs for an NSA development project. He actually commissioned an updated version. I'd never heard of any projects with the NSA, and besides, none of their top brass dealt directly with me. I knew something was up."

So you figured you'd had him over a barrel," Blankenchip says. "Get something out of it."

"I know how the game is played, Aaron."

"Now you've given Ramsey the key to destroying a whole nation."

"What are you talking about?"

"What Ramsey conveniently omitted was the fact that he was using the designs to manufacture a whole line of armor to start a war in Lemalia. He had one of his associates manufacture them and ship them off to Lemalia to help overthrow the current regime."

"You serious?"

"As a heart attack."

CHAPTER FORTY-TWO

RUSH

August 30th
Mediterranean Economic Summit (MES)
State Opera House
Athens, Greece

Legaud wraps up the opening session of the MES as its last speaker. The country has been ostracized under his policies and he is slowly seeing the downside of his economic nationalism. His speech will be direct... the Lemalians need to re-establish economic relations with their Mediterranean neighbors or else they face total economic collapse.

He steps up to the lectern and reaches for the microphone. His voice is steady as he begins outlining his plan for renewed ties with the Mediterranean Economic Council. As he reaches the conclusion of his speech, shouts erupt in the back of the auditorium. Two representatives from the Greek and Cyprus contingents get into a verbal sparring match, which escalates into a full-fledged fistfight. The security staff intervenes and, in the turmoil, a gun is fired into the crowd.

Immediately, Legaud's four-man security detail rushes him offstage. As they make their way, one of the guards taking the rear is shot in the chest. Legaud turns to see him crumple to the floor. Knowing that the bullet was intended for him, his mind is instantly flooded with thoughts that this assassination attempt is being implemented by the same person who killed Mohann Aldessa. Legaud's lead security guard radios for the limousine to pull around to the side exit door. They make their way hurriedly down the steps leading to the exit. Legaud's lead guard kicks the exit door with the heel of his functional dress shoe. With his head down and smothered by his guards, Legaud is ushered into the vehicle.

The rest of Legaud's entourage follows close behind, including a second limousine with his extended security detail, and two police escorts on motorcycles. During the confusion they fail to notice the unmarked black SUV trailing them. As the convoy rushes down Akadimias street, they are slowed by a traffic pile-up. Legaud's driver tries to back out of the congestion to find an alternate route of escape.

At that moment, a man positioned on a rooftop just above the convoy removes a shoulder-mounted rocket launcher from its carrying case and trains its sights on Legaud's caravan. A member of the secondary security team sees this and warns his compatriots as he reaches for his assault rifle. The missile is launched before he can grab hold of his weapon, and in an instant the trailing limousine is obliterated. Shrapnel from the explosion kills the flanking police escorts. The ensuing shockwaves from the blast reverberate through the area. The man on the rooftop readies his weapon to take another shot when he is blasted from behind by a solid energy force beam. He lands headfirst into the hood of one of the cars below.

Legaud's limousine speeds down Vasilis Sofias road and turns down a side street off Platia Monastiraki. The street dead-ends. Right behind them is the black SUV, which turns broadside to completely block their exit. Six men step out of the vehicle with weapons at the ready. Legaud's driver ducks under the dashboard before the men begin firing their semiautomatic weapons at the limousine.

In that instant, an oscillating yellow energy field surrounds the limousine, deflecting the bullets.

The assassins are momentarily bewildered. Just as they begin to walk toward

Legaud's limousine, they hear an ominous sound from above. Morrison, his molecular density altered to granite, comes down from the adjoining rooftop and smashes into the assassins' SUV, completely demolishing the vehicle. The impact of Morrison's fall flings some of the assassins to the ground.

A few of the assassins recover and start firing their weapons on Morrison who transitions from granite to titanium. The bullets bounce off of his metallic body. He grabs the two assassins lying on the ground next to him and flings them into the concrete wall behind him. Another comes from behind Morrison and swings a knife down on him, but the knife breaks once it strikes his neck. Morrison turns and grabs the assassin, takes him by his shirt collar, and hurls him into another assassin who is shooting at him.

The last pair of assassins, seeing that firing on Morrison is useless, turn their attention back to Legaud's vehicle. As they prepare to shoot, their weapons begin to superheat and turn crimson red. The assassins quickly drop their guns. They look up to see Arrowhawk standing on the hood of Legaud's limousine.

The newly unarmed assassins reach into their coat pockets for their handguns, but Arrowhawk connects with a right cross to the jaw of one of them before he can reach for it. The second assassin swings at Arrowhawk, who ducks the blow and quickly counters with an uppercut that knocks the assassin out cold.

Seeing that Arrowhawk has taken out the last of the assassins, Legaud's guards begin to get him out of the vehicle. As they open the door the driver reaches into the glove compartment to remove a silver Beretta with a silencer on the tip. The partitioning glass slides down, and the driver quickly shoots both of Legaud's security guards. As the assassin starts to pull the trigger on Legaud, a beam of pure energy rips through the front windshield and blasts him through the back windshield. He crashes to the ground behind the limousine, unconscious.

Morrison and Arrowhawk walk up to the driver's body splayed out on the ground.

"Nice shot."

"Thank you," Arrowhawk responds.

The two men help the visibly shaken Legaud out of his limousine. "Mr. President, are you all right?" Morrison asks.

"Ye-yes, I am. Who are you?" Legaud inquires.

Arrowhawk turns to Morrison. "We have got to get a new publicist."

"I thought you were dating her," Morrison says slyly.

He ignores the remark and looks at Legaud. "Mr. Legaud, my name is John Arrowhawk and this is Terrell Morrison. We're a part of Vigil."

"But I thought that you had become criminals?" Legaud exclaims.

"No, sir. We're still the good guys," Morrison assures him.

Arrowhawk presses a button on the small remote he pulls from his uniform's outer coat, and the Avian uncloaks just above them.   "Terrell, we gotta go," Arrowhawk says, reminding Morrison of their tight schedule.

Morrison extends his hand to Legaud. "Mr. President, you should be safe here. The police are on their way."

"Yes. Thank you, thank you very much for saving my life," Legaud says, shaking Morrison's hand.

"You're welcome, sir."

Rappelling lines descend from the Avian's hull. The two men hook themselves in with the attached harnesses before the rappelling lines retract.

As they make their ascent, Arrowhawk says, "That was too close. If we had come one second later, Legaud would be dead right now."

"Thankfully we got here in time."

"I hate to admit it, but I kind of wish Cynthia was in on this op."

"Alicia had other plans for her," Morrison replies.

"Do you think she made the right decision about Cynthia?"

"I'm beginning to trust Alicia's decisions," Morrison replies, evidencing a change of heart. "I don't always agree with her methods, but she gets results."

CHAPTER FORTY-THREE

THE DROP

August 31st
Montgomery County Department of Child Welfare Services
Rockville, Maryland

Case officer Maurice Hodges is sitting in his cubicle, thanklessly inputting case logs into his computer, when his phone rings. Hodges looks at the Caller ID screen with a jaundiced eye. He notices that it reads "Restricted." He lets the phone ring one more time before reluctantly picking up the receiver.

"Child Welfare Services, Maurice Hodges speaking," Hodges answers, his voice breaking.

"Don't talk, just listen," an electronically altered voice on the other end of the line says. It was the kind of voice that you would hear from a disguised informant on "Dateline." "I have the evidence that will win you the Conrad case."

"Excuse me, who is this?" Hodges replies, this time with a little bass in his voice. Suddenly his voice matched his age.

"You're not very good at this following directions thing, are you?" the person answers wryly. "I said don't talk. If you want the evidence, meet me in the parking garage of the Rockville AMC movie theater in twenty minutes."

Hodges does not respond. He just clutches the phone close to his ear. After a few awkward and agonizing seconds the caller speaks.

"OK, this is the part where you can talk."

Hodges hesitates before saying, "Yes, I understand."

The caller hangs up, leaving Hodges sitting in his office chair, bewildered.

* * *

First floor parking garage
AMC Movie Theater
Rockville, Maryland

Hodges waits by his fuel efficient compact car for his mysterious benefactor to arrive. He grows impatient and starts checking his watch. Just as he is about to reenter the car, the barrel of a H&K P30 pistol presses against the back of his neck.

"Don't say a word." It's the same eerie voice he heard on the phone earlier.

"Slowly, without turning around, unlock the doors."

Hodges complies.

"Get in."

Hodges eases his way into the driver's seat. His mysterious benefactor makes their way into the seat directly behind him, still holding the gun to the back of his neck. The benefactor drops a legal-sized manila envelope onto the front passenger seat next to Hodges.

"Take this directly to the county attorney's office. A tracking device is in the lining of the envelope, so don't try anything cute."

Hodges instinctively goes into bureaucrat mode and begins babbling. "But county policy says—"

The benefactor forcefully strikes the back of Hodges's head with the handle of the pistol. Hodges elicits a gut level groan.

"What did I say about talking?! Mr. Hodges, you do not want to make me angry."

"Like you weren't already?" Hodges mumbles to himself, half in sarcasm and half in fear.

"Did you say something?"

Hodges furiously shakes his head from side to side to indicate that he did not.

"Good. Don't leave until five minutes after I vacate this vehicle. Understand?"

Hodges nods in acknowledgement. Hodges's benefactor leaves the car and walks briskly to the nearest exit. As they descend down the stairs, they remove their facial prosthetics and transdermal voice scrambler to reveal the face of Lauren Price.

Meanwhile, Hodges slowly gathers himself and reaches over to the passenger seat to pick up the envelope. He opens it and pulls out a photo that makes him gasp.

CHAPTER FORTY-FOUR

NUCLEAR OPTION

September 2nd
Yegevny Nuclear Weapons Facility
Aral, Kazakhstan

"Go! Go! Go!" Fighting Bull screams as Conrad and Blankenchip jump out of the Avian at a height of 30,000 feet. As promised, the young CIA agent is marooned to a support role on this assignment. She is none too pleased, but begrudgingly complies with her orders.

The wind rushes through the opened hatch as the duo leaps out. High Altitude Low Opening jumps are old hat for these veteran Special Forces operatives. Aiming to evade Popov's radar, the two pick up velocity as they tumble through the cold roaring winds.

As soon as the pair hits 3,000 feet, they open their parachutes and land in the reservoir leading into the facility. They dislodge their parachutes after landing. The perimeter guards don't spot them as they move silently to the main sewage line at the end of the reservoir. After removing the grating over the main sewage line entrance, they split up to deactivate Popov's nuclear warheads.

"We'll rendezvous at the central annex in fifteen minutes," Conrad radios to Blankenchip.

"Copy that."

Conrad goes to the east wing and Blankenchip the west. Sweat beads up on her forehead as she sprints down a long corridor. The exit doors explode open as she bursts through them. She leaps and grabs on to the crossbar of the stairwell and flips herself into the landing below. As her feet touch the ground she encounters two armed guards who reach for their rifles.

Before they can fire a shot, she runs up to the guards and delivers a Muay Thai knee strike to the first guard's chin which snaps his neck back. She then connects to his wrist with a closed hand blow that dislodges his gun. She torques her torso around to the second guard and throws small spikes into his forearm. Then, in one fluid motion, she roundhouse kicks the first guard and backhand punches the second. Both guards fall, unconscious.

Conrad hustles down the rest of the stairs, barely winded by her previous encounters. Finally arriving at the lower-level silo bay, she confronts four armed guards stationed at the entrance. Upon noticing her, they open fire. Bullets ricochet off of the old silo walls as Conrad dodges them with an acrobatic cartwheel. In mid-air she reaches for her Glock pistol in her back holster. She lands hard on the ground but still manages to return fire with her own salvo of bullets. A scream is heard from the lead guard as a bullet pierces his left shoulder, while another bullet makes its way into a second guards thigh, severing his femoral artery. Immediately the second guard collapses to the ground. Unabated, the last two guards continue shooting. Rolling off of the ground she reacquires solid footing and continues firing back as bullet shells empty from her expiring magazine. The intent was to create space between her and her adversaries to allow for her to get a running start toward them. Although she could have eliminated them easily by just shooting them, she didn't want that, that would be too easy. She would rather take them out with skill. She does a front flip toward one of the guards and delivers a drop kick that slams him to the ground. The last guard points his rifle at her, but before he can even let off a shot she delivers a side kick to his lateral knee, throwing him off balance and then delivers a follow-through roundhouse to his face.

Barely moments after the last guard's head hits the floor, she overrides the door locks and enters the silo. As she moves in, she pulls out a small circular device about three inches in diameter from her tactical webbing and places it on the missile, which scrambles the command and control relay system. Then, she rushes off to disarm the second missile.

Blankenchip, meanwhile, is in the process of installing the same jamming device on the third missile. After completing his task, he heads toward the west central silo to disarm the fourth. As he's making his way, he encounters a six-man roving patrol. The guards immediately begin firing on him, and Blankenchip instinctively returns fire. A majority of the bullets deflect off his armor. "Dammit, Cynthia, you could've warned me there were hostiles around the corner!" he shouts as he quickly shoots three of the guards. The remaining three take cover.

"Thermals are iffy at best, they have the building pretty well shielded from any type of imaging," Fighting Bull replies over the radio.

"That's no excuse!"

"Hey here's a tip, don't get your head blown off." She notices thermal outlines of two guards turning in Blankenchip's direction, "Watch your back Aaron!"

The two guards shoot at Blankenchip sporadically from behind the support pillars in the hall. Blankenchip opts to use the thermal imaging view on in his own heads-up display to determine the location of the guards. Then he fires a laser beam from his gauntlet at the pillar one of the guards is hiding behind. The pillar collapses onto the guard.

A second guard continues shooting. Using his targeting computer, Blankenchip finds a weak point in the ceiling and fires at it, causing part of it to collapse on the second guard. The last guard rushes from his cover to the alarm switch on the wall adjacent to him, and pulls it.

Blankenchip turns around immediately. "Oh damn."

The guard turns and shoots at Blankenchip in a last-ditch attempt to kill him. Blankenchip quickly shoots the guard in the neck, then radios Conrad.

"Alicia, I've been compromised."

"I kind of figured that from the alarms. What's your twenty?"

"I'm about five hundred meters away from the west central silo."

"I'm finishing up here. See if you can get to it and meet me at the secondary extraction point in ten minutes."

"Copy that."

The alarms initiate the facility's automatic lockdown. Nicolai Popov and his men are in the control room as this happens.

One of his men alerts him to the cause of the alarm. "Sir, we have intruders."

Popov looks at the security monitors to see both Conrad and Blankenchip making short work of his security force.

"This changes things." Popov looks to the launch coordinator. "Initiate the sequence."

"Three of the missiles are offline, sir. They must have deactivated them."

"And the fourth?"

"It's still operational."

"Start the sequence."

"But, sir, we weren't scheduled to launch for another hour."

"I don't pay you to talk back," Popov barks back. "Do it now."

The launch coordinator sheepishly complies and initiates the sequence.

The countdown is broadcast over the facility's public announcement system. Even though the countdown is in Russian, both Conrad and Blankenchip know what it means.

"You get to the last nuke?" Conrad radios to Blankenchip.

"Negative. I encountered more guards before I could get there."

"OK, I'll take care of it."

"Are you crazy, Alicia? The nuke launches in less than two minutes, and you're on the opposite end of the building. There's no way you're going to make it in time."

Conrad begins running in the direction of the last missile silo.

"I can make it," she says assuredly.

"No, you can't," Blankenchip exclaims. "I don't care if you can run faster than Carl Lewis; you're not going to make it. Activate the SBL protocols now!"

"And have a megaton yield of radioactive material scattered over the countryside? That's pure genius, Aaron."

She pulls out a pair of goggles and gloves with miniature adherens points on the finger pads from her tactical webbing and puts them on. As she reaches the entrance to the silo, she encounters four more guards. She slide tackles the first guard; as he falls over, she grabs the back of his head and drives it into the ground like a piston. A second guard trains his rifle on her and fires—she avoids the shot and kicks the rifle out of his hand with a Capoeira move. She follows with a blow to his face from the bottom of her right boot. Conrad's suddenly thrown off balance from the impact of a bullet from the third guard hitting the flank of her body armor. She recovers with a leaping roundhouse kick to the head of the guard, splaying him on the ground in front of her. Conrad then pulls out her Glock 17 from her side holster and swivels her body around to face the fourth guard. Three bullets pierce his right shoulder and thigh and he drops to the ground with a thud. Then she trains her pistol on the door lock and obliterates it with one shot. Lowering her shoulder, she rams the silo-door open—taking it off of its hinges.

The missile launches just as she enters the silo. Propulsion exhaust flames engulf the area as the missile begins to ascend. She uses part of the broken silo door to shield herself. Conrad leaps onto the side of the missile and holds on tight as it bursts into the sky. At that moment Blankenchip radios her.

"What's your twenty?"

"I'm on the missile."

"What the hell!" Blankenchip yells. "Do you have a death wish?"

"If I died, then you'd be in charge! I couldn't let that happen now, could I?"

Conrad switches her radio channel from Blankenchip to Fighting Bull.

"Cynthia, I need you to bring the Avian under my comm signal in thirty seconds."

"Copy that, Captain."

Conrad silences her radio earpiece. She strains against the relentless shearing winds to peel back the cover panel of the missile guidance system and attaches the signal jammer to it. Before the missile reaches maximum ascent, Conrad leaps off backwards.

As she free-falls through the sky, the Avian uncloaks just meters beneath her. Fighting Bull deploys one of the rappelling rope lines, which snags Conrad at the waist, then retracts to tow her into the ship.

All the while the missile spirals out of control. It splashes down into the Aral Sea.

As Conrad is ushered into the ship she turns her radio earpiece back on. The sounds of Blankenchip's continuing ranting welcome her.

"Alicia, you pull more stunts like that, and the twins won't just be parentless anymore."

Conrad seethes at this comment.

"I got the job done, right?"

"Yeah, but you're not indestructible."

"But I'm the closest thing to it," she replies defiantly.

CHAPTER FORTY-FIVE

LIBERATION POINT

Four hours later
Oman, Jordan

The information Fighting Bull previously gathered from Danforth traced the intricacies of Haq's elaborate human trafficking operation. Haq pulled from his US and Mideast trafficking operations to a common staging area in the outskirts of Oman. Incidentally, Haq used an abandoned prison work camp as a base.

He intended to supply the Lemalian rebel effort with fresh bodies for military, labor, and less savory purposes. The final destination for Haq's human cargo was Kalaran, Lemalia. If any of the captives resisted, they would be killed or worse.

Morrison and Arrowhawk had gone ahead a few days earlier to set up surveillance, making note of the transport and exchange routes. As the Avian lands a few meters outside of the camp, it assumes cloaking mode.

"Terrell, what's your twenty?" Conrad asks over the Avian's radio link.

Perched on an old observer tower, Morrison peers through a pair of tactical binoculars. He watches as armed guards move chained children by the dozens into a cargo hangar housing three transporting Mac trucks.

"We're at the observer station," Morrison answers over his earpiece. "They're loading the first group into the trucks now."

"Are the charges in place?"

"Yes, ma'am."

"Good. Cynthia will be in position in ten."

"Copy that, Captain."

Conrad taps her earpiece and grabs her weapons before exiting the ship. Fighting Bull looks in Conrad's direction and nods in acknowledgement. She straps on her tactical webbing before making her way to rendezvous with Arrowhawk.

A few minutes pass as the trafficked children, chained together arm to arm, are ushered into the first of the trucks. Blankenchip inches up behind the rear guard of one of the trucks. Before the guard can bring down the trailer's rear latch, Blankenchip snatches him from behind and tasers him in the neck. The guard immediately slumps to the ground, convulsing before he finally loses consciousness.

The driver of the truck is oblivious to what has just happened. He climbs into the driver's side and is greeted by a Glock 36 in his face courtesy of Conrad. The driver feigns surrender by raising his hands. He eases out of the driver's side. Conrad directs him to clasp his hands behind his head, and as she reaches to handcuff him, he twists his body around to bat the gun out of her hand, much to her surprise. Conrad briefly mentally chides herself for being so careless. The driver follows through with a right cross, which Conrad blocks with her left forearm. She returns the favor with a direct, closed-fingered blow to his windpipe. She follows with a knee to his abdomen and a judo throw across her right hip.

In the midst of this conflict one of the guards posted just outside of the hangar entrance notices the commotion. He radios the other two trucks.

The trucks take off, bolting through the hangar doors down a half-paved driveway. That driveway was the only exit route to the shipping port where the children are going to be loaded and sent off to Lemalia. Along the side of that road is Arrowhawk. He uses his binoculars to focus in on the second truck. His fingertips crackling with yellow energy, he points his hands in the direction of the truck's tires and emits a broad band of high intensity plasma energy, which sears through the eighteen wheels. Immediately the truck comes to a grinding halt as its tires are completely incinerated, but still having some forward inertia, the truck's haul of children flips forward. Before the trailer can hit the ground, Arrowhawk erects an oscillating force field cushion to buffer the children inside. The second truck sharply swerves around the now debilitated 18-wheeler. It speeds on ahead to its destination.

Conrad radios Fighting Bull. "Cynthia what's the twenty on the last truck?"

Fighting Bull pulls out a detonation device from her tactical webbing. She stands just a few meters off the roadside as the last truck barrels past her.

"Right where I want it to be," she answers.

Fighting Bull presses the detonator button, and immediately the explosives, planted earlier by Morrison on the truck's fifth wheel coupling, ignite. The explosion frees the trailer from the tractor unit. The trailer skids on the semi-paved road, sparks flying violently as it comes to a stop. Fighting Bull runs quickly to the trailer, pulls out her pistol, and shoots the locks off the latches. She lifts up the sliding door to find the chained children jostled about, but otherwise safe.

As what's left of the truck hurries away, the driver eyes a singular figure in the middle of the road. His compatriot in the passenger seat sees him too.

"What's wrong with that fool?" the driver says in Arabic.

"It doesn't matter. Run him over," the other smuggler responds.

The truck accelerates from fifty to sixty to sixty-five miles an hour. As the man in the middle of the road comes into closer view, they see his body take on a metallic glint. The man cocks back his right fist.

"It's one of them—" the driver blurts out. His words are cut short by the impact of a titanium fist through the truck's front grill. The men are thrown through the front windshield as the truck is brought to a forceful stop. Shards of glass tear through the men's clothes and skin as they are jettisoned out of the truck. The smugglers bounce awkwardly a few times on the road behind Morrison. He walks over to check their pulses to see if they are still alive.

Fortunately for the smugglers, the impact of the blow did not kill them but they wouldn't be walking any time soon.

"Should've worn your seatbelts," Morrison says before tapping his earpiece. "Alicia, the last of the smugglers has been contained."

"Good work, Terrell," Conrad says. "John, how far out are the Jordanian authorities?"

"On the way now," Arrowhawk responds as he listens over the communications scanner embedded in his tactical gear. "Should be here in about ten minutes."

"Excellent, we'll leave them to take out the trash."

CHAPTER FORTY-SIX

TRUTH OF THE HEART

Two days later
Hart Senate Office Building
Washington, DC

Just down the hall from the Senate Majority Leader's office is the office of the senior senator from Louisiana, Matrice Malveux. She also served as chairwoman of the Joint Committee on National Security. She's hard at work on crafting new national surveillance security legislation with her staff members at a wide board room style table in center of her office. The cell phone on her desk rings.

"Max, hand me my phone please."

Max Golding, her long-time assistant who first served as her page in the House of Representatives, complies.

She hears a familiar voice on the other end of the line.

"OK, I'll be there," she responds.

Malveux ends the call and addresses her staff. "That's enough for today. We'll start again tomorrow after morning session."

Once her staff has left, she puts on her blue suit coat and leaves the office for Union Station.

* * *

Union Station
Washington, DC

After picking up her meal of General Tso's chicken from P.F. Chang's Express, Malveux scans the food court for a suitable place to sit. She comes across a person alone in a corner booth reading the Metro section of the Washington Post. The newspaper obscures the person's face.

"Excuse me, is this seat taken?" Malveux asks, motioning with her right forefinger to the seat across from the person.

The newspaper page comes down to reveal Conrad's face.

"For you senator, it's always open."

Malveux smiles, and the two women embrace.

Senator Malveux sits. "When you called I was surprised. I hadn't heard from you in a while, and I was getting worried. Is everything OK?"

Conrad folds the newspaper in two and puts it aside. "I'm fine," she replies unconvincingly.

"They're saying you guys have gone rogue," Malveux continues. "Since I hadn't heard from you in so long, I was beginning to wonder if this was true."

"You of all people know you can't believe everything you hear."

"Good point. So what's really going on?"

Conrad pulls out the metal briefcase at her side. She places it before Malveux.

"What is this?"

"Open it."

The senator pauses for a moment, then unlocks the side latches. The briefcase pops open. Before her eyes is a plethora of pictures and documents detailing Ramsey's illegal activities. Malveux is momentarily speechless in the face of what she sees.

"We've been compiling evidence against Chandler Ramsey since we discovered he was involved in Vásquez's drug smuggling operation," Conrad says.

"Emmanuel Vásquez, the Paraguayan deputy foreign minister?"

"Yes, they're both part of an organization called 'the Network.' They've been involved in everything from economic espionage to genocide."

"How long has Ramsey been a member?" Malveux asks.

"He's one of its founders." Conrad leans forward intently. "Senator, with all due respect, you need to get this to the JNSC immediately."

"We just got back from summer recess and already have a full slate of hearings ahead of us."

"This can't wait. The Network plans on inciting a civil war in Lemalia."

Malveux's eyes widen. "What? Why?"

"Why does any outside power want to start a civil war? To profit off resources and use them for their own ends."

"Lemalia's a failed state. Why would anyone want to take over that country?"

"Because the Network sees the current administration's economic stance as a detriment to their agenda, and they're willing to go to whatever lengths necessary to get that agenda accomplished."

"I'll see what I can do," Malveux says.

"Thank you, Senator."

"So, how are you doing?".

Conrad responds hesitantly. "I'm fine," she says. Fatigue is evident in her voice, and this is not lost on Malveux.

"Look, Alicia, I've known you since you were a baby. I can tell when something's going on; what is it?"

Conrad relents. "Montgomery DCWS is on my case again."

"About the twins?"

"Yeah."

"You know I've always been willing to help."

"Yes, but I don't want to…"

"'…break up our family.'" Malveux says, completing Conrad's sentence. "I know, Alicia. You can be as obstinate as your mother sometimes."

Malveux's history with Conrad's mother, Constance Akosua Conrad, goes back to their days as roommates in college at LSU. Back then, Malveux knew her better by her nickname, Akos. In fact, Conrad had Malveux to thank for her very existence. It was Malveux who introduced her parents to each other. Over time, Akos and Malveux grew very close.

"But you understand…?"

"I'm your godmother, Alicia. You and the twins are as much my kids as Justin and Perry are."

"I know, but the whole thing is just…"

Malveux once more completes Conrad's sentence. "Overwhelming?"

"You know, you finishing my sentences gets old after a while," Conrad says, trying to add some levity to the moment.

"I can't help it, child," she says in her Louisiana accent, "you're as predictable as a skipping record."

"What's a record?" Conrad asks jokingly.

Malveux gives her a look of exasperation.

Conrad smiles and laments, "I've been so busy running around trying to save the world, but I can't even hold my own family together."

"I know," Malveux replies empathetically. "You ever stop to think what if you didn't try to do it all on your own?"

"Yeah." She looks away briefly before making eye contact with Malveux. "But I made a promise to my mother keep watch over the twins."

"But you don't have to do it alone. You never were alone," she says, tapping the table with her right hand. "You chose to go it alone, honey."

"Yeah, but like you said: I can be hard-hardheaded sometimes."

"'Sometimes?!'" Malveux jokes. "Anyway, how are Cam and Camille taking it?"

Conrad glances down before responding. "Cam hates my guts, and Camille puts on a brave face, but I know she's terrified. I try to reassure them that everything'll be OK, but I'm beginning to doubt my own rhetoric."

"Alicia, listen to me." Malveux grasps Conrad's right hand. "You are one of the most capable women I know. You can and will get through this. I have faith in you."

"You do?"

Malveux squeezes her hand tightly. "Yes. Great people shine through adversity and this is your moment, Alicia."

Conrad nods. She glances at her wristwatch and realizes she's late for her meeting with her siblings.

"I have to go; I'm meeting the twins for lunch."

"All right."

"Thank you, Senator," Conrad says, returning to her formal military mode of speech.

"Alicia, we're not at a Senate hearing. You can drop the formalities."

Conrad smiles and relents. "Thanks, Aunt Mattie."

"That's my girl. Give the twins my love."

"Yes, ma'am, I will."

CHAPTER FORTY-SEVEN

SIBLING DISSENT

The National Zoo
Woodley Park
Washington, DC

Camille and Cameron are sitting on a park bench in the food pavilion. Camille eats a Caesar salad while Cameron consumes a slice of pepperoni pizza. The elder twin, by exactly two minutes, watches the news on his phone.

"Reports are coming in that the situation in Lemalia is becoming worse as tensions between supporters of current president Emerante Legaud and loyalists of Mohann Aldessa clashed in the Center Square in the heart of Lemalia's capital, Delohar," Leslie Michaels from HM News reports.

"In other news, new information has leaked linking Vigil member John Arrowhawk to eco-terrorist organization The Pangaea Consortium," Vincent Lowell, her co-anchor, adds. "Apparently, agent Arrowhawk's brother, Alan Arrowhawk, an operative within the organization, facilitated bombings of animal research facilities, as well as attacks on multiple oil refineries worldwide. Emails and phone records have been obtained that show that Agent John Arrowhawk provided classified FBI intelligence to his brother to help him avoid capture..."

Camille, frustrated with what she's hearing expresses her displeasure. "Shut that off, Cam."

"Why? Isn't Alicia always telling us we should be informed?"

"They're lying—they're making it look like Alicia and her team is a bunch of criminals, but they're not."

"Who said?" Cameron fires back.

"She told me when I talked to her a couple days ago."

"And you believed her?"

"Of course—she's my sister."

"She's my sister too, Camille."

"I can barely tell by the way you're acting," Camille chides. "Can't you even give her the benefit of the doubt?"

"Why should I?"

"Because she loves us."

Cameron gives her a crass smile. "If she loved us so much, why did she leave us for two years while she dealt with her mental issues?"

"That's cold, Cam!"

"Am I lying though? We were in three different foster homes while she was gone."

"That's not fair," Camille says defensively. "Grandma took care of us—"

Cameron cuts her off before she can complete her sentence.

"For like six months before her visa expired. Think about it, have we ever really been a priority in her life? She couldn't even show up on time to meet us today."

"You know that's not fair. She has a real important job…"

"And it's more important than us? We've always come second to 'national security,' whatever that means."

"Cam, this is Alicia we're talking about. I know she's not perfect and I know what she did to *both* of us. So, stop acting like you're the only one who was hurt! But I choose to give her the benefit of the doubt. Look at how she turned around and gave up having her own life to take care of us after mom and dad died."

Cameron looks her in the eye. " Do you even remember them?"

Ruffled, Camille responds, "Does it matter if I remember? All I know is, Alicia stepped up to take care of us."

"Nobody asked her to take care of us. I mean, so many people were willing to take us in; but Alicia was too stubborn or selfish to let them."

"She wanted to keep us together."

"A lot of good that's doing us now. I just wish she'd be there when we need her."

"I'm here now, Cameron."

The twins are startled by their sister's sudden appearance. She's been listening, unnoticed, to the last few moments of their conversation.

"Oh! You scared me, Alicia," Camille says.

"Sorry."

Camille fully embraces her older sister while Cameron gives Conrad a side hug, the kind you give someone to be polite, not one given in love.

"Sorry I'm late," Conrad says. "I had to make a stop before coming here. Have you been waiting long?"

"Yes!" Cameron blurts out reflexively.

Camille smacks her brother on the arm. "No, not really."

"Has Mrs. Perkins been stopping by like I asked?"

"Yeah, but I don't see why," Camille answers. "It's not like we're kids anymore; we can take care of ourselves."

"We've *been* taking care of ourselves…" Cameron says under his breath, but low enough that his older sister can't hear it.

"Just because you *just* got your license does not mean you're grown, little girl."

Camille and Conrad both chuckle at the remark.

Conrad turns to her brother. "How's it going, Cam?"

"I'm fine," he replies flatly.

"Look, guys, I'm sorry I've been scarce the last couple of weeks, but we've been working on stopping a bad guy in the government."

"I didn't know there were any good ones," Cameron comments flippantly.

"Well, it's taken more time than I thought, and I apologize for not being around."

"That's OK," Camille says reassuringly. "Are you safe though? On the news they said something about you guys stopping an assassination."

"I'm fine."

Conrad lightly touches Cameron's right forearm. "Cameron, I want to say that I'm sorry. I know I haven't been the big sister that I should be, but I want you to know that I love you and Camille very much."

He looks down at Conrad's hand on his forearm and moves it away.

"You have to show it, Alicia."

"I know."

"You have to decide what matters most to you."

Trying to break the tension, Camille interjects, "You think you'll be done in time to testify?"

"What?"

"Mr. Phillips was going to call you to testify before the trial ends. Didn't you get his calls?"

"I probably did, but I've been so busy I haven't checked my messages. When is it?"

"Two weeks from today. You'll be there, right?"

"I wouldn't miss it."

Conrad's phone rings. She pulls it out of her right coat pocket and sees Arrowhawk's name on the caller ID. She answers it.

"Hey, John, what's up?"

"You have a T.V. close by? There's something you should see."

Conrad asks her brother if she can use his phone.

"Can I see your phone?"

"Why can't you use yours?"

"Because I can't talk and operate the T.V. app at the same time."

"You need to get an upgrade then."

Conrad turns down the corners of her mouth. Cameron relents and gives her the phone. There's a slight shock when she grabs it.

"Ow," Conrad says as she shakes her hand then turns on the T.V. application. She sees a report on the rebel assault of the Lemalian port city of Kalaran. Her countenance immediately changes. "Put the Avian on auto pilot and send it to pick me up."

"Got it."

Conrad hangs up and turns to her siblings.

"I have to go."

"We understand," Camille answers for the pair.

"Don't worry, I'll be in court."

"OK," Cameron replies gruffly. "You have to go, Alicia, so go."

"I love you guys, don't ever doubt that."

Camille nods, but Cameron evinces no response as Conrad leaves them.

PART FIVE

DECONSTRUCTING THE NETWORK

CHAPTER FORTY-EIGHT

FRAMING THE ARGUMENT

September 5th
Kalaran, Lemalia

Under a backdrop of heavy mortar fire and artillery rounds, embedded foreign correspondent Peter Wallace reports from the front lines of the Lemalian conflict. He wears a flak jacket and helmet to protect him from the foray of weapons fire. Gathering up his wireless microphone, he begins speaking.

"The people of Lemalia have suffered greatly under the Legaud regime. Over seventy percent of the populace suffers from malnutrition. The transition from a free market to a socialist system has cost the Lemalian economy close to half a million jobs. Numerous sanctions have been levied against the country and trade embargoes have even been establish by the UN. Needless to say, economic aid is scarce. In response, the United People's Front has launched an uprising against the Legaud regime. To explain, we are joined by UPF spokesman Mr. Lussad Vassen."

A portly man, no more than five feet, five inches tall, steps forward to stand beside Wallace. Vassen's helmet covers his receding hairline and graying sideburns.

"Thank you for joining me, Mr. Vassen."

"It is good to be here," he responds.

"What does the UPF plan to gain from this uprising?"

Vassen answers, looking straight at the camera, "We plan to correct the actions taken by so-called 'President Legaud'."

Wallace moves his microphone closer to Vassen. "Tell us how you plan to do this."

"Well, we have set up feeding centers and shelters for those who have lost their jobs due to his nationalization plan. The UPF has also built new schools and vocational training centers to educate and prepare our children for a changing economy. We also plan to re-establish ties with many of our former allies."

"That's great that you're trying to make a difference," Wallace says, smiling with admiration. "What has the government done?"

"Ha!" Vassen laughs. "This government doesn't care. Especially with a leader like Legaud. He is not even the rightful president. Mohann Aldessa won the election…"

Wallace interrupts Vassen before he can complete his sentence.

"Right, before he was assassinated at his inauguration. Have there been any new findings in the investigation?"

"I do not know."

"Mr. Vassen, what kind of change does the UPF plan on implementing if they gain power? What is their vision for Lemalia?"

"Legaud has failed Lemalia. The United People's Front plans on restoring this nation to its former prominence."

CHAPTER FORTY-NINE

CRACKS IN THE FAÇADE

The Metropolitan Apartments
Bethesda, Maryland

Price is running late for work. She has to make a quick pit stop at Dunkin Donuts for her morning pick-me-up coffee before she heads off. As she reaches for her cell phone to check her email, she gets a call from the front lobby.

"Dammit, not now," she says to herself. She answers the call.

It's the front desk attendant. "Good morning, Ms. Price, we have a package for you to sign."

"Aren't you supposed to have a concierge service down there?"

"Yes, ma'am."

"Then do your job and hold it for me. I'm running late for work."

"I'm sorry, but apparently it's time sensitive and can only be signed by the addressee. The deliveryman won't let us sign for it."

"Can't they come back another time?"

"I'm sorry, ma'am, but they insisted that the package is time sensitive."

Price reluctantly caves in. Besides, she is late anyway, what's another five minutes?

"Alright, I'm coming down."

She leaves her fifth-floor apartment and takes the elevator down to the lobby. As soon as the doors open, she steps into the midst of a gaggle of FBI agents. Startled, Price initially backs away from them, but her access to the elevator is blocked by one of the agents who quickly steps behind her. The lead agent in charge, Lee Johnson, steps forward. Standing six feet tall, with a head of red hair, he casts an imposing shadow over the much smaller Price.

"What is this?" she asks.

"Ms. Price, you are under arrest for three counts of espionage, one count of drug smuggling, two counts of domestic terrorism, three counts of money laundering, and forty counts of destruction of federal property."

"This is insane! What evidence do you have?"

Johnson motions with his right hand to another agent. They pull out a tablet computer and hand it to Johnson, who quickly taps the screen and places it in front of Price.

"You signed the shipping manifest for a plane that shipped over 10,000 kilos of cocaine to Paraguay. We also have evidence that you stole classified military technology. The schematics of the National Mall were uploaded to the hard drives of the drones that attacked Washington from your personal server. Do you need me to go on?"

Price lowers her head in dejection. She knows she has no way out of this situation. Looking back, she also knew that this could happen. Cleverly, Ramsey allowed her to deal first-hand with all of his schemes to afford himself the option of plausible deniability. And now, after being so faithful to Ramsey, Price realizes that if the tables were turned he would not be as faithful to her. With the possibility of facing a steep jail sentence, Price relents.

"OK. What do you want to know?"

* * *

The Louvre
Paris, France

Laurent Messier's term as the executive director of the Louvre's Board of Trustees is up at the end of the year. This is the board's last quarterly meeting, and thus the last one he'd be presiding over. It's bitter sweet as he concludes the meeting and each of the members, which includes Chase and Duvalier, wishes him well. Chase quickly pushes away from the board table and retreats to his office, while Duvalier stays behind to congratulate Messier.

"Good work, Laurent. Too bad you can't stick around for me to be a pain in your ass anymore," Duvalier says.

Messier kisses her hand. "I wouldn't have had it any other way Lorraine."

Duvalier smiles at the remark. Her cell phone buzzes. She looks to see that it's a text message from Chase: "Main office in ten minutes."

Duvalier bids farewell to the other board members before heading towards the Denon wing. She enters the office to see Chase sitting at his desk with a disconcerted look on his face. The pair have been good friends for the past twenty years, and Chase rarely wears his emotions on his sleeve.

"Abner, what is it? Why the sad look?"

Chase gets up from his chair and pulls down the wall-mounted painting behind him.

"After our office was broken into," Chase says, "we were focused solely on the data that Vigil pulled from our computers."

He presses his hand against the wall and a sliding panel opens to reveal a safe. He unlocks the safe and throws the door open. Duvalier walks closer to see what's inside. Within are a few stacks of euros, a first edition of the *Alchemist*, and a gold statuette.

Unimpressed, Duvalier says, "And the problem is? I don't see anything missing."

"You're not looking close enough. They left everything except for the Phase Two proposal."

"Are you sure? You probably misplaced it."

"Unlikely. The thing never moves but the few feet between my desk and this safe."

"And you *had* to put one of our most important documents in an old safe from the last century?" she says half-jokingly.

"I could do without the brow-beating, Lorraine. This is serious; the Phase Two proposal was the next step after Hegemony…"

"And without it our whole plan crumbles," Duvalier says, finishing his thought. "I know, Abner. Why do you have to be so dramatic? Look, this all could have been avoided if you had let me put it on one of my servers with a million-bit network encryption. Instead you wanted it as a hard copy."

"Now what difference would it have made anyway? Vigil's busted through every technological firewall and safeguard we've put up so far."

"So, what are you suggesting?" she says as she folds her arms defensively.

Chase moves slowly to his desk chair and sits. "We have to let the others know that the Phase Two proposal has been compromised."

"And come off looking as incompetent as Chandler?" Duvalier says with disdain. "Not a chance. Look, we keep this to ourselves. For now."

Chase gives a look of unease to Duvalier. "I don't think that's wise…"

"No, it's exactly the smart thing to do. Look, the UPF forces have already started their attack. Let's wait until we have Lemalia in hand before alarming the others to what's happened."

"It just doesn't seem right."

"Trust me on this one, Abner. Have I steered you wrong before?"

"No," he says grudgingly.

"Then trust me."

"OK, I'll keep quiet for now."

"That's what I like to hear," Duvalier says with a smile.

CHAPTER FIFTY

RUBICON

Aboard the Avian

"I don't understand, are you saying the UPF is backed by foreign interests?" Legaud's chief of staff Leonid Tourgassa asks, as his image is projected on the Avian's widescreen monitor.

Onscreen, in full view of the team, Tourgassa is surrounded by the rest of Legaud's defense council, which includes the Defense Minister, Commander in Charge of Armed Forces (CINC), and the Foreign Minister.

"Exactly," Conrad replies.

"Captain, what other information can you give us?" the Defense Minister asks.

"We've just transferred all the files we have to your main server, everything from the details of the UPF's financial and military support to their direct connection to the PNDP."

"We appreciate that, but we are in immediate need of military support," the CINC says. "Preferably, the superhuman kind."

"We'll be willing to help on the condition that you grant us a face-to-face meeting with President Legaud."

Tourgassa reacts to this demand. "That will be difficult to arrange."

"If you tried hard enough, I'm sure you could make it happen," Conrad replies assuredly.

Tourgassa recoils for a moment, but then answers, "I will see what I can do."

"Good. Contact us once the meeting is confirmed. And Commander?"

"Yes, Captain."

"We have reason to believe that you have a mole in your command."

"How can you know?"

Conrad glances at Fighting Bull.

"I have my sources."

"How do I find this mole?"

"I suggest checking the military datanet to see if there's been any unauthorized activity."

"I understand," the CINC responds.

"Mr. Tourgassa, we will be waiting for your call," she concludes.

The chief of staff nods in acknowledgment. The screen goes to black as the video feed disconnects.

"I'm not sure if helping Legaud is the right move, Cap," Arrowhawk says.

"Why?"

"Because we'd be legitimizing his presidency."

"Didn't you and Terrell just save him from being assassinated?"

"I never said the man didn't deserve to live, but I don't think he deserves to be president."

"This isn't up for debate, John."

"The bigger question is: What will we do after this is over?" Fighting Bull interjects.

"Our objective is the here and now. We'll worry about that when the time comes," Conrad responds.

"Well, I have two words for you, Cap: 'Exit Strategy,'" Arrowhawk says. "If anything, recent history's shown us that foreign interventions without an exit plan can end in disaster."

"You sound like a talking head on *Meet the Press*," Blankenchip chimes in. "Whatever happens happens. We get the job done and get out."

"It's never that simple," Fighting Bull says. "Assuming we help them win this war, they're going to look to us to help rebuild in the aftermath."

Arrowhawk adds, "The flip side of that is if we overstay our welcome, we'll be looked on as unwanted occupying force. And nobody likes one of those."

"Enough," Morrison says, finally joining the conversation. "Look, we have a duty to stop this war before it destroys more lives. There's a verse in scripture that says, 'For our struggle is not against flesh and blood, but against the rulers, against the authorities, against the powers of this dark world and against the spiritual forces of evil in the heavenly realms.'[10] It relates perfectly to our situation. We have to look beyond Legaud's presidency and even what happens after the war to see what this fight is really about." Morrison scans the faces of his teammates. "It's about the Network and what they represent. That's where our focus should be."

The team takes pause at Morrison's bold statement.

A few moments later Conrad breaks the silence. "I couldn't have said it better myself."

---

10 From Ephesians 6:12 in the New International Version of the Holy Bible

CHAPTER FIFTY-ONE

OFFENSIVES

September 7th
UPF headquarters
Ansora, Lemalia

The 1970s-era bunker that serves as the UPF's headquarters is an anachronism compared to the technology that lies inside it. The Network has outfitted them with the latest computers, integrated network capabilities, and real-time video relay feeds. Within the central operations room, Erosin Analaise provides the Network Principals with the latest status report. His image is projected on a large screen as the Principals listen intently from their Rome headquarters.

"Kalaran is secured," Analaise explains. "We have units advancing from the west. An additional heavy armored battalion will advance from the south."

"What about Sumani in the north?" Angella asks.

"The area is heavily fortified. The dam is the main source of power for the military as well as two-thirds of the country."

"We'll send air support," Dankwah interjects. "Air strikes will cripple their defensive capabilities, and then you can move your men in."

"Understood."

"Is the provisional cabinet in place?" Ramsey asks.

"Yes, Mr. Ramsey. I have them secured in a bunker 120 miles from here.

We'll be prepared to establish a functioning government immediately after we eliminate Legaud."

"Great, and CoBALT is providing security for them, right?"

"Yes."

Angella, always thinking about the bigger picture, adds another caveat. "Remember to leave the mining and manufacturing infrastructure intact. There's no reason to destroy the very things we're trying to save."

"Yes, Mr. Angella," Analaise responds obediently. "But, what about civilian casualties?"

"That will be all, Mr. Analaise," Angella says, ignoring Analaise's question.

The video feed disconnects, and the Principals begin talking among themselves.

"Things seem to be going as planned," Haq contends.

"Except for your botched shipment of child soldiers to the field," Duvalier says.

"A minor set-back," he counters dismissively.

"Granted, there are still some loose ends that have to be tied up," Angella says. "Lawrence, what is the latest on the Aldessa investigation?"

Holmes pulls a few papers from his slim briefcase and puts on his black-framed reading glasses.

"My investigators have confirmed that it was in fact an American operative who killed Aldessa. The identity of the person hasn't been confirmed, but they suspect they were highly trained—possibly CIA or Special Forces."

"Are you aware of any US operatives in the field, Chandler?"

"There were no ops being run in Lemalia at that time. If it was an American, then they were working off the grid."

"And the custody situation?" Chase inquires.

"The evidence is in the county's hands now."

"Excellent," Angella responds in delight.

"I'm proud of you, Chandler. You continue to disprove the theory that you're nothing but incompetency personified," Duvalier says, delivering another one of her signature acerbic remarks.

"Go to hell, Lorraine," Ramsey snaps back.

Angella intercedes before the argument can escalate. "Enough!" He turns to Pei. "Are there any updates from the UN?"

"My Security Council contact has convinced the rest of the members to hold off on military engagement. He has also persuaded the secretary general to withhold aid to Lemalia for the time being."

"That's good to hear," Angella says. "Make sure it stays that way."

CHAPTER FIFTY-TWO

OPPORTUNE TIME

The Presidential Office
Presidential Palace
Delohar, Lemalia

"Your terms are unacceptable!" Chief of Staff Tourgassa shouts after hearing Vigil's terms of assistance. Behind him stand the defense council and President Legaud.

"Please, be reasonable, Captain," the defense minister pleads, voicing his concern as well.

Conrad responds calmly yet unequivocally. "Our terms are non-negotiable. You can either take them or leave them.

"This is preposterous; you want our president to step down from office?!" Tourgassa says.

Conrad does not meet his tone, but instead reacts coolly. "Yes, in exchange for our help. After this is over we want new elections monitored by the UN. Mr. Legaud may run if he so wishes, but all election processes should be fair and open."

Legaud finally steps into the conversation. "I want to discuss this privately with my ministers."

"Certainly, Mr. President," Conrad answers.

The team is escorted out of the president's office. After they're gone, Legaud and his defense council discuss the proposal in their native Ludvaric language.

"I've never seen such arrogance in my life!" Tourgassa vents. "These Americans always try to dictate to other countries."

"Don't forget," Legaud reminds him, "it was 'these Americans' who saved my life in Athens."

"I understand, but there must be some other way—" Tourgassa begins, before he's interrupted by the defense minister.

"But what other choice do we have?"

Legaud turns to the CINC. "Commander, can we win without them?"

"I've run through every possible scenario, sir, and honestly, we will be wiped out without their help."

Tourgassa once more inserts his opinion. "What about our allies? They could—"

"Our allies have all abandoned us," the foreign minister says, abruptly cutting him off. "Even the UN has washed their hands of us."

"What is your recommendation, Commander?" Legaud asks.

"I would agree to their terms, sir," the CINC answers. "We truly have no other options."

Legaud turns to his defense minister.

"I agree with the Commander," the minister answers. "I see no other choice."

Legaud nods, then turns to Tourgassa.

"Leonid?"

"I disagree. You should not have to sacrifice your presidency for the sake of some American's misguided sense of democratic idealism."

Legaud reclines in his chair and clasps his hands behind his neck. He thinks deeply about the situation. He takes a few moments to makes his decision.

"I will agree to their terms."

"You can't be serious!" Tourgassa shouts.

"We will be overrun by these rebels if they don't help us," Legaud responds. "And if what they say is true, then we will become the subjects of corporate neo-colonizers. That, I will not allow."

"But, sir, you must think this through!" Tourgassa pleads.

"I have, Leonid, and I will make whatever sacrifice is necessary to maintain my country's sovereignty." Legaud's statement heartens everyone except for Tourgassa.

The team is called back into the president's office.

"After discussing the situation with my advisors, I have decided to agree to your conditions."

"Good." Conrad motions to Arrowhawk, and he hands her a manila folder. She removes a form from the folder and places it in front of Legaud.

"This is a memorandum of agreement outlining the terms."

"I understand." Legaud quickly reads the document and signs it.

"What is your battle strategy?" the defense minister asks.

"We've been monitoring UPF communications for the last twenty-four hours, and we've located their main supply line." Conrad motions to Fighting Bull to hand her the holo-tab. She taps the screen, and a holographic schematic of the Desian region pops. "A train from this area supplies weapons, vehicles, and food to their ground forces. We first need to cut off this supply line before reinforcing the three other fronts."

"What about reconnaissance and intelligence gathering operations?" the CINC asks.

"That gets to my next point. Were you able to locate the mole?"

"Yes, it was one of my top generals, General Daisona. We have him in custody."

"Good. Have him contact his superiors in the insurgency."

"I don't understand."

"Have you heard the term 'bait and switch'? We have to give the perception that he's escaped."

"And what will we do then?"

"My intelligence officer, Cynthia Fighting Bull, will take his place. She'll infiltrate the insurgent command center and relay information to us."

"How would she do that?"

"Agent Fighting Bull can perfectly mimic every aspect of an individual. The general's own mother wouldn't even be able to tell the difference."

"What about the three attack fronts?" the minister of defense asks.

"You'll have to give us provisional command of your ground forces," Conrad says.

"Granted."

"Agent Morrison will be in charge of securing Delohar. Lieutenant Blankenchip will lead the northern counter-offensive in Sumani, and Agent Arrowhawk will back the forces in Kalaran. I'll lead the Desian counter-offensive."

"I will need to get the mission parameters to my field generals," the CINC states.

Conrad taps the screen on her holo-tab. "It's already done. We've uploaded them to your server. They should be going out to your generals' smart tablets as we speak. My team needs time to prep; then we can deploy within the hour."

CHAPTER FIFTY-THREE

CHOKE POINT

Four hours later
Desian Region of Lemalia

Aten-car supply train barrels over the railroad intersecting the
mountainous Desian region. The train is filled with artillery, combat
vehicles, and assault weapons. Sunlight gleams on the steel skins of five F/A-
18 Hornet fighter jets as they swoop in diamond formation just above the
locomotive. Two jets fall back close to the rear cars of the train, and three fly
ahead. The two rear jets fire Hellfire missiles at the railroad tracks, destroying
the quarter mile of tracks. The forward three jets fire missiles at the half-mile
stretch of railroad ahead of the train. With their task complete, the jets retreat
back to base, making way for the Lemalian ground forces to advance.

The train's engineer slams on the brakes bringing the locomotive to a
screeching halt. Conrad, along with a full heavy-armored brigade of Lemalian
soldiers, encircles the train. The rebels in the middle three supply cars open
their sliding doors and begin firing.

"Take cover!" Conrad yells over the communication line.

The Lemalian forces return fire, killing seven of the rebels. Lemalian snipers
provide cover fire as a group of soldiers lay down a miniature portable dry
support bridge to the train car entrance. Conrad hurries up the bridge with
five Lemalian soldiers into the lead supply car, just behind the engineer's cabin.

Once inside, they are greeted with weapons-fire from four of the rebels still onboard the car. Conrad drops to the ground to take cover beneath one of the jeeps on the car. She trains her rifle on the legs of the rebel firing on her and shoots. The rebel tumbles to the ground screaming. A fellow UPF rebel sees his comrade down, pulls the pin off a grenade, and hurls it toward one of the Lemalian soldiers.

"Grenade!" Conrad shouts. She instinctively leaps at the soldier to protect him from the blast.

The explosion hurls Conrad and the soldier out of the car. Shrapnel permeates the confined space, killing two of the Lemalian soldiers. Conrad lands on the ground with a thud while still holding onto the soldier. She removes his flak jacket to see shrapnel embedded in his side. She radios for immediate medical evacuation as she applies pressure to the wound.

The three remaining rebels jump into the jeep and make their way off the supply train. They escape into the surrounding mountains. The last two Lemalian soldiers hotwire one of the jeeps and go after the fleeing rebels. Unbeknownst to the pursuing Lemalian soldiers, the terrain was heavily scouted by the UPF and is littered with explosive ordnance.

Using her enhanced mental perception, Conrad sees this and warns them over the comm-line, "Do not pursue, I repeat, do not pursue the hostiles!"

The soldiers ignore her warning and continue chasing after the escaping rebels, who zigzag across the terrain, making sure they avoid the land mines. As the soldiers gain ground on the rebels, they drive over a hidden land mine. Within an instant, the Lemalian soldiers' lives are taken by the explosive ordnance. The reverberation from the blast temporarily knocks the rebels off-course, but they manage to continue their escape.

Conrad observes what happens. "Lieutenant Manesha, secure the train. I'll deal with the rebels."

With her wounded soldier safely in the hands of the medic, she leaves them to seek cover behind a pile of twisted metal track thrown up by the rail explosion. She aims her Colt Commando rifle in the direction of the rebels.

With the help of her enhanced mental perception, she shoots at the rebel jeep's rear tires. The tires rip open, and the vehicle starts spinning. The rebel driver frantically tries to regain control of the jeep, but instead it flips on top of one of the planted landmines. The explosion instantly kills the rebels.

Conrad turns her face away from the brightness of the explosion. Clouds of smoke and dust billow up from the blast. After the dust settles, she looks back and pauses at the sight of the wounded and fallen Lemalian soldiers around her. She then radios her lieutenant to come and secure the bodies of their slain comrades.

CHAPTER FIFTY-FOUR

ROCK AND HARD PLACE

Sumani Hydroelectric Dam
Northern region of Lemalia

"**G**et down!" Blankenchip shouts, as he and the Lemalian forces are peppered with machine gunfire.

The UPF forces have launched their strike against the Sumani Dam. Their aim is to take over the main grid for close to one-third of the country, as well as the Lemalian military.

UPF Harrier jets pound the Lemalian ground troops with missile after missile.

"What about air support?!" Blankenchip asks Commanding Lieutenant Genadi Surin, who's huddled next to him behind the remains of a damaged Lemalian tank.

"They are scrambling to get here, but they are still five minutes out."

"We'll be dead by then!" Blankenchip pulls back the sliding panel on his right gauntlet and presses a button on the underlying touch screen. Two hundred yards away the Avian's engines start rumbling. Within seconds it's streaking through the air to the epicenter of the fight.

As a Lemalian tank rolls to the front of the defensive perimeter, a UPF Harrier jet fires on it. The tank commander sees this on his telemetry screen and yells at his crew to get out. Just before the incendiary hits, it's intercepted by the Avian's high-intensity laser. Then the Avian tails the UPF jet that fired the missile. The jet's pilot deftly banks a sharp right to get the Avian off his trail, but it follows right behind. The Avian's targeting computer locks onto the jet and fires. The jet explodes in a spectacular fireball.

Doubling back, the Avian zeroes in on the remaining UPF jets. The pilot of one of them picks the Avian up on his radar and radios the others in his squadron. Within seconds the Avian swoops in fast on top of it, firing its lasers at the jet, which banks sharp left and then right to avoid the laser fire.

Meanwhile, as the Avian pursues the rebel jet, the rest of the squadron flies in behind the Avian. The lead UPF jet that's being pursued by the Avian turns sideways to slip in between two concrete support beams attached to the dam wall. Before the Avian can turn sideways as well, a UPF rebel missile hits it from behind, damaging one of its engines. The Avian's left wing scrapes the side of the dam wall as it tries to regain altitude.

A second UPF jet fires on the Avian, but this time the Avian's force shield activates to deflect it. The Avian's defensive effort drains energy from its navigational controls. As a result of this, the aircraft begins spiraling toward the dam's lower outflow reservoir and plunges into the water. The UPF rebel jets fly in and hover above the reservoir, looking for any signs of the Avian.

"Do you see anything?" the rebel squad leader asks one of his squad members.

"Nothing on visuals or radar."

"It's gone, let's head back."

"Copy that."

As the UPF jets make their way above the dam's main wall, they're greeted by the Avian. Six high-intensity lasers tear through them. The Avian had feigned defeat by sinking itself in the water. In fact, it actually used its water-proof propeller turbines to make its way through the reservoir penstock and the lower control gate and out the upper intake reservoir.

Damaged but still flyable, the Avian heads back to rejoin Blankenchip and his group on the front lines. As Blankenchip looks up to see the Avian coming into view, a land-based UPF rocket launcher fifty yards from his position fires on it. The missile pierces the Avian's force shield, damaging its left wing and laser cannon.

"Dammit!" Blankenchip says to himself. He reaches for his grenade launcher and fires at the UPF rocket launcher, destroying it. Shrapnel from the explosion flies everywhere, endangering some of Blankenchip's soldiers. He shields one of the Lemalian soldiers from the blast, but a large piece of shrapnel smashes into Blankenchip's lower back.

He screams. The shrapnel has hit him in the same area as his previous spinal injury. He falls to the ground.

"Are you OK?" one of the Lemalian soldiers asks.

"Yeah, I'm fine," Blankenchip says, mentally chiding himself for not thinking through his actions.

He pulls himself up. The damage assessment summary appears on his heads-up display. His power core is badly damaged. Even with his back-up battery he doesn't have enough power to fight much beyond a few days, but he does have more than enough to complete this battle.

CHAPTER FIFTY-FIVE

STRAIN

Zikhana Mine
Kalaran, Lemalia

Arrowhawk and his detachment are in a tight spot. They are trapped at the valley floor by UPF forces shooting down on them from the surrounding hillsides.

Zikhana Mine is the major mining hub for Duritium and now is completely under UPF insurgent control. One by one Lemalian soldiers are being picked off by the UPF rebels. There is little cover for them as they try to forge ahead. Arrowhawk creates a dome-sized solid energy force field around the remaining men in his detachment. The shield allowed bullets out and but none in. The UPF rebel bullets deflect off his energy shield, giving the soldiers some semblance of protection. Some of the Lemalian soldiers fire their weapons upwards at their attackers, eliminating a handful as they make their approach to the UPF's stronghold.

As the Lemalian soldiers advance, a UPF commander perched at the base of one of the surrounding hills removes a detonator from his tactical webbing. When the Lemalian soldiers are within fifty yards of the UPF stronghold, a devastating explosion overtakes them. The underground mines had been booby-trapped by the UPF soldiers. The sinkhole created by the explosion swallows up the leading column of Arrowhawk's detachment. With just a smattering of Lemalian soldiers left, they try to advance again. Some of the soldiers attempt to help their fallen mates, but it is of no use because they are buried under a sheet of rubble.

Arrowhawk looks up to see a group of Crawler Dozers lining up on the hills just above. The dozers plow mounds of mining shavings and debris down the hill. It takes Arrowhawk mere moments to realize that the UPF rebels plan to bury the Lemalian soldiers in a pile of debris. He quickly raises his fists in the direction of the line of dozers to his right and emits a focused high-intensity plasma blast, instantly destroying the machines. Arrowhawk is a little uneasy letting loose, but he knows this situation calls for it.

A wave of UPF soldiers comes streaming down the surrounding hillsides, along with the remaining dozers. Arrowhawk's eyes begin to glow and his entire body crackles with energy. He expands his energy force field to deflect the UPF rebel weapons-fire, and then returns the favor with a focused energy blast. The impact of the blast kills or incapacitates dozens of rebels. But Arrowhawk must temporarily lower his shield as he emits the energy blast, allowing for some UPF bullets to come through to kill a dozen of the Lemalian soldiers around him.

He's angered that his brief failing has cost the lives of his soldiers. Before he can collect himself to refocus, a UPF rebel riding on one of the dozers launches an RPG in Arrowhawk's direction. His heart races as the grenade closes in on him. His attempt to erect a protective energy force field comes up short. He's blasted back thirty feet into a heap of rubble and twisted metal. Arrowhawk gashes his head on a piece of metal shaving as he crashes awkwardly onto his right arm. Blood streams down Arrowhawk's face as his vision gets blurry. All he can see are UPF rebels aiming their guns at him before he loses consciousness.

CHAPTER FIFTY-SIX

THE TROUBLE WITH DOUBLES

Network Headquarters
Rome, Italy

The Network Principals receive continuous streams of data on the war. They are engrossed in the satellite, video, and photo imagery projected on their wall-sized LCD monitor. A news report from behind the rebel lines comes on-screen. Embedded reporter Peter Wallace provides a vivid account of the battle at Kalaran, embellishing greatly.

"The United People's Front is engaged in a pitched battle with the Lemalian army. These rebels fight not only for themselves, but also for the poor, the hungry, and the destitute who yearn for freedom from Emerante Legaud's oppressive regime."

As the Principals watch, Ramsey makes a comment. "I'm loving this. You said it best, Taryn: 'All reality is media reality.'"

Bewildered by Ramsey's comment, Marunowski responds, "What are you talking about, Chandler?"

"You said that the other day when you called."

"That's a clever line, but I never said it."

"Of course you did," Ramsey insists. "You called me a couple of days ago."

"About what?"

"Remember, you forgot the specs on the Lemalia op."

"Why would I call you about the Lemalia op when I was at the meeting? I may be getting up there in age, but I'm not senile."

"Look, I remember distinctly that you called me. Your call came over the secure line. It was you."

"How? My phone's been on me the whole time," Marunowski says.

Angella brings up another possibility. "Perhaps your phone was cloned?"

"It was her voice that I heard on the line!" Ramsey exclaims.

Then he pauses because he has just recalled something.

Angella asks, "Chandler, what's wrong?"

"Fighting Bull."

"Excuse me?"

"It was Cynthia Fighting Bull. That shape-shifting waif impersonated Taryn to get intel from me."

"Then our operation has been compromised more than we thought," Angella says ominously.

CHAPTER FIFTY-SEVEN

COUNTER STRAIN

Lemalian army field trauma unit
Kalaran, Lemalia

Once behind a sheltered area the chief medic examines Arrowhawk. He grimaces noticeably as they remove his protective body armor. The medic does a bedside abdominal ultrasound on him.

"H-How did I get here?" he asks.

"The remaining soldiers in your detachment pulled you out," the medic responds. "Hold still."

The medic moves the ultrasound probe to Arrowhawk's left flank.

"OK, Mr. Arrowhawk, you have a bruised kidney and based on the X-rays we did before you regained consciousness; you've also suffered four broken ribs and a broken arm. We have to get you back to the central med-unit immediately," the medic tells Arrowhawk.

"No," Arrowhawk responds.

"You are in no condition to go back into battle."

As the medic argues with Arrowhawk, his eyes catch a glimpse of the news footage on the monitor behind the medic. It shows the Lemalian forces losing ground. The remaining Lemalian forces are being decimated by the UPF rebels.

As more Lemalian soldiers rush forward to the front line to provide reinforcement, the UPF rebels begin to pull back. As the Lemalian forces surge forward to attack they are intercepted by a wall of 100 C.A.T. armored UPF rebels. The armored rebels unleash a barrage of machine gun fire on the Lemalian forces.

The UPF rebels rip through the Lemalian forces with ease. With the Lemalians pushed back to a defensive position, their situation is dire. Witnessing this, Arrowhawk struggles to his feet.

"You are in no condition to fight. You need to lie back down and wait until we can get you medivaced out of here."

"Look, they need me out there," Arrowhawk answers.

"But you might die," the medic argues.

Arrowhawk responds cavalierly.

"Yeah, that tends to happen in armed conflict. Now, do you have a helicopter?"

"Yes, we have a Chinook in reserve."

"Good, I'm going to need it."

* * *

One hour later

Arrowhawk and the pilot of the Lemalian Chinook helicopter fly roughly twenty feet above the advancing UPF forces. He radios the regiment lead commander.

"Are your men in position?"

"Yes, we have pulled back 200 yards from our previous position, as you asked."

"Good. Be ready to move in two minutes."

Arrowhawk cuts off the transmission, looks at the pilot, and motions for him to get lower. The pilot drops down another ten feet, and Arrowhawk jumps out of the helicopter. He lands in the midst of the armored rebels. He lets out a mild groan as he lands—the impact irritates his cracked ribs.

The rebels immediately encircle him. As they raise their weapons to fire on Arrowhawk, he lifts up his head. His eyes crackle with energy. According to the intelligence that Blankenchip gathered from Raines, the armor can't withstand an electromagnetic pulse on the wavelength of 500 GHz. Arrowhawk has to focus his electromagnetic pulse wave precisely. He stretches out his arms wide and unleashes a broad range electromagnetic pulse. The energy engulfs the rebel forces within the immediate area and the armored rebels are rendered helpless. Not only does the pulse freeze the armored rebels in place, but it also shuts down all of the rebels' electrical equipment.

The Lemalian soldiers make their move as the non-armored UPF rebels start to retreat. Arrowhawk smiles, knowing that he has given the Lemalians a fighting chance.

CHAPTER FIFTY-EIGHT

COURSE CORRECTION

UPF Rebel Command Center
Ansora, Lemalia

The Kalaran offensive goes sour, and the UPF forces in the northern region are defeated. The data from all these defeats floods across Analaise's computer screen. Sitting at the UPF central command console, he relays the status to the Network Principals.

As he disseminates the information, his senior-level officers mill around in the background, gathering intelligence reports and coordinating a counter-offensive strategy. Unbeknownst to Analaise, Fighting Bull is among these officers, masquerading in the guise of General Daisona. She sits at the adjacent computer station filing a report while listening to Analaise's conversation with the Principals.

"Where do we stand, Erosin?" Angella demands.

"We have sustained considerable losses," Analaise answers. "Our units in the northern region and in Kalaran have been defeated."

"And the eastern offensive?"

"They mobilized their air force and intercepted our planes. Ninety percent of our fleet has been destroyed."

"Were all of the C.A.T. units utilized in the Kalaran strike?" Dankwah asks.

"No. We still have 100 units remaining, including the two Omega units."

"What is our estimated troop level?" Angella asks.

"Currently 30 percent of our original fighting force remains."

"We have decided to alter our attack strategy. Redirect all remaining forces to Delohar."

"Mr. Angella, with all due respect, that is a disastrous choice. Hundreds of civilians will be killed in the fighting."

"Are you having a sudden attack of conscience?" Angella asks mockingly. "Erosin, make no mistake—you serve at our pleasure. Even though we've given you some semblance of authority, we decide the final course of this war, and ultimately the fate of Lemalia."

Angella's statement angers Analaise, but he forces himself to keep his displeasure hidden. "Understood. It will take some time to regroup and organize a viable attack plan for this operation."

"How long?" Angella asks.

"Redeploying the remaining forces and drawing up the attack parameters could take us two days."

"Make it one, and I want a draft of your attack plan within the hour."

"Yes, sir."

The video feed disconnects, and Analaise goes back to work. "So, what did they say?" one of his first lieutenants asks.

"They are homicidal idiots," Analaise responds. " They want a full-scale attack on the capital."

"What? Hundreds of civilians will die!"

"Ask them if they care."

Fighting Bull then slips out of the room to make contact with Conrad after hearing this interchange.

CHAPTER FIFTY-NINE

THE BEST DEFENSE

September 9th
The Presidential Office
Presidential Palace
Delohar, Lemalia

President Legaud, his advisors, and three of the five members of Vigil gather within the confines of the Presidential Office. Arrowhawk is in a nearby hospital recovering from the injuries he incurred during the Kalaran battle, while Fighting Bull is still embedded with UPF forces.

Conrad presents the intelligence gathered on the UPF forces to the assembled group. "The UPF rebels have retooled their strategy. They've pulled back their forces from the three battle fronts and have organized them for a direct attack on Delohar."

She taps the screen of the holo-tab on Legaud's desk. A holographic image of the rebel attack plan appears on the display wall in front of them.

"Agent Fighting Bull sent me these specs yesterday."

"Is she still in the rebel command center?" CINC Deladin asks.

"Yes, she'll extract herself before the rebels launch their attack. They're planning a direct attack in three waves. What's left of their air force will come in first. They'll be targeting our communications towers and land-based missile defenses. UPF ground forces will come in next to engage our ground troops.

Following close behind them will be the final wave of remaining C.A.T. units." Conrad puts on her THIGs, walks to the holographic display, and taps on the image of the Presidential Palace. "These units will be targeting the palace."

"Why the sudden change in their attack plan?" the defense minister asks.

"Trying to cut their losses and concentrate their remaining forces on a winnable target."

"This is their Hail Mary play," Blankenchip adds.

"Hail Mary?" Tourgassa asks, unfamiliar with American football analogies.

"Forget it," Blankenchip says flatly.

"When do they plan on attacking?" Legaud asks.

"Within the next eight hours."

"Do you think our defenses will hold?" the CINC asks.

"Don't worry, our defensive strategy is sound," Conrad says reassuringly.

"And the armored units?" the CINC asks.

Conrad smiles. "Leave that to us."

CHAPTER SIXTY

WARZONE

Eight Hours Later
Outer Gates of Delohar

The UPF forces attack the capital city with the first wave of air strikes. As a squadron of UPF Joint Strike Fighter jets tear through the sky they fire their laser guided missiles on the roof-mounted communications towers. The missiles are countered by those of the Lemalian fighter fleet. Six of the rebel planes are shot down, but not before they eliminate seven of the Lemalian F/A-18 jets. The remaining quartet of rebel planes hits its targets—destroying two communications towers and four land-based missile launchers. As the dogfight ensues, debris from the conflict descends on the inhabitants of the city.

A portion of a rebel fighter jet wing crashes into one of the city walls, causing a torrent of brick and metal debris to descend on the fleeing civilians. A woman and her husband flee the onslaught. He trips over a small steel beam, right under the path of falling bricks. Morrison shields them with his molecularly altered titanium body before the debris can crush them.

Within moments of the air strike UPF ground troops approach the city gates and engage the Lemalian military. The Lemalian army puts up a valiant effort with the help of Blankenchip and Conrad leading the charge. The Lemalians take the upper hand. During the course of the battle, the warning light on Blankenchip's heads-up display starts blinking.

"Dammit!" he says loud enough that it can be heard over his comm-link.

"What?" Conrad asks.

"I'm running low on juice."

Conrad responds jokingly. "You have a multimillion dollar combat suit and it decides to give out now?"

"Well with my power core being damaged from the fight in Sumani, you should be happy it's gotten this far."

"How much power do you have left?"

"I'm at 15 percent. I won't be able to go much longer than twenty minutes, maybe half an hour max."

"OK, pull back. Have one of your men relieve you. We've pretty much got this thing under control."

Blankenchip informs the on-site Lemalian commander that he's going to retreat back to the Lemalian base of operations.

As the Lemalian forces finish off the last of the UPF ground forces, the remaining armored rebels move in. The Lemalian air force zooms in to confront them, but half their planes are shot down by the armored rebels' superior fire power.

Seeing this, Conrad radios Morrison. "I need you at the front gates now!"

"I'm on it."

He jumps into an abandoned Lemalian Humvee and slams on the gas. He drives toward the outer gates and aims the vehicle straight into one of the armored rebels. Morrison's skin turns into steel as he accelerates. The ensuing crash ignites an explosion. He emerges unscathed from the wreckage, carrying the unconscious and severely burned rebel. Then Morrison alters his molecular structure from steel to titanium in anticipation of the oncoming armored rebels. Noticing their downed compatriot, the remaining armored rebels turn their attention toward Morrison.

He kneels down, grabs a steel I-beam from the debris of a collapsed pillar and hammers two of the rebels squarely in the chest with it, sending them hurtling through the air.

A group of twenty armored rebels encircles Morrison. He grabs one of the downed armored rebels and swings him in a circle, using him to knock down opponents like bowling pins.

From thirty feet away, a pair of the rebels fires two grenades in Morrison's direction. He's blown back off his feet into a pile of destroyed armored Hummers. One of the rebels who fired on him jumps on his chest and directs his rifle at Morrison's forehead. Before he can pull the trigger, Morrison grabs a part of the wrecked Hummer's door frame and swats the rebel away. Behind him another rebel directs his laser sight to the back of Morrison's head. He barely gets one shot off before Morrison tosses the door frame into his abdomen. A smattering of the remaining armored rebels unloads their rounds on Morrison. The bullets deflect off his metallic skin. Morrison sees that they have taken refuge under a half-destroyed apartment building with an unstable overhanging balcony. He raises his arms to the sky and brings his fists down forcefully. The very ground trembles, destabilizing the apartment structure just above the rebels. They quickly lose their footing and fall as the remains of the building they took refuge under collapses on them.

Thinking that he's defeated all of his opponents, Morrison lets his guard down and alters his molecular density back to its normal state. Twenty feet behind him, an armored rebel raises his weapon in Morrison's direction, but as the rebel readies the weapon to fire, a UPF jet fires on him. The blast startles Morrison, who reflexively alters his molecular state to steel. He looks back to witness the aftermath of the explosion. His eyes trace up to the sky to see Fighting Bull in the cockpit of the rebel aircraft.

She radios him. "Got your back, Terrell."

Morrison gives her a thumbs up.

A pair of armored rebels recover from the rubble and fire on Fighting Bull's jet. "Cynthia, look out!"

The rebel's bullets rip through the jet's fuselage. Telemetry alarms scream in Fighting Bull's ear as the jet spirals to the ground. She quickly pulls the ejector lever. The jet's glass canopy flies open as she's jettisoned from the aircraft. The rebels continue firing on her as her parachute opens.

Morrison tackles one of the rebels and rips his weapon away from him. The rebel punches him in the face, but it does nothing but anger Morrison. He strikes the rebel in the face and then flings him into the second rebel— knocking both of them out cold.

Fighting Bull lands about ten feet from Morrison. He walks over to help her out of her ejector seat.

"Thanks for the save."

"One good save deserves another," he answers.

Morrison helps her out of her seat. As they are getting their bearings, they look up to see two AC-130 gunships flying in. Sixty-foot tall robotic versions of the C.A.T. armored units are attached to them. The couplings anchoring the armored units detach, and the mechanized constructs descend to the battlefield. These robots begin to unleash an onslaught of high-intensity lasers on the people below, firing indiscriminately on civilian and soldier alike.

The lasers sear through the ground just feet behind Morrison and Fighting Bull as the pair runs for cover. Fighting Bull eyes an abandoned rebel Armored Personnel Carrier.

"Over here!" She grabs Morrison's arm. They get into the APC with the heat of the high intensity lasers on their backs.

"You know how to drive one of these things?" Morrison asks.

"We're about to find out."

It takes just moments for them to regroup with Conrad and Blankenchip on the Presidential Palace balcony.

The robots continue tearing a bloody swath through the city as they witness the destruction. With Arrowhawk injured and the Avian damaged, they were left with only one option to end the bloodshed.

Blankenchip looks in Conrad's direction. "Alicia…"

She looks on the destruction. "I know."

She pauses for a moment, knowing full well what she has to do. "Please, God, forgive me."

Conrad slowly pulls out a small rectangular control panel from one of the side slips in her modular tactical vest. She presses the center button on the device and activates the SBL.

A few thousand miles above them, the Vigil Satellite Defense System laser cannon comes to life. The cannon calibrates its coordinates to Conrad's signal. Within seconds, a high-powered laser beam rips through the cloudless sky. The beam lances through the robots, completely incinerating them, along with the remaining UPF forces in the immediate area. In just a blink of an eye, there's nothing left but smoldering ash and melted metal.

CHAPTER SIXTY-ONE

PROPORTIONATE RESPONSE

Office of the Secretary General
United Nations Headquarters
New York, New York

UN Secretary General Anurak Chankul observes the events in Lemalia live from his office. He is deeply unsettled by what he sees. Never before has he witnessed such an unbridled show of destructive forces in his life. As the images continue to stream across his TV screen, he's transfixed and appalled.

His phone rings. It's Chinese UN Security Council Representative, Ambassador Yuen Li Shang.

"Good afternoon, Mr. Secretary. I am assuming you're watching the situation in Lemalia?"

"It's a sad thing."

"This is very disconcerting. You know that what they've done is in direct violation of the OST[11] of 1967."

"Yes."

"They have opened up a Pandora's box, Mr. Secretary."

Chankul nods and clicks on a file on his computer screen titled: *Guardsmen Protocols*. "I agree. Something must be done."

---

11 Outer Space Treaty

CHAPTER SIXTY-TWO

ALL FALLS DOWN

September 11th
NSA Headquarters
Fort Meade, Maryland

Chandler Ramsey leaves the parking lot to enter his office building. As he passes some of his colleagues in the hall, they quickly become quiet. An uneasy feeling comes on him as he enters the foyer leading into his office. When he opens his door, he is greeted by an assortment of FBI agents rummaging through his files and packing away his computer.

"What in the... what's this?!" Ramsey demands.

One of the agents walks up to Ramsey and shows him his badge. "My name is agent Lee Johnson. You are under arrest for ten acts of terrorism against the United States, a hundred counts of human trafficking and twenty counts of drug trafficking. You have the right to remain silent—"

"Wait a second. 'An act of terror against the US'? Your allegations are baseless!"

Johnson motions to the agent to his left, who quickly removes a manila dossier from his briefcase and hands it to Johnson. Johnson shows the documents within to Ramsey.

"We have a sworn confession from your assistant, Lauren Price, linking you to an assortment of illicit activities, including the attack on the National Mall, the drug smuggling operation with the Paraguayan deputy foreign minister, money laundering, human trafficking—"

"Enough. You actually believe that ungrateful quim? This is ridiculous. She's a lying witch."

Agent Johnson motions to the agents to place Ramsey in handcuffs. He tries to push them off, but they force him against the wall and clasp the cuffs onto his wrists.

"You have no idea what a mistake you're making. This is not over by any stretch of the imagination," Ramsey says.

* * *

Marunowski Residence
2172 Stratford Circle
Bel Air, California

Marunowski is resting comfortably in bed when she's woken by a commotion just outside her mansion gate.

"Huh, what's going on outside, Allen?"

"I don't know. Let me check it out."

Her husband, Allen Madison, gets out of bed and puts on his robe. He tightens the belt and walks to the bedroom doors. When he opens them he is greeted by a squad of FBI agents, with Agent Cristina De La Vega at the forefront.

"What the hell is this?"

She flashes her badge in Madison's face.

"Agent De La Vega, FBI." She points to Marunowski, who sits up in the bed. "We have a warrant for Ms. Marunowski's arrest."

The accompanying agents move Madison aside. De La Vega pulls Marunowski out of the bed by her left arm.

"Ms. Marunowski, you are under arrest for ten counts of money laundering, thirty counts of telecommunications fraud, and a hundred counts of human trafficking, to start."

"Get your damn hands off me!" Marunowski screams in protest as she's being restrained. She frees up her right hand and cocks back her fist to punch De La Vega in the face. De La Vega stops the blow with the palm of her left hand. Marunowski pulls her hand back violently and shakes it in pain.

"Owww! Your hand's like freaking ice, you stupid whore!"

"Not the first time I've been told that," De La Vega answers with a smile.

Marunowski is read her Miranda rights as she's handcuffed and led out of the bedroom.

* * *

September 12th
CNN Headquarters
Atlanta, Georgia

"The country of Lemalia is recovering from the civil war that ended yesterday," longtime newscaster Darrell Lewis reports. "The Legaud administration was successful in its defeat of the rebel uprising, with the help of Vigil."

"The reaction internationally has been mixed," his co-anchor Annette Sutton adds. "Many of Lemalia's neighbors are relieved that the war has ended, and others are calling for Vigil to be brought up on war crimes."

"In related news, there's been a global dragnet of arrests in relation to the Lemalian war," Lewis says. "Through a joint effort coordinated by Interpol, security and police agencies worldwide have taken into custody many of the individuals thought to be behind the civil war. Included among them is Taryn Marunowski, CEO of multi-media conglomerate Halcyon media, as well as high-level NSA official Chandler Ramsey. It has also been revealed that Mr. Ramsey was involved in the Fourth of July National Mall attack."

"In addition," Sutton continues, "more information is coming to light regarding Ramsey's longtime involvement in global crime. Now that Ramsey has been taken into custody, a congressional investigation has been initiated to look into allegations of treason and espionage on his part."

CHAPTER SIXTY-THREE

THE THIRD ELEMENT

September 13th
J. Edgar Hoover Building
Washington, DC

Arrowhawk sits in FBI director Martin Stansfield's office waiting for the director to say anything. Arrowhawk favors his right side just a bit—he's still healing from the broken ribs he sustained in Lemalia. Director Stansfield takes his time reading through Arrowhawk's debriefing report. Having finished, Stansfield lowers his eyeglasses and looks in Arrowhawk's direction.

"What can I say, John? Good work."

"Thank you sir."

"You're really making a name for yourself—first Kerrington, now this. Are you trying to be the next Eliot Ness or something?"

"Not at all, sir," Arrowhawk responds with a smile.

"The intelligence you gave us on Price, plus Vásquez's sworn testimony, helped bring down Ramsey's house of cards."

"Thanks, sir. And I'm glad you were able to coordinate with Interpol to dismantle the rest of the Network."

"Thanks to you, son," Stansfield replies. "Now we have most of them in custody. I think the only two on the run are Harada and Haq. But we'll leave that up to their local agencies."

"Music to my ears. Now, sir, about my brother and the leak…"

Stansfield raises his hand before Arrowhawk can say any more. "We know none of it's true. Apparently someone hacked our internal server and they falsified your email and call records. We traced it back to an IP address in France, likely linked to Duvalier's people. The LGN[12] is handling that. You're clear."

"Thank you sir."

"Anytime, but you know he's still a wanted a fugitive."

"Yes, sir, and I will do everything I can to make sure he comes to justice."

"No worries. Look, I just want you to be careful. What you and the rest of Vigil did… you pissed off a lot of people."

"I know the Network is just…"

"No. I mean here—at the CIA, the Bureau, Congress. I just want you to be careful, all right?"

"Yes, sir."

"Now get out of here."

With that Arrowhawk promptly leaves his seat and exits Stansfield's office. As he's walking out, his cell phone rings. He puts the handset to his ear to be greeted by the saccharin voice of Agent De La Vega.

"Hey, John, it's me."

"What's up, Tina?"

"Well, I looked into your mystery men at the Louvre. They're ex-special forces from the 102nd Airborne division—part of a unit code-named the Eagle's Talon. Apparently they've been working as mercenaries for the last five years."

"What did you find out about their latest assignments?" Arrowhawk asks.

"I pulled the call records from their cell phones and found recurring calls from a number out of Naknek, Alaska."

"Alaska? Seriously?"

"Obviously it was a fake phone number. The calls were rerouted and encrypted through a number of cell towers."

---

12 La Gendarmerie Nationale- French Policing Agency

"Were you able to decrypt it?"

"Yeah."

"Great. What about the palace security video I sent you?"

"After doing some image modification I was able to get a clearer picture of the shooter. I cross-referenced it with the database and came up with a guy named Frank Spencer. Same background as the others: ex-special forces, a member of the Eagle's Talon."

"Couldn't be a coincidence, could it?"

"I highly doubt it."

"Good work. Could you send me those call records?"

"I'm faxing them right now," De La Vega responds.

"Thanks, Tina."

"Anytime."

Arrowhawk hangs up and goes to the fax machine. He picks up the document from the tray and glances through the list. He comes upon something that causes him to take pause. "Oh, wow."

Arrowhawk picks up his phone and calls Conrad.

"Hey, Cap, it's me."

"What's up, John?"

"We found Aldessa's killer."

"That's good news."

"That's not all, but I don't want to discuss it over the phone. Is there someplace we can meet?"

CHAPTER SIXTY-FOUR

STILL RIGHT HERE

Conrad Residence
Silver Spring, Maryland

After finishing her conversation with Arrowhawk, Conrad hangs up and walks to the living room where her siblings are seated watching the news.

"Who was that?" Camille asks.

"Someone I work with."

"Was it that girl who can change into anybody?" Camille says.

"No, it's the guy who can shoot laser beams from his hands."

"The one who looks like an Abercrombie model? He's kind of cute."

Amused by her sister's comment, Conrad smiles. "Yeah, Camille."

"What did he want?" Cameron asks.

"That's not important right now. Can you turn off the T.V. for a minute?"

Cameron presses the remote's "Off" button. Conrad makes herself comfortable on the loveseat.

"I appreciate that you've been patient with me over the last couple of weeks, but I'm going to have to ask you to be patient with me a little longer."

"What's wrong?" Cameron asks.

"I've been called to testify before a congressional committee. Unfortunately, it's on the same day as the custody hearing."

"Ain't that about a…" Cameron says in exasperation.

"You're not going to make it?" Camille asks.

"My congressional testimony is a couple of hours before the custody hearing. If all goes well I should be able to make both."

Camille pulls back a little, trying her best not to show her disappointment. Cameron, on the other hand, has no problem letting his older sister know how he feels.

"Listen to yourself, Alicia. You're asking us if it's OK for you to—once again—blow us off in favor of your job. What do you expect us to say: 'Go ahead, screw us over one more time, we don't care'?"

"Cameron..." Conrad intones.

"I'm done listening," he says as he puts his hand up in his sister's face. "I've had it with all of your nonsense. It's obvious that you don't give a damn about us."

Conrad gets up from her seat. "Wait a minute, Cameron!"

"No, I'm through listening to your excuses."

He gets up to leave. It's at this point that Conrad decides she's tolerated his petulance long enough. She grabs his right shoulder and shoves him back onto the couch.

"You're absolutely too old to be throwing tantrums like this. Look, I know you're angry and hurt, but don't you think I am too? I'm tired, Cameron. What do you want me to do, not go to the hearing? If you don't want me to, then I won't."

"Are you serious?" Camille asks.

Conrad turns to look at her sister. "Yes."

Cameron and Camille look at each other with sullen expressions, then Cameron looks at Conrad.

"How serious is this thing?"

"Dead serious."

Cameron pauses for a moment. Camille looks at him, then turns to Conrad.

"If it's helping people, then do it."

"You sure?" Conrad asks.

"Yes."

Conrad looks at Cameron for confirmation. He nods in agreement.

CHAPTER SIXTY-FIVE

A TEAM FOR ALL SEASONS

Joint National Security Committee Hearing
September 15th
The Capitol Building

The team is held in an isolated waiting area before the hearing is to start. Conrad constantly looks at her wristwatch as they wait. She flips through the committee report the team filed to make sure that she memorized the highlights. Fighting Bull sees her and walks over.

"Alicia, you OK?"

"Yeah, just want to make sure I have my facts straight so I don't look like a total idiot when I get in there."

"Gotcha, and does that have anything to do with you checking your watch every ten seconds?"

"You noticed that, huh?"

"Yep, it was pretty obvious."

"Ten seconds though? I'm not that bad."

"Uhm, I timed it, and you ran pretty regular—every ten seconds."

Conrad smiles at the remark.

Fighting Bull leans in closer to Conrad's ear. "I know you need to get to the custody hearing. We don't all have to be here. I can take your place here if you want. They couldn't tell—"

"No. I have to do this, Cynthia. It's my responsibility and my duty."

Fighting Bull nods in acceptance. She turns to see Arrowhawk looking in a mirror and adjusting his tie.

"Let me help you with that," Fighting Bull says as she walks over to him.

"I was never good with a Windsor knot."

Fighting Bull re-knots his tie. "I must say, you showed some cojones back there in Kalaran. You saved that regiment from worse casualties."

"I know. I'm the man."

"Uh, keep dreaming. But I must say, that confidence to let go is kind of attractive."

"Just admit it, Cynthia, you want me."

She slides the knot up tight around his neck, making him gag.

"Nope," she says with a smile as he loosens the tie.

Morrison looks on in amusement at the two. His cell phone vibrates. He reaches into his left vest pocket to retrieve the phone and sees a text message from Danielle wishing him good luck at the hearing. He smiles and starts to dial her number, but stops himself. Senate aide Brooke Renault walks into the room.

"They're ready for you now. Please follow me."

As the team members begin to file out of the room, Blankenchip lingers behind, looking over a photo of his children. Morrison pats him on the back.

"Aaron, you ready?"

"Yeah. Let's do this damn thing," Blankenchip says.

Camera flashes nearly blind the members of Vigil as they file into the room, making their way to the rectangular table with chestnut colored chairs.

Typically a hearing concerning a high-ranking intelligence officer would be closed to the media, but due to the high-profile nature of the case, the committee has decided to allow broadcast of the proceedings.

The purpose of the hearing is twofold. The first is to determine the extent of Chandler Ramsey's treason and the second is to discover if there was further unsanctioned US involvement in the Lemalian civil war. The team is sworn in before taking their seats.

Senator Malveux begins the questioning. "Captain Conrad, could you please explain your relationship to Mr. Ramsey?"

"Yes, Madame Chairwoman, Mr. Ramsey served as Vigil operations officer."

Representative S. Elizabeth Lavdis asks Conrad the next question.

"In your report, you state that Mr. Ramsey was involved in the illicit drug smuggling operation of Mr. Emmanuel Vásquez, who I believe was the former Paraguayan deputy foreign minister." Lavdis pauses for a moment as she flips through the pages in her briefing report. "Could you elaborate on this?"

Conrad pulls the microphone close to her mouth. "Mr. Ramsey facilitated the transport of over 10,000 kilograms of cocaine to Paraguay under the guise of humanitarian aid."

"And you were in no way aware of this?"

"No, ma'am. Upon entering Paraguayan airspace, we were intercepted by the Paraguayan authorities. It was then that we discovered the truth about Mr. Ramsey's involvement with Minister Vásquez."

Senator A.R. Wilson interjects. "In your report you state that Mr. Vásquez implicated Mr. Ramsey in a number of his illegal activities. Was there any evidence supporting these accusations?"

Conrad looks in Fighting Bull's direction.

"Yes, Senator," Fighting Bull says. "Included within our report is a detailed list of financial transactions between Vásquez and Ramsey pulled directly from Justice Department and CIA files."

Senator Malveux addresses Conrad.

"From my understanding, Captain, you set up surveillance on Mr. Ramsey shortly after discovering his involvement with Mr. Vásquez?"

"Yes, ma'am, that's right."

Senator Wilson comments again. "And on whose authority did you establish a surveillance program on a high-level NSA officer?"

Arrowhawk intercepts that question. "We obtained a sealed warrant from a district judge to set up surveillance, sir."

"The question was addressed to Captain Conrad, Agent Arrowhawk," Wilson snaps back. "When I want your input I will ask for it."

It is no surprise that Arrowhawk receives the stern rebuke that he does. Wilson was one of former Senator Fred Kerrington's closest friends.

"You also implicate Mr. Ramsey's involvement in trading sensitive national security information and a number of other illicit activities," Malveux says, trying to get the discussion back on task. "You state that he's done this within the context of a larger organization. Could you elaborate on this?"

This time Conrad defers to Morrison, who responds, "Yes, Senator, Mr. Ramsey is a part of a clandestine organization that calls itself 'the Network.' Mr. Ramsey has provided this organization with classified intelligence and military technology."

Representative Vince Davidson interposes. "According to your report, this organization, 'the Network' as it's called, was directly responsible for initiating the civil strife in Lemalia?"

"Yes. As you've probably witnessed from the news, its members include powerful corporate and government figures," Conrad answers. "These individuals have a large economic and political stake in Lemalia. They saw the current administration as a threat to their collective interest. In response, they organized and funded a rebel movement to topple President Legaud's government."

CHAPTER SIXTY-SIX

THE EVIDENCE

Montgomery County Circuit Court

Trenton Phillips looks anxiously at his wristwatch as he awaits Conrad's arrival. The twins are seated behind him.

"Did Alicia say she would make it in time after the congressional hearing?" he asks them.

"That's what she said," Cameron answers.

"She'll show up when it's time," Camille adds, trying to reassure both herself and Phillips. She gently strokes the *Gye Nyame* necklace her grandmother gave her. A slight spark comes off the necklace as she strokes it. She quickly pulls her hand away and looks up at the clock in the courtroom.

"I hope so, because she's our only shot at winning this thing," Phillips says.

Before making his closing arguments, county lawyer Devin Mayes asks the judge, "Your honor, may I present a new piece of evidence that has recently come to my attention?"

Phillips quickly responds. "Objection, Your Honor! Counsel did not provide us with access to this evidence beforehand."

"Sustained," the judge responds.

"Your Honor, I received this evidence just moments ago," Mayes states. "Considering its content, I believe it is very pertinent to this case."

"Let me see," the judge demands.

Mayes approaches the bench and hands him an 11x14 photo. The judge reacts in shock to what he sees. After collecting himself, he hands the photo back to Mayes.

"You may proceed, counselor."

"Thank you, Your Honor," Mayes answers.

Phillips reacts. "Your Honor, this is unfair!"

"The content of that photo speaks to Ms. Conrad's ability to serve as an adequate custodian to her brother and sister. Continue, counselor."

"Thanks again, Your Honor."

Mayes turns to the jury. "Ladies and gentlemen, we have argued over Ms. Conrad's fitness to serve as a guardian to her siblings. As we all know, the issues of moral character play an important role in determining whether an individual will be a good guardian. We as a society value a certain moral standard, and there are just some things we deem morally wrong. Things like stealing, lying, killing, and torture."

Mayes places the photo under the light projector brought in by the bailiff. The image of the photo is projected onto a drop-down screen in clear view of both the jury and the courtroom gallery. The photo depicts Conrad, during her days with the CCI unit, waterboarding a man chained to a wooden chair. Reactions to the photo are a mix of disgust, surprise, and horror.

Camille turns to her brother and cries in his arms. Phillips puts his head down and covers his face with his right hand.

Cameron voices his disbelief. "My God, Alicia. How could you…?"

CHAPTER SIXTY-SEVEN

THE VIGIL DOCTRINE

Joint Committee on National Security hearing
Capitol Building

The committee continues grilling the team over their actions during the past few weeks. Senator Jim Daniels in particular continues antagonizing them, especially Conrad.

He holds up a copy of his report. "It says here that you got involved in the Lemalian civil war without the authority of the United States government."

"That's right, sir."

"You made a unilateral decision to assist the Lemalian government even though the United States does not formally recognize the Legaud administration. You openly defied every policy directive and sanction against Lemalia. Would you say that this is a correct characterization, Captain?"

"That is correct, Senator," Conrad answers once more. "We believed that we had a personal responsibility—"

Daniels interrupts her mid-sentence. "What was that?"

Conrad glares at him as she completes her thought. "Personal responsibility to help the Lemalians."

"'Personal responsibility'?" Daniels says mockingly. "I doubt your intentions were altogether altruistic, Captain." Daniels pulls down his eye glasses to peer at another set of documents handed to him by one of his aides. "We've received reports that you forced President Legaud to hold new elections in exchange for your help. Is that correct, Captain?"

"I wouldn't characterize what we did as forcing, sir."

"You made him sign a memorandum of agreement to that effect!" he says, raising a copy of the report.

"Yes, sir, but we were giving them something that they sorely needed."

"And what was that?"

"Hope."

"Humph, you mean hope that they wouldn't be slaughtered if you didn't help."

"Sir, we did what we felt was necessary for the country's long-term well-being and survival."

"You can't just impose American-style democracy on a sovereign nation, Captain."

"Why not? It's been done before."

The comment incenses Daniels, as evidenced by the redness of his face. He throws the report down.

"You people seem to think that the rules don't apply to you. Even the way you went about gathering your evidence was suspect—hijacking a federal spacecraft, breaking into NSA headquarters, impersonating private citizens. You even unleashed a weapon of mass destruction on foreign soil! This is just a sample of the long laundry list of unorthodox and border-line illegal actions you undertook to accomplish your goals."

"As the saying goes, Senator, sometimes you have to break a few eggs to make an omelet," Conrad responds.

Daniels is visibly angered by her flippancy. "You've got some nerve, Captain. Do you have any idea of the impact your actions have on this nation? What gives you the right to engage in these types of actions? Tell me Captain, what makes you so special?

She takes a slow sip of her water before answering.

"Truman said it best," she states. "He said, 'I believe it must be the policy of the United States to support free peoples who are resisting attempted subjugation by armed minorities or by outside pressures.' The people of Lemalia needed us and we answered the call. We have decided not to sit by as injustices are committed against any group of people: American, Lemalian, or otherwise. We will be there, wherever we are needed. And frankly sir, to those who have a problem with this, I pose this question: 'Do you think you can stop us?'"

"Are you trying to make some sort of threat, Captain?" Daniels asks.

"Never threats, sir; just promises."

CHAPTER SIXTY-EIGHT

VENDETTA

The steps outside the Capitol Building

Roughly twenty minutes after the conclusion of the hearing, the Vigil team leaves to go to their vehicle, a late-model Ford Excursion. As they exit the Capitol Building, a throng of news reporters, narrowly being held back by DC Metro Police, bombard them, throwing questions at the team in rapid-fire succession.

A reporter from the Washington Post is able to break through. "Captain Conrad, many would interpret your final comments in the hearing as inflammatory. Could you clarify what you meant?"

"What I said was not meant to be a threat but an assurance that we will fight for and defend all people from injustice no matter who they are. Thank you."

The team is ushered into their SUV as the cameras continue flashing.

A man in an office in Virginia watches these events on his television. Littered across his desk are photos of members of the Network and Mohann Aldessa, kill orders for Aldessa, photos of Frank Spencer, and schematics of the Louvre. His secretary, Ava Staples, calls him over the phone intercom.

"Sir, the coffee is ready."

"Thanks, I'll be right up."

The man gets up from his leather chair and walks toward the TV for a closer look. The shadows retreat from Secretary Hanahan's face as he looks at the TV screen with an assured expression.

"Well done Alicia, well done."

EPILOGUE

CONTINUATION OF POLITICS BY OTHER MEANS

Office of the Secretary of Defense
The Pentagon
Arlington, Virginia

In the room just outside of his office, Hanahan sips his cup of freshly brewed coffee.

"This is some good stuff, Ava," he tells his secretary.

"Thank you, sir," Staples replies. "Oh, before I forget…"

She pulls out a stack of documents from her bottom left desk drawer and hands it to Hanahan.

"Here's the initial defense budget proposal for the upcoming fiscal year."

Hanahan grabs the stack of papers as he balances his coffee cup in the other hand.

"Thanks," he replies half-heartedly.

"Just a little light reading for you," Staples says with a smile.

Hanahan flips through the pages with a free thumb. He walks up to his office door and pushes it open with his left shoulder. As the door opens, he hears a familiar voice.

"Hello, Mr. Secretary."

He looks up from the pages to see Conrad sitting at his desk, surrounded by the rest of the team.

"Alicia," Hanahan says in acknowledgment, almost as if he was expecting her.

"Have a seat please, sir," Conrad continues. "I'll keep this brief: there are ten FBI agents just outside this office waiting to take you into custody for the assassination of Mohann Aldessa."

"Let me guess—my boys got sloppy," Hanahan says.

"We got security footage from the Lemalian inauguration showing Frank Spencer leaving the scene," Arrowhawk says. "Cell phone records show a call out to you via an encrypted line."

Conrad leans in and asks, "All I want to know is, why?"

Hanahan places the defense proposal on the coffee table in front of him. He takes a moment before speaking. "Aldessa, as you already know, was just a front man for the Network. Their plan went beyond Lemalia."

"What do you mean?" Conrad asks.

"Lemalia produces about seventy percent of the global supply of Duritium. The other thirty percent is split amongst a number of other countries. The Network's aim was to control the worldwide supply. They wanted to create a global monopoly through a consortium of Duritium-producing nations."

Conrad motions to Fighting Bull to hand over the manila folder clasped under her left arm. "Is this what you're talking about?"

She throws the file onto the coffee table in front of Hanahan. The cover of the file reads: *Proposal for the formation of the Duritium Exporting Countries Association,* with Duvalier and Chase's names listed below as authors.

Hanahan picks up the document and flips through the pages.

"That was on one of your men in Paris when Cynthia intercepted them," Conrad says.

With a disconcerted look, Hanahan fixes his gaze on Conrad.

"Alicia, they were going to create their own twisted version of OPEC. Can you imagine how devastating that would have been to our economy? The world's economy? They would've controlled everything from the mining, refining, distribution, and price of Duritium."

"So you resort to political assassination instead?" Conrad fires back.

"It was a start," Hanahan answers. "You guys finished the rest."

"So, you've been the puppet master this whole time, huh?"

"If you want to call it that," Hanahan says. "With Lemalia out of play the whole thing would fall apart. No monopoly, cheaper Duritium. Everyone wins."

"How long have you had this in motion?" Conrad asks.

"For the past four years."

"And your selection of Ramsey as our operations chief was obviously intentional."

"Of course, Alicia," Hanahan replies matter-of-factly. "You've known me your whole life. When have I ever done anything without an end objective in mind?"

Conrad knows that he speaks the truth. She's just disappointed that this is coming from one of the few people she trusted unequivocally.

"So you knew Ramsey was involved with the Network. You positioned him where you could keep a close eye on him."

"Not only that, but I had to have someone I could trust in a position to take him and his band of brothers down."

"So the team…" Conrad starts to say.

"Again, was not a random act," Hanahan finishes her thought. "The NSC was gonna do whatever I told them to. I essentially hand-picked each of you. You all had the skills, powers, and know-how to take down the Network."

He points with both forefingers to each member of the team in turn.

"Arrowhawk can practically obliterate anything in his way with those energy powers of his. They couldn't come anywhere close in terms of raw power. Plus, he had the investigative curiosity to find out about the Network.

"Fighting Bull is the perfect covert agent. I knew the Network had no chance when it came to counter-intelligence. She could easily infiltrate any insurgency cell.

"Morrison is virtually indestructible, and I knew because of his religious convictions he would never let you guys cross certain moral lines. Making it legal and making the charges stick.

"Aaron is as stubborn as a goat but a technical genius. He figured out the flaw in the cybernetic suits that the UPF was using.

"And you, Alicia, you were my ace in the hole. You were the only one I knew who could bring this all together. You have no idea how important you and the twins are. No idea," Hanahan says, finally completing his laudatory speech.

"So you set into motion the beginnings of a civil war, all for what? Cornering the market on a precious metal?!" Conrad responds angrily.

Hanahan leans in and says, "War is the..."

"...continuation of politics by other means," Conrad says, completing his sentence, a paraphrasing of a quotation from Carl Von Clausewitz.

"Exactly," Hanahan says with a smile.

Conrad turns to Arrowhawk and nods her head. He taps his earpiece reflexively.

"We're ready," Arrowhawk says.

A group of FBI agents enter the room and converge on Hanahan. Handcuffs are quickly clasped on his wrists. Before he is taken out of the room he turns once more to Conrad.

"Alicia, you have no idea how much you and your family are caught up in this, do you?"

"What are you talking about?"

"The Network wasn't the only one funding the rebels in Lemalia. Someone very close to you and your family was involved too."

Blankenchip interjects, "He's just psyching you out Alicia, don't listen to him."

"Am I, Aaron?" Hanahan says with assuredness. "It's the same person who was involved in your parents' murders."

Conrad is temporarily stunned by his statement. For all of her adult life she has believed her parents' deaths were the result of an accident. The thought that they could have been murdered brings a sick feeling to her stomach.

"Just promise me, Alicia, no matter what happens, you never lose your resolve," Hanahan says as he is led out of his office.

"Alicia, snap out of it," Blankenchip barks. "We gotta get you out of here. Your custody case, remember?

Conrad picks up her beret from Hanahan's desk and places it firmly on the crown of her head.

"Let's go."

-THE BEGINNING-

THANKS AND A SNEAK PEEK

I hope you enjoyed reading the first book in the *Vigil* saga. As a thanks for reading it, I would like to share with you a preview of *Sovereign*, the second book in the series. Enjoy!

With gratitude,
P.B. Obeng

PROLOGUE ONE

December 5th
Shibuya District
Tokyo, Japan

Raindrops pelted Kaori Fujihara's smooth, oval face as she squeezed her way through the evening throng of people walking across Shibuya Scramble Crossing. Her thumping heartbeat drowned out the screams of her pursuers calling on her to halt. Five men adorned in light, hooded jackets with grey, camouflaged BDU pants with combat boots, followed quickly behind her. The gap between them shrunk to a hair's width. Rain mixed with the tears streamed down her face as she felt them gaining on her. She cut her eyes to the subway station entrance. Her pace quickened as she darted in the direction of what she hoped would be her salvation.

Her pursuers barreled past pedestrians with little regard for their wellbeing. One of the men with a buzzcut and tattoos at the base of his neck, shoved a small, five-year-old girl into the path of an oncoming transit bus. The bus driver violently yanked the steering wheel to the right. As Kaori ran through the subway entrance, she glanced back to see the young girl, feet away from losing her life. Kaori's pupils emitted a cool, azure glow. The bus's electrical braking system activated, bringing the vehicle to an immediate stop. The forward momentum of the vehicle jostled the bus's occupants out of their seats, but they were none the worse for wear. The little girl stared in amazement as her parents quickly collected her from the middle of the intersection. Without breaking her stride, Fujihara continued through the subway entrance.

She pressed her way through the congested escalator. A gloved hand latched on to the back of her thin, right wrist like a vice grip. Kaori swiveled her head around to see the man with the buzzcut's firm hand grasping her own. She frantically wriggled her wrist backward and forward but to no avail. Kaori's eyes traced down to a bulge in the man's right thigh pocket. Sparks exploded from his BDU pants as an azure glow beamed from her pupils. The man screamed in anguish as he collapsed to the ground. Seizing the opportunity, Kaori yanked her right arm away as the man released his grip to tend to his injured thigh. She moved with alacrity to the subway platform at the base of the escalator, slipping lithely through the bustling crowd.

"Dammit, I told Jenkins to leave his phone behind," shouted one of the wounded man's fellow compatriots who followed close behind. He reached for a plastic, archaic looking walkie-talkie in the side compartment of his jacket. "Stiles, this Shepherd. The target is headed toward the Hachiko exit."

"Copy that. So, five grown men couldn't catch a twenty-three-year-old girl?"

"Now's not the time for your crap Stiles," the man spat back through the walkie-talkie receiver.

Stiles snickered, "I'm on it."

Kaori slipped through the gleaming, metallic sliding doors leading to Hachiko square. She was welcomed by the unrelenting rain as she exited the station. A crowd of people surrounded the statue of the loyal Akita dog that was the square's namesake. She slowed her pace, trying to mix in with the group. A person in the crowd offered her their dome-shaped umbrella to share as they walked toward Adores Game Center. Kaori obliged, taking shelter under it. The pursuing men followed closely behind. They pushed aside many of those in the crowd as they furtively looked for the young woman. An on-duty policeman noticed the commotion and accosted one of the men.

Another pursuer with a silky, black mohawk pulled out a taser from his thigh pocket. He firmly thrust the end of the weapon into the policeman's chest. 50,000 volts coursed through the hapless officer. He convulsed violently and began foaming at the mouth before slumping to the ground. Bystanders looked on in disbelief at what they were witnessing.

Kaori used the momentary distraction to break away from the crowd to make a beeline to Adores Gaming Center. Her red, Adidas tennis shoes sloshed heavily against the pavement as the Gaming Center's entrance came into view. Her mind drifted back to when she was a little girl; her father brought her there as a reward for her good grades at the end of each school semester. She frequented the Center so often she virtually knew it like the back of her hand. The rain-soaked pursuers, now whittled down to four, split off as they entered Adores Gaming Center. Two broke to the opposite sides of the Center with the remaining two following directly behind Kaori.

Fear quickened her thinking. She made her way between two unattended crane games she saw in the corner of her eye. Kaori shivered as the cold from her drenched clothes seeped into her body. With her heart beating a thousand times a minute, she tried to calm herself. Fujihara used a technique that helped quell her pre-game jitters before high school soccer matches. Thoughts of how her younger brother made her laugh before family dinners by plugging his nose with noodles, and how her father's warm embrace made her feel before she left for her first year of university flooded her mind. Her heart rate started to steadily come down.

Two of the flanking pursuers fanned the crowd looking for her. One of them grabbed his walkie talkie. As he clenched the device, his sleeve receded back to accentuate a tattoo of an eagle grasping lightening and a rifle in each talon.

"This is Cane. I have no sign of her," the man said. "Duval and Shepherd what do you see?"

"Me and Shep have got nothing," the bearded pursuer responded. "Faulk, you got eyes on her?"

Faulk scanned the crowd like a hawk, noting every facial detail, mannerism, and movement of those around him. He took his time before responding. "Nothing yet." He reached for the holstered 9 mm M9 Beretta on his right hip, sliding back the holstering strap. Faulk turned the corner to the cluster of crane games hiding Fujihara. Hearing the lurch of his footsteps drawing nearer, she lets out a small gasp. He immediately drew his weapon. The barrel of his gun led his advance.

As Faulk turned the corner around a *Pokémon*-themed crane game, its glass casing shattered in his face. He fell to the ground with a face marred with glass shards. He yelled in pain as the errant crane claw retracted back from where it shattered the glass. Immediately, Kaori shot out of the cluster of games and through the crowd of people gathered at the latest *Dance Dance Revolution* game.

Picking out the bloody shards from his face, Faulk radioed his teammates, "The target's on the move." Through blood-streaked vision he saw Kaori making her escape. "She's headed for the north side exit."

"How'd she get past you?" Shepherd asked.

"She activated one of the games on me. Threw me for a loop with a face full of glass."

"You ok?"

"Better than that bitch will be in a few seconds."

Fujihara looked back to see she'd shaken off her pursuers. A sense of calm fell over her as she slowed her pace. The crowd in front of her thinned out the closer she got to her exit. Her feet barely made it through the exit doors when she was met with a stiff, clothesline strike to her throat. The force from the strike laid her flat on her back. Her shoulder-length hair flopped in the air as her occiput slammed hard into the drenched pavement. She gasped, as she struggled to catch her breath.

Kaori tasted a faint hint of iron on her lips as she wiped the blood coming out of her left nostril. An overwhelming shadow hovered over her. Glancing up, she saw Stiles leaning over her with the barrel of a Heckler and Koch P30 pistol pointed squarely in her face. Stiles struck an imposing figure, standing over five-feet-ten inches in height with shadows obscuring most of her facial features. The spikey black hair and her spiraling dragon tattoo around her neck sent chills down Kaori's spine. Reacting instinctively, Kaori's eyes began to glow. Stiles' left arm started to spasm violently, causing the pistol to jerk out of her hand. Before Kaori's eyes reached full luminescence, Stiles delivered a quick karate-chop blow to Kaori's right temple—knocking her unconscious.

Kneeling over Fujihara's body, Stiles grabbed her gun from the ground, returning the weapon to the right shoulder holster hidden underneath her hooded jacket. She winced slightly as she grabbed her left arm and looked back down at Fujihara before reaching for the walkie talkie hooked on her back waistband.

"Target neutralized," Stiles said, as she spoke into the device.

CHAPTER ONE

UNFINISHED BUSINESS

Nine months later
Tokyo Institute of Technology
Minato City
Tokyo, Japan

Automated beeps emanated from the metallic entryway into the geological research lab as it slid open. A female lab assistant outfitted with thin-rimmed glasses and a hip-length baby blue lab coat entered. She scanned the expanse of the lab as she entered its inner sub-chamber.

The young woman carefully placed a sleek cell phone sized device against the casing system's glass exterior. Red lights on the side of the device lit up sequentially. A slight hissing sound—like a pressure release valve—was heard as the glass casing slid back. The smell of fresh leather filled her nostrils as she pulled her gloves on. She reached into the glass casing, carefully pulling the tectonic module and agitator from their clamps. Her hands quivered slightly as she placed the device into her duffle bag.

The light steps from her flat-soled shoes were barely heard as she left the lab and walked down the long hallway. She quickly made her way through the labyrinth of winding halls and corridors. As she exited the building, she brushed past a thin man wearing sunglasses, and a bespoke pinstriped suit. She gently passed the duffle bag over the man without breaking her stride.

The man in the tailored suit carefully slid the duffle bag over his right shoulder. He eventually walked down a cobble-stoned winding path through a crowd of bystanders, toward the ornate temple of Zojo-ji in Shiba Park. Sweat beaded up on the back of his neck as the afternoon sun began to break through the clouds. He walked up behind two women—one with a pixie-cut and the other with shoulder-length hair.

"Madame Harada, we have the device," the man said.

The woman with shoulder-length hair turned to glance up at him.

"Very good work, Seiji," Codai Harada replied, as she lowered her Dolce and Gabana shades.

The freckle-faced Yakuza boss looked spritely considering she survived the collapse of the Network just over a year ago.

Seiji passed the duffle bag to the Harada's assistant with the pixie-cut. Her assistant carefully pulled the zipper back. With gloved hands she placed the devices into a large foam lined, carbon-fiber reinforced suitcase.

"Should I meet you at the rendezvous point?" Seiji asked.

"Yes." Harada said as they began walking toward the stretch limousine waiting for her just outside of the temple. As her assistant stretched her hand to open the door for her, the hairs on Harada's neck went erect. She quickly turned around.

"Is there something wrong, Madame?" her assistant asked.

"Give me your weapon."

Her assistant nodded and pulled a Ruger SR9C pistol from her shoulder holster and handed it to Harada. After placing the weapon in her coat pocket, Harada quickly made herself comfortable on the limousine's plush, leather seating.

Unbeknownst to Harada, Captain Alicia Conrad observed everything below. She used her high-powered binoculars to zero in on Harada's limousine from the Top Deck of the Tokyo Tower. Standing at approximately 1,093 feet, it served as the perfect perch for Conrad. Harada's limousine was flanked by four leather jacket-clad men on all black Suzuki Hayabusa motorcycles.

Conrad pulled out a rifle that bore a slight resemblance to an AR-15 from her tactical bag. She firmly planted the butt-end of the weapon against her right shoulder. Conrad brushed back the few thin dreadlocks as she looked down her rifle's laser scope. She pulled the trigger. The rifle hardly made a sound as she fired the tracer disc directly at the limousine's rear bumper. Harada's entourage didn't even notice the device as it assimilated to the shape and color of the vehicle.

"Got it," Conrad said over her earpiece radio link.

"Don't be so cocky Alicia, just 'cause you made the shot," Lieutenant Aaron Blankenchip retorted. His dark brown hair peppered with gray was illuminated by the noonday sun coming through the windshield of his Silver Dodge Charger. He shifted gears from park to drive as he moved in behind Harada's caravan.

"You know I've always been a better shot than you, Aaron," Conrad responded with a roguish smile.

"Get the hell out of here! I coulda hit that shot with my eyes closed and right hand behind my back!"

"I need you all to focus," Agent Cynthia Fighting Bull interrupted, with a schoolteacher-like tone. "We've been tracking Harada for the past year. This is the best chance we've had. Outside of Weiping Pei, she's the last Network Principal still on the run."

"I thought keeping the team on task was my job, Cynthia?" Conrad said.

"I guess you're rubbing off on me, Alicia."

"Isn't that a good thing?"

"Depends on who you ask," Fighting Bull said.

"You all set at Shinagawa train station?"

Fighting Bull shook her head and smiled. "Come on now. Don't forget who you're talking to here."

Conrad smiled at her remark as she packed the rifle in her tactical bag. and carefully slid her legs into her sturdy, leather lined rappelling harness and rappelled down the Tower's steel girded elevator shaft. Conrad made it to the ground floor and sprinted to the Harley Davidson Livewire motorcycle stowed away a block south of the tower.

Meanwhile, Blankenchip maintained a distance of three car-lengths behind Harada's entourage while Conrad's tracker signal displayed on the screen of his center console. Appling light pressure to the accelerator, he moved closer to Harada. Several car lengths ahead, a fender-bender brought traffic to a standstill.

Blankenchip patiently kept his distance. After a few minutes, the traffic began to lighten. He continued to follow behind Harada—tucking himself behind a bluish Nissan and a small Corolla.

One of the four motorcyclists that flanked Harada's limousine saw the out-of- place Charger in his rear-view mirror. He tapped his helmet and nodded to his partner. Immediately, the entourage split off in three directions—two motorcyclists headed east, another two to the west, while Harada's limousine continued south.

"Dammit, I think they spotted me," Blankenchip shouted within earshot of the team's communication line.

"I see what's happened," Conrad said as she saw the real-time satellite images on her motorcycle's display screen. "Stay with Harada, I'll tail the Gijo Hei going east."

The motorcyclists that accompanied Harada were her elite Honor Guard, or Gijo-Hei. These men were Harada's specially trained bodyguards, as deadly as any Navy Seal or Army Special Forces operative.

"Copy that, Alicia."

The Charger's Hemi engine rumbled as Blankenchip stepped on the gas in pursuit of Harada's limousine. Forty, then thirty, then twenty feet separated him from his target. Blankenchip's heartrate sped up, almost matching his car's acceleration as he drew nearer. As the distance narrowed to ten feet, his rear tire blew out.

The exploding tire sent the Charger careening headfirst into a nearby light pole on a crowded street. The Charger's front windshield and passenger windows shattered into multiple pieces. Many people scattered the scene. Blankenchip suffered whiplash from his neck bouncing off the exploding airbag, aggravating an old injury he incurred in the field many years ago. The airbag's impact cracked the bridge of Blankenchip's nose, leaving him bloodied. Blankenchip looked out of the cracked driver's side window to see Harada's motor cycled Gijo Hei shoving clips into their weapons.

"Careless, Aaron!" Blankenchip thought to himself, as blood flowed from his nose and mouth. He struggled to reach for his left wristband tucked under his sleeve---or more like a forearm bracelet (although he Blankenchip was too macho to call it that) to activate his exoskeletal suit. The bands covered the lengths of his wrists and forearms.

After they dismounted from their vehicles, they crept toward Blankenchip's damaged vehicle. They methodically screwed on silencer tips to their Sig Sauer pistols. They stood just feet outside of Blankenchip's damaged passenger door. Aiming their weapons in his direction they unleashed multiple rounds on the Dodge Charger with little regard to injuring any bystanders. Shell-casings of the spent ammunition littered the ground beneath the gunmen as they emptied their clips on the vehicle. They left the remnants of the vehicle resembling Swiss Cheese.

One of the gunmen inched closer to the destroyed Charger. As he reached for the driver's side door handle, the door flew opened explosively. The gunman fell backward, landing hard on his mid-back. After he briefly gathered himself, he looked up. Blankenchip, in his black hexagonal patterned exoskeletal armor, stood over him with the barrel of his modified H&K MP7 submachine gun pointed squarely at him. Being the wiser, the man raised his hands up.

"Put your hands behind your head!" Blankenchip shouted down to the man in Japanese—finally utilizing the translator suggestion that Conrad suggested over a year ago.

The assailed Gijo-Hei complied and clasped his fingers behind his head. Blankenchip tapped the side of his right thigh and an interlocking sliding panel opened, revealing a holstered H&K SFP9 M pistol. He plunged his hand into the thigh compartment, removed the weapon and pointed it at the second Gijo Hei who was about to fire on him.

"Get on the ground!" he screamed to the second one. Just as Blankenchip was briefly distracted, the first downed Gijo Hei opened his mouth. His vocal cords vibrated and unleashed a sonic scream that rocketed Blankenchip off his feet. He was slammed him back into his destroyed Charger. He shook his head before tapping the side of his feline-looking helmet to activate his armor's onboard countermeasures analysis. It was intended to automatically activate on his own, but it still had a few bugs to work out. Blankenchip's heads up display went crazy with streams of data that scrolled across his field of vision. Data about his assailants' abilities and vital statistics popped up.

"So, we have an Augment and a cyborg," Blankenchip said. Blankenchip's HUD immediately ran counter-measure protocols; none too soon as the sonic screaming Gijo-Hei got up from the ground and unleashed another sonic blast. Immediately, Blankenchip leaped out of the way, landing on his right side. As he tried to recover, he bumped into a young man trying to escape the havoc. Blankenchip pushed him out of the way just before he was walloped by an uppercut punch from the second cybernetically enhanced Gijo-Hei. The blow lifted Blankenchip diagonally off his feet and slammed him through the wall of an adjacent pharmacy. Blankenchip winced as his lumbar spine slammed against the wall. He grabbed the area where his old surgical scar was. As he looked through his helmet's cracked view screen, his HUD spat out gibberish.

"Aw hell, let's do it old school." Blankenchip ripped off his helmet and fired two rounds into the ground, just past the charging cybernetically enhanced Gijo Hei. The bullets ricocheted off the ground and struck the sonic screaming Gijo Hei in the torso and right thigh—severing his femoral artery. As blood gushed from his leg, he let out a sonic scream. The ensuing sonic scream blasted the advancing cybernetically enhanced one off balance and in Blankenchip's direction.

Dread came upon the Gijo Hei's face as he bowled toward Blankenchip's pointed weapon. Three bullets ripped through his midsection and another through his right shoulder, taking him down for good.

As he leaned over the dead Gijo Hei, Blankenchip noticed exposed wiring and metallic plating underneath his right shoulder. He used his armor's enhanced strength to rip off a piece of the metallic plating underneath the Gijo Hei's skin. He observed the intricate circuitry and silicon wafers. Flipping over one of the wafers, he saw a Japanese name etched on its surface.

Blankenchip crept toward the wounded sonic screaming Gijo Hei. He pressed his right knee into the Gijo Hei's wounded thigh while creating a seal over his mouth with his left hand. Blankenchip then firmly planted the barrel of his weapon in the center of the Gijo Hei's chest.

"You even dare let off a sonic scream and I swear I will leave a crater in your chest."

The Gijo Hei's eyes widened as sweat beaded up on his furrowed brow. Blankenchip released the tight seal over the man's mouth. Blankenchip lifted the silicon wafer to within an inch of the Gijo Hei's face.

"Tell me where you got these enhancements."

As he felt the firm thrust of Blankenchip's weapon in his chest, his eyes looked down worriedly at the barrel and then up to Blankenchip's menacing face.

"Saisentan."

"Thanks."

Blankenchip struck him in the face, with a forceful enough blow to knock him unconscious. He radioed Conrad.

"Alicia, watch your ass. Harada's upgraded her personal bodyguards."

"Yeah, I see that," Conrad responded as she swerved to dodge a bio-electric pulse blast from one of the motorcycled Gijo Hei. The blast seared through the front grill of the black Toyota Land Cruiser behind her. The downward impact flipped the vehicle over in mid-air, right above Conrad's head. As the vehicle somersaulted over her, Conrad glimpsed the occupants of the SUV through the vehicle's windshield. They were barely older than her siblings.

The male driver and female passenger were thrown about inside the vehicle's cabin. As their world became a jumbled mess, the driver didn't notice the windshield shattered. Suddenly, he felt his seatbelt release as Conrad cut it. Conrad stabilized him with a scissor leg hold while she reached for the other passenger. With a speed that defied comprehension, the passenger side seatbelt was quickly cut by Conrad's Night Force knife. Conrad attached a metallic disc with numerous drilled holes on the young woman while the SUV was still airborne. The disc released a grayish-colored microencapsulated polymer that encased the woman in an expanding foam composite. It made the woman resemble something like a human puffer fish. She was thrusted through the passenger side door as the protective foam casing rapidly expanded. Her composite encased body bounced lightly into traffic as many drivers veered out of the way to avoid her. Some couldn't avoid her but she ping-ponged from some of those cars without any harm to herself or the other passengers.

Conrad pressed the center button of her tactical belt which released thin metal filaments from the belt's side compartments, entangling the man close to Conrad. She pulled a grappling gun from her thigh pocket and fired a high tensile strength grappling line through the shattered windshield. The electrostatic grappling hook latched on to one of the light poles that aligned the freeway.

Conrad and the driver were immediately yanked away out of the tumbling SUV. As they retracted out of harm's way, she pulled another metallic disc from her harness and threw it in the direction of the tumbling vehicle. The damaged SUV was suddenly encapsulated in a foam composite as well, keeping the vehicle from causing more damage to the other oncoming vehicles on the freeway.

Conrad and the SUV driver came down from the light pole on the freeway shoulder. Emergency service vehicle sirens suddenly immersed the area. She unstrapped the driver. A quick visual observation showed some minor cuts on his face from the broken windshield glass but no other major wounds.

She asked the passenger if he was ok, trying her best in broken Japanese. He acknowledged he was fine. An ambulance quickly pulled up just feet beside them. As the paramedics brought out their stretcher, Conrad looked up to see Harada's Gijo Hei had already sped off.

* * *

Fifteen Minutes Later
Shinagawa Train Station
Tokyo, Japan

Harada was quickly ushered out of her limousine through the train station's Konan entrance by her four Gijo Hei bodyguards who were in the limousine with her. Their way was impeded by the mob of shoppers. As they pushed aside bystanders, they caught the attention of onlookers as well as an observant transit police officer.

"Stop. Put your hands up!" the transit officer screamed.

Harada and her entourage momentarily paused at the command. Within moments, a squad of five more transit police officers converged on Harada's location. Three of the officers formed a perimeter around Harada and her Gijo Hei, which blocked them from ascending to the first-floor JR platform.

Harada looked in the direction of a member of her Gijo-Hei who wore a brown leather jacket, shades, and gloves. He nodded in her direction and removed his shades---behind them were glowing eyes crackling with power. A pulsating circle of red energy began to form in the palms of his hands. He raised his hands to unleash a bright red bioelectric blast as the three officers returned fire.

Meanwhile, on the upper platform, Fighting Bull heard the cacophony on the floor below her. She checked the shoulder holster underneath her fitted beige trench coat to make sure that her Sig Sauer P365 and glasses were in place. Fighting Bull ran toward the first-floor platform. She leaped over turnstiles and in between screaming crowds fleeing the scene. As soon as her feet touched the ground, she saw the fire fight.

Bullets buzzed back and forth between the transit police and the Gijo-Hei. One transit officer wounded the super-powered Gijo Hei. As he fell, he emitted an errant energy blast that hit a horizontal fluorescent light fixture. The fixture descended upon a large crowd of civilians below. A little girl with an incredibly over-sized *Hello Kitty* backpack was left behind as the crowd scattered. Fighting Bull's heart raced as she moved swiftly to move the child out of harm's way. As she grabbed the girl, she pulled the child close to her chest and tumbled forward in a front roll. Fighting Bull let out a slight grunt as her back slammed against the platform handrails.

After they recovered, the girl's parents quickly ran to gather her. With the girl safe with her parents, Fighting Bull immediately morphed into one of the transit police. She aimed her Sig Sauer P365 pistol on her target. Her aim was fixed on the Gijo Hei who fired his Beretta. She let off three shots. They hit their mark and pierced his chest wall and neck. Since the Lemalian war, she honed her action-shooting skills to almost, but not completely, rival that of Conrad's.

Another Gijo Hei saw his comrade felled by the flurry of Fighting Bull's bullets. He then trained his pistol on Fighting Bull, firing errantly. She took cover behind a news stand as she morphed into Agent John Arrowhawk's form. She immediately erected a broad band energy shield to deflect the bullets that were being fired up on her. Due to recent upgrades to her uniform, she was able to store the abilities of the people who she morphed into for a 15-minute window—something the tech division called "tactile memory."

As Fighting Bull defended herself, Harada rushed up the escalator to platform 23, for the Shinkansen train to Kyoto. Noticing Harada making her escape, Fighting Bull directed a broad bright blue energy blast from her left hand that knocked the gunman out. She quickly morphed back to her natural form as she raced up the escalator behind Harada. As soon as she hit the platform, Fighting Bull saw Harada slide into one of the forward train cars. She swiftly made her way through the sliding doors of the train car immediately behind Harada.

Fighting Bull put on the dark-tinted glasses with metallic black frames that she had previously tucked away. Thankfully, those weren't affected by her multiple metamorphoses. The glasses provided her with heads-up display-like schematics on everyone on the train. She scanned the train car intently. As she looked around, every detail popped up on the lens of her glasses—everything from height, age, and gender were laid bare for Fighting Bull to see. She walked down the nicely carpeted aisle to make her way through multiple train cars until she got to the Gran Class, or high-class section of the train.

Around the fifth row from the train car entrance a matched heat signature popped up. With her target acquired, Fighting Bull folded the glasses and put them back in her coat pocket. As she made her way toward Harada, her original face melted back to reveal the face of a young Japanese woman. Fighting Bull took a seat in the luxury chair across from Harada. To her right was a port window. She saw Harada with her leg crossed and the suitcase with the tectonic agitator. Harada had placed her coat over the edge of her armrest, to give herself some breathing room. Fighting Bull looked unassumingly at Harada, eliciting a small smile.

"Nice weather today isn't it?" Fighting Bull asked in Japanese.

Harada nodded, trying not to look too frazzled, "Yes, it is."

"Too bad they say a heavy storm is coming this evening."

"What was that?" Harada asked.

"A storm is supposed to be coming," Fighting Bull said, with an intonation that was slightly off, something Harada clearly picked up on. Fighting Bull may have looked like a native-born Japanese woman, but she didn't sound like one.

Harada gently uncrossed her legs as they continued speaking. She abruptly got up from her chair and grabbed her coat and suitcase. Fighting Bull reached out to grab Harada's right wrist. Harada in turn, plunged her free hand into her coat pocket and pulled out the Ruger SR9C compact 9 mm semi-automatic pistol. She trained her weapon on Fighting Bull—hitting her squarely in the chest with three rounds. The impact of the bullets laid Fighting Bull flat on the ground. Other civilians in the train car immediately ran for cover at the sound of the gunshots. Harada quickly grabbed the suitcase and rushed in the opposite direction.

Struggling to get up, Fighting Bull winced in pain. Thankfully, even though her uniform morphed with her, it still retained its protective and impact-absorptive properties. The intrinsic mesh of biosteel and Duritium held. She turned to see the deformed bullets from the Ruger pistol laid on either side of her. Thankfully her glasses weren't damaged by the gunfire, so she placed them on the bridge of her nose and tapped the right rim of the glasses. A schematic of the train cars popped up on her lenses. Within seconds, Harada's location was triangulated two train cars down.

As Harada ran rapidly between cars, she looked back to see Fighting Bull just a few feet behind her. Her Ruger was still in her hand and she made good use of it as she fired wildly in Fighting Bull's direction, hitting a side panel and a handrail. Fighting Bull ducked out of the way of the bullets. Running at her current stride, she wouldn't have dared return fire with her Sig Sauer for fear of hitting civilians.

Harada hurried to the next train car. As she slid the door open, a transit officer came into clear view. The transit officer cautioned her to stop. She fired one bullet straight through his chest. The Yakuza boss barely broke her stride before one of the civilians, ducked under their seat, extended her right foot into the aisleway. Tumbling forward Harada lost the suitcase with the tectonic agitator. As Harada tried to pull herself from off the ground, she heard Fighting Bull's voice.

"Don't move."

Harada's eyes darted around the floor looking for her gun.

"Looking for this?" Fighting Bull said with her foot on the suitcase. She pointed the Ruger and Sig Sauer in Harada's direction.

Harada cautiously rolled around from her prone position with her hands up...

SCAN THIS CODE TO BUY 'SOVEREIGN'

ALSO BY P.B. OBENG

A SUPER-TEAM STRUGGLING TO KEEP THE WORLD IN ORDER. A TECHNO-ORGANIC VIRUS THREATENING TO REWRITE ALL OF HUMANITY.

Captain Alicia Conrad isn't sure she's on the right side of the coming cyberwar. As she leads her team of superhumans on their quest for global safety, she's conflicted by the compromises she's forced to make. And when a technopath vanishes, it isn't long before she suspects a powerful corporation, led by the enigmatic Dennis Stroud, is behind the abduction.

Desperate for answers, Conrad and her team are horrified when their hunt for the truth reveals a whistleblower and his family's brutal slaughter. And with shadowy powers rising to claim everything she holds dear, she discovers a terrifying menace waiting to be unleashed: a revolutionary man-made virus jeopardizing all of humankind.

Can one leader expose the ugly reality before the planet falls to a madman's warped vision?

Sovereign, Book 2 of the Vigil Saga, is available now to *buy in paperback, hardback and Kindle from Amazon. (*You can scan the QR code opposite to do so).

VIGIL MERCH AVAILABLE NOW ON TEESPRING!

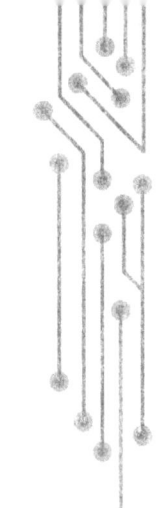

SCAN ME

ACKNOWLEDGEMENTS

I would like to acknowledge Marti Kanna with New Leaf Editing and Katherine Stephen for their assistance in editing this manuscript.

ABOUT THE AUTHOR

Paa-Kofi B. Obeng is a full time internal medicine physician who lives in Virginia with his family.

Vigil is the first novel in series. The inspiration for his novel comes from his love of comics, family dramas as well as current events.

You can reach him at **www.pbobeng.com**.

You can also connect with him via the following social media:

www.facebook.com/authorpbobeng

www.instagram.com/author_pbobeng

www.ingramcontent.com/pod-product-compliance
Lightning Source LLC
Chambersburg PA
CBHW031139120726
47905CB00006B/1741